Praise for the writing of Terri Pray

Focused On Love is an absolute page-turner. The poignant heart-tugging characters touch the heart in such a way that it is hard releasing them once the book is finished. Dani and Steven make such a delightful couple and the way they seek to conquer the odds stacked up against them is well-written. Ms. Pray pens a sharp and intense read that keeps the reader mesmerized.
 -- Linda L., *The Romance Studio,* on *Focused On Love*

Ettore's Women is a beautifully written and perhaps deliberately fragmented story of women who work in a brothel. Terri Pray's voice fascinates me. I want to read more.
 -- Catherine H., *Novelspot,* on *Ettore's Woman*

The novel flows extremely well. There is never a dull moment and the sex is blistering hot. *Sweet Deceptions* is a great way to spend a lazy afternoon. Full of intrigue it keeps you wondering what is happening and who did it.
 -- Leyna, *Fallen Angel Reviews,* on *Sweet Deceptions*

...[A]n enjoyable fast read with the premise of being able to unleash the magic within yourself, if you have enough faith.
 -- Aggie Tsirikas, *Just Erotic Romance Reviews,* on *Green Dreams* (Mojocastle Press)

Scratching Post

Terri Pray

Terri Pray

Warning

This book contains sexually explicit scenes, graphic and adult language and may be considered offensive to some readers.

Dedication

To my Sam, thank you now and always for your help, love and support.

Chapter One

The smell of the bar hit her before the noise did, but combined, they acted like a brick wall, striking her senses full force.

Why the hell do I put myself through this every single month? She hated this, hated what her body forced her to endure and yet it was the only safe option.

Emmie Byron had already learned all too well that ignoring the call of her body was dangerous. It couldn't be shut down, and hunting close to home would've been a mistake. Here, amongst the one-night stands, the men and women looking for little more than bump and grind, she would be able to find a man who would take what she offered and be thankful for it. Her body ached for the touch of a man, any man. Just enough to take the edge off the hormones that now wracked a devastating path through her body.

Here, in the city, amongst the anonymous, she had a way of dealing with the cycle her body endured each and every month. Her home had been carefully chosen, away from the throngs of people, and for the most part, she had been able to stay hidden away from the males of her kind. Only now and then did she catch a faint hint of their presence, their travels bringing them close to town but never fully into it.

She'd been lucky. Just how much longer that luck would hold out, she couldn't be sure. But, for now, she pushed that thought to one side and gave in to the call, the demand for sex her body screamed out for. She'd find the answer here. A man to sate her needs, to bring her body through the fires that even now threatened to push her into the depths of insanity.

Emmie lifted her head up and turned, walking into the bar. Their aroma hit her. Men. Men hungry for sex. *Yes. God, yes.* Delicious, there was no other way of describing it, their hunger, their desires all crowded her, demanding attention, feeding into her own needs.

Her body reacted before she could prevent it. Her nipples tightened beneath her dress. Her core clenched, pulse quickening as she entered the bar. Her skin tingled, anticipation building with every breath. She knew what it was they saw in her. She was the walking answer to their hunger, a way of sating their needs, if they could only get her to pick one of them. Or two. Most of the men there wouldn't have minded sharing, just as long as they had their turn with her sweet, pliant body.

A dozen sets of gazes turned her way as Emmie walked into the bar. They stripped away the thin, short dress, peered at the thigh-high boots, and wondered just what it would take to get into her panties. They saw her as the prize, little knowing that one amongst their number would become her prey.

Twin desires battled instantly within her. She needed this. But her human side demanded that she leave, find a man who would be with her always. Not one who would simply sate her needs but once and then be abandoned.

Her core rippled, clenching. Her body was tight, thrumming with a hunger that would no longer be denied, and with that, the small human voice within her found itself gagged. Emmie lifted up her head and let a long, sensual roll claim her hips as she walked farther into the bar.

"Hey, darlin'! Can I get you something?" The blond, tall, well-built man who stepped into her path smelled of concrete dust and sweat. Delicious. Yes, that was a fitting term for him. He looked like every woman's dream, one who could easily delight a partner.

She took a half step toward him, inhaling deeply, a slight frown creasing her brow. Something else there. A smell she had come across before. Sickness? Yes, one that would be passed on if he was the careless type. No, not a risk she was willing to take, even though the risks of it being passed on to her were slim. "Thanks, but no, thanks."

"Not to your taste? Come on, girl, I can change your mind if you give me a chance. You don't know what you're missing." He grinned, reaching out for her arm. "I'll rock your world, and you'll never look back after a night with me."

Emmie leaned forward, her lips almost touching his ear. "I know what I'm missing out on, and believe me, a case of the clap is not to my taste." Heat flushed across the man's face as he stumbled back and walked away from her through the bar without another word. Getting rid of him had been almost too easy. The construction worker hadn't been the first one she had come across who carried with him the scent of sickness, nor would he be the last. Most reacted like this one, they turned away and slunk back through the bar.

Some put up a fight, either physical or verbal. At least she had been spared that this time. This time. But there would always be a next time. Another cycle to go through alone. Another push to enter the city and find a partner for the night, and with that there would always be risks.

She smiled and headed for the bar, settling onto a stool there, and ordered a glass of wine from a tousle-haired bartender with a gold ring in his left ear. The tender flashed a smile as he set down a paper napkin, the glass resting easily on top of it. He leaned against the polished wood surface, chatting for a few minutes, his voice slightly higher than it needed to be, the sway of his hips and the way he used his hands designed to suggest that he was gay.

An act.

If the tender was gay, then she was the great goddess, Bast. Still, he did a good job of playing the role; she just had to figure out why he was doing it.

She glanced at his finger, searching for some reason behind the act; then she spotted it. The group of gay men at the end of the bar. Big tippers by the looks of things. Ah, well, the man had to earn a living, and tips were the only way a tender had of making a good and legal wage. Pity, though, it meant that the tender was automatically out of the running.

Emmie sipped the glass of dry white wine, then turned on the stool, her gaze moving over the assembled barhoppers. A typical Friday night crew in the busy downtown area of the city; the bar was just one of over twenty within a four-block strip

For close to half an hour, Emmie sat at the bar, watching the swarms of humanity slip past. Men, women, cross-dressers, and pre-ops all mingled together. Only her sense of smell saved her from one mistake after another until she saw him. Not too tall, not too short, a slight ridge on his nose, which was just enough to keep his glasses from slipping down. His full lips quirked in a merry smile, and although he appeared content enough to sit at the table that his colleagues had staked out for the night, she couldn't help but notice the almost wistful look in his deep brown eyes.

Heat surged through her core as she took in every inch of his body. *Strong. Yes, very strong. This is the one.* But there was something else about him. An unspoken hope. One that called to her, begged for her attention. Cute and shy. The type of man many women, especially in bars, overlooked. What was the old saying? Good guys came last?

Well, not tonight.

Emmie set the glass down on the bar, ran her fingers through her hair, and made her way across the crowded room. His eyes widened as she neared the table, and he glanced around, expecting her to walk past him. When she slid onto the stool next to him, he blanched, then found his voice.

"Are you looking for someone?" His voice soft, trembling as he looked at her, his hands tightening around the half-empty glass in front of him.

"I've found someone, I hope. Unless you're waiting for someone?" *Come on, take the bait. I don't bite. Well, not that much.* "If you are, then I can leave."

"I -- I'm sorry. I don't have the money to..." Twin points of color burned instantly into life in his cheeks.

"Ah, I think you're a little confused. I'm not a working girl."

Scars

Shit, I didn't dress that slutty tonight, did I? No, if they had thought she was working the bar then the tender wouldn't have been so friendly with her, or he'd have laid down the rules for working the bar. She'd made that mistake once before. Never again.

"Sorry, I just assumed that -- oh, did one of the guys send you over?" A frown touched his brow. "It's a lousy joke if they did. They know better. Sorry if they've wasted your time. Did they tell you I'd laugh and go along with the joke?"

Emmie swallowed a sigh. This wasn't exactly going according to plan. Odd, she had never had such a problem in approaching a man before. "I'm not a hooker, and your friends didn't send me over." She leaned in, resting one hand on his arm as she looked directly into his eyes. "I'm hitting on you."

"You -- oh?" The smile that claimed his lips danced into his eyes. He pushed his shoulders back, straightening his back as he stared at her, finally letting go of the glass. "I just assumed that the guys were playing a joke on me again."

Again? No wonder he'd had to be told just what she was doing there. "Sounds like your friends are real gems. Have they done that to you often? Sent someone over, I mean, as a joke? Or have they ever tried to really set you up with someone?"

"They just like messing around, that's all." He shrugged and looked over the dance floor. "They're over there, by the edge of the bar. And it's been done, erm, three times now. Always as a joke. Guess they think it's funny. Maybe you should head over there and talk to them yourself?"

"I see, but I'm not interested in them." *Why was he making this such hard work?* Had she misjudged him? He hadn't done anything to suggest that he was gay. "Would you prefer if I left you alone? Maybe I came over at the wrong moment, or I'm not your type?" She reached out and gently teased one finger over his arm, smiling softly as she saw the skin tighten beneath her light caress. At least that was one thing. He wasn't gay. Just uncertain and nervous of what was happening around him. Or what she might want from him.

"No. No, it's not that. Just. Well. I'm not sure what you want with me." Heat flushed across his face as he looked at her, then looked away quickly. "Not when there are others around who are -- well, more your speed. I'm just -- Well. I -- God."

Oh, my God. A virgin! No wonder the man was so nervous. "Well, let's see where this goes, then. I'm Emmie, and you are?"

"Brian." He reached for his drink, taking a large swallow before he looked back at her. "Sorry for making those assumptions earlier. Just, well, normally I don't get hit on that often, and it's normally a joke one of the guys has set up, and I've told you that already. God, you must think I'm an idiot."

"No, I don't. And, well, I give you my word. I'm not a joke, or here to hurt you." *No, I'm just here to fuck your brains out and then vanish into the night when the matter is done. But I'll leave you with a memory of delight, passion, and the hope of more to come.*

Theron Grave stopped in his tracks as the woman tangled her fingers into the hand of the trembling man and led him toward the door. Her aroma hit him hard, threatening to send him to his knees in the middle of the room, her image imprinted onto his heart, mind, and soul alike.

Shifter. Female. Feline and in heat. All thought about just what had brought him to the bar fled with the walking temptation she offered him. Beautiful. Seductive. Sex on legs as she walked away from him. No. He couldn't let her just walk out on him. Not with the promise of what she was, the pleasure her body offered, so blatantly on display for his senses. He took a step toward her, his gaze focused on her sensually curved form.

Her long, dark hair was a living tail in human form as it snaked about her shoulders. God, it would have been so very easy to pull her away from the man, wrap his fingers into her hair, and claim her. Fully. His. Not the human's. She didn't belong with their kind.

Scars

What was she doing with him? Couldn't she smell another of her own kind here in the bar? Or was she so wrapped up in the human that she knew nothing else? Whatever was going on it would end. Now.

His body tightened, his cock thickening within his jeans. He wanted to move to her, to take her into his arms, but even if she had not been with another man, there was a crowd around them. Their path to the door was half blocked as one man stopped the human male she was with, laughing and joking with him.

Theron edged closer, ignoring the light touch of a woman who attempted to attract his attention. Whatever the women here wanted, or his reason for entering the bar, those now paled as he watched the female of his kind move away through the crowd.

Where was she from?

What had brought her to the bar? No, that part he knew and understood all too well. The cycle had hit her; the need to mate ruled her decisions.

Now it called to him, demanded his attention and affection.

A low growl spilled from his lips as he moved forward through the bar, but they had already left, vanishing through the door. He couldn't push past the men and women quickly enough, yet they appeared hell-bent on keeping him trapped within the bar itself.

No. I can't let her go. She's mine. She doesn't belong with humans. They're not worth her attention or the touch of a female in heat. They don't even know how to arouse a woman of their own kind fully, let alone welcome the hungry beast of a woman like this.

He yanked open the door and hurried out into the night, but they were gone from sight. Only the soft, lingering scent of her arousal remained in the air. Tempting him, teasing him with her existence. He had to find her. She couldn't have gone far. Not with the human, the man she had chosen to spend the next few hours with. It wouldn't take much to track her down, not with the way her body left such delicious signals in the air.

His pulse raced as he lifted his head, sniffing the air, searching for a sign of where she had gone, which direction she had walked, but the myriad of strange, chemical-heavy smells combined to reduce his chances of locating her. No. It couldn't be this way. Not with the years he had spent as a hunter, a tracker; those skills couldn't fail him now. The hateful smells of the city combined to battle against him, but he had to try and follow her, track her down. He couldn't just sit back and let her walk out of his life.

Whoever she was, she belonged to him.

If only for the night.

No. Not just for the night. For longer...

God. What has gotten into me? Longer than a night? Has it truly been that long since I slipped between the willing thighs of a female in heat? Have I forgotten just how they call out with their soft smells, their delicious bodies? Have I been denied their touch for that long?

If so, he was lost in a way he had never expected could happen to him.

"Hey, Theron. Are you just going to stand there all night? I thought we had a job to do." Buck rested one hand on Theron's shoulder. "Lloyd is going to get away from us if we just stand out here all night."

Lloyd. Fuck. Where had the man vanished to? That a female's heat could pull him away from a job he had sworn to complete sat ill with him. *Damn woman. Fuck it. There'll be others. There are always others.* "Sorry, distracted for a minute, that's all."

"He's still at the bar, chatting up some pretty young thing working the crowd."

"Human?" Theron tried to put all thoughts of the female shifter out of his mind, but even as he turned his attention back to the job, he couldn't quite shake off the pull of her natural perfume.

"Yeah, this time he's found a human woman to pick on." Buck jerked his head toward the bar as the two men walked back into the building. "Not sure how he hooked up with our client's daughter last time, but we can't run the risk of him doing it again. If he..."

"It could have been worse. At least he didn't see her in full shift, and as I understand it, he assumed it was part of a drunken hallucination until Momma Bear walked in on them." Theron shook his head, forcing his attention back to the job. To the man, Lloyd, and the problems he had caused. Men like that gave the rest of them a bad name. Oh, he had a good idea just what he did in order to bring the women to their knees, compliant, stunned, and unable to protest.

And if he was right, that man had to be stopped.

"He screamed like a girl, so I hear, and then he ran out into the night, gibbering the entire time." Buck grinned and tapped one finger against his belt. "Pity Momma Bear didn't get her claws into him, at least then it would have looked as though he'd angered a wild beast. Not far off the truth, but -- no, neither she nor her daughter would have been able to live with that."

Theron suppressed a chuckle and fixed his gaze on the steadily drinking form that, even now, rested one arm around the shoulders of a nervous-looking woman. "And he probably thinks he was seeing things, but I understand we can't take the risk of the man blabbing that he saw two women shift into bear form right in front of his eyes."

"Not just that, he's a danger to any woman; even their women don't deserve the sort of shit he pulls. Date-rape drugs are no laughing matter. It's just lucky that your kind tend to have a stronger resistance to the drugs than my people do." Buck rubbed the back of his neck but didn't shift his gaze away from the man at the bar.

"Human weaknesses. There will always be others of your kind who will find a way to prey on your people, and yet they call my kind the monsters." Theron growled; out of all the humans he'd dealt with through the years, only Buck had proven himself to be worth the time and effort to try and understand. Date-rape drugs. Yes. He'd assumed it was something like that the man used. How else had he been able to control a shifter, a female shifter? But he wouldn't have been expecting the woman to burn it off so quickly or to remember what had happened. That, at least, had played in their favor.

There would be one less monster roaming the world by the end of the night, if he had his way. But what about the others? The ones he didn't have leave to deal with. They could kill each other off for all he cared. But when he was given an assignment, or a client found him, then these monsters gave him a way to pay the rent of whatever motel room he needed for the night. And this one was no different. Just, they weren't allowed to kill him, not this one -- too many important friends. Not that it showed to look at him.

Pity, really.

Instead they were to use another option, one Theron disliked at the best of times. With the aid of a witch, they had come up with a pretty little spell-laced pill that would steal the man of his memories, if they could just get it into him and give him the right commands. But it wasn't always that easy.

He would have preferred to slit the man's throat, leave him bleeding on the ground. But no, he would play the hand dealt to him and find a way to get the pill into the drunken sot, drag him into a quieter area, and command him to forget everything he had witnessed.

"Distract the woman, we need to get her away from him before it's too late. Before he slips her something that we will be left to deal with. She doesn't need to be affected by those damn drugs he uses on them." Theron's jaw clenched as he watched how Lloyd traced his fingers down the woman's back, the way his greedy eyes took in every part of her body and silently stripped away her clothing.

Animals. That's what they called his people, but men like Lloyd

Scars

were the true animals.

Chapter Two

"God!" Brian hissed against her lips, his body warm and eager beneath her touch. "I can't believe this is happening. Not to me. I keep expecting them to turn up and tell me it's a joke."

"Believe it." Emmie wrapped her arms about his neck and pulled him into the small hotel room, kicking the door closed behind them. "This is real, no dream. Not a joke. Not some cruel game. Just you and me -- and the bed."

He trembled in her grasp, closing his eyes as she nibbled across his lips. He tasted sweet, clean, and gentle. This one would be easy to control. Her core rippled, eager to feel him deep within her being. Human or not, he would satisfy the need that had tormented her even before she had slipped into the car and headed for the city.

"Why me?" he groaned, his eyes closing as she licked across his neck. The beast within her craved his body, and it would not be denied. "Why me out of all the men in the bar?"

"Because you're the one. The one I choose for tonight." She pushed him back toward the bed. Why couldn't he just shut up and enjoy it? "Trust me. Let me show you what I enjoy."

He swallowed hard and stumbled back across the room, his eyes alight with a newfound hunger. She could almost hear the thoughts running through his head. This was happening, really happening. Someone had chosen him. He was finally going to get laid. He'd know what it was like to feel his cock slide into the warm, welcoming body of a woman instead of being teased into release by his own hand.

Emmie tugged out his shirt, unbuttoning it quickly before she tossed it onto the floor and turned to look at him again. His skin was smooth across his chest, no hairs, just silken skin pulled taut over tight muscles. His cock surged against his jeans; a low groan filled the air as he trembled under her caress.

Innocent. There was something intoxicating about an innocent. She'd be his first, the one to show him the delights of a woman's body. The one to corrupt him, change him, seduce him. The beast deep within her growled in sheer joy at the thought. It struggled to find a way free, but she slammed the door closed on the change.

A wicked smile claimed her lips. Turning into a large, black cat was not the best way to introduce a man to sex. Not even when the cat had this sudden urge to turn him into a human ball and bounce him off the walls. She couldn't help it. It was a cat thing.

"Close your eyes." She pressed one hand against his chest, forcing him to lie down on the bed. Brian didn't even complain. He closed his eyes and settled onto the bed, his heart pounding so loudly she could hear it. Emmie trailed her hand down his chest to his jeans, unbuckling his belt before she slid it out of the denim loops. "Don't move unless I tell you to."

He nodded, pressing his lips together in a thin line as he lay there. She couldn't help but smile. He'd quickly learn that he was about to be introduced to not just sex, but the delights of a darker nature. She looped the belt about his wrists, binding them quickly before she pushed his hands above his head. She bound one end of the belt to the headboard, all before he fully realized what she was doing.

"Wh-what are you doing?" His eyes snapped open, fear dancing within them.

"I said trust me. I'm not going to hurt you." Emmie brushed her fingertips over his eyes. "Just close them for me No harm will come to you. You'll enjoy this night and everything I show you. The delights of the flesh, the way a woman's body can feel, and your cock -- yes, your sweet cock -- pressed deep within my body."

He groaned at her words, a soft tremble working through his body as she teased her fingers over his chest. There was something about him, this human she had picked out from the crowds. Not just his innocence, but something more. The way he reacted to her light touch, the caress of her fingers over his flat nipples, the tightening of his skin over his chest and abdomen; he held so much promise, and yet no woman had been drawn to him.

What was it about this man that he had passed beneath the attention of others?

For a moment she almost stopped, wanting to know more about the man she had chosen to spend the evening with. The man she would take into her body, but the beast, the hunger that had forced her into the city in the first place, now demanded that she sate her desires.

She leaned forward, pressing soft kisses along his chest, lapping gently over one flat nipple as he groaned beneath her touch. Reason fled. She knew now that only the desires of her body counted. With the leather binding his wrists and his own passions now invoked, he would no longer fight her touch, or her desires.

She tugged on the edge of his jeans, pulling them down over his hips, leaving them to catch about his ankles, instead of removing his shoes or socks. His shirt lay open, baring his chest to her gaze, and with his eyes closed, she took the moment she needed to strip away her panties and dress. His cock thickened as she watched him, surging into life until it stood upward, away from his body; the head of his thick erection throbbed openly, small beads of desire glistening on the swollen tip.

She leaned down over the bed, brushing her tight nipples over his chest. Heat flushed through her body, coating her inner walls, her clit throbbing as she watched him lying there on the bed. His hips rolling, his body ready for her touch, her sex, anything more that she would be willing to grant him.

"Please." His voice became little more than a whisper, his muscles tight across his shoulders and chest as he turned toward her. "I need -- need to know what it is like to be with you."

"And you shall." With her boots still on, she eased onto the bed, straddling his hips in one easy motion.

"You're still wearing your boots." He whimpered as she settled over him. "Oh, God!"

A wicked smile claimed her lips as she rolled her hips, brushing her naked sex across the tip of his erect cock. For a moment she almost forgot herself. Her core rippled; silken, sweet need coated her inner walls. A moment, that's all it would take, just a moment, and she could slide down onto his erection and bury him deep into her tight, eager body.

Control. She would control it, not be ruled by it. She might have the beast within her, the ability to change into the great, black cat, but she was not owned by it. Emmie closed her eyes, trembling as she took a deep breath, bringing her desires back under control, focusing until she knew it would not force her to act in haste.

He waited. Helpless by both the leather on his wrists and the need to see this through, he didn't even open his eyes as he lay there beneath her, the tip of his cock teasing between her lower, silken, lips. She waited only a moment longer before she slowly eased herself down onto his waiting erection.

Brian arched instantly, thrusting up into her core, his hips shuddering as he rolled beneath her body. She wanted to tell him to be still, but he'd pressed into her so fully that her ability, her desire to yell *cease,* had vanished. Her inner walls tightened on him quickly, claiming him, pulling him farther within her being as she tipped her hips and welcomed him fully.

Lost. She was lost. He needed this, wanted it, and her body answered his need with a hunger of her own. Heat rippled through her body, a pressure she could not deny now built in the pit of her being, she whimpered, hips dancing down on his cock, circling, tipping, only to tighten and press down as he writhed, all but helpless beneath her.

Emmie bit into her bottom lip, fighting to keep silent, to cover the sounds she wanted to make. Just a man, a body, a way to sate the hunger, a man she would leave and forget come the morning. Not a slow, loving time, not a passion that would be remembered through the ages, just a way of sating two hungry bodies.

More. She needed more than the simple act of his body, his cock, buried within her being. She reached down, scratching her nails across his chest, teasing his flat nipples, urging him to move, to rock upward, to press his thick cock deeper into her body. *Yes. Oh, God, yes!*

So close.

"Going to -- oh, please. I have to..."

"Cum for me," Emmie cried out, grinding her hips down against him, taking him, owning him, her body alive, the need controlling her. "Cum for me now!" Just a body to help ease the terrible drive, if only for a day, a night. Just this once, enough to grant her a few hours of sleep.

He screamed, pressing upward, his heels digging into the bedding as he released into her body, never even stopping for a moment to see if she was ready. Young. Hungry. Eager. It didn't matter, that trigger was enough, this once it was enough.

Liquid heat rippled along her inner walls, coating his cock, answering his release with one of her own.

Yes, for now her beast was satisfied.

Tomorrow would be another matter.

"Well, that was easy enough to deal with. I expected him to put up more of a fight, but..."

"And the woman he was with?" Buck frowned slightly as he glanced back at the bar. "She looked a little frightened when you led her away. I thought she was going to scream at one point."

"She calmed down when I showed her the pill Lloyd had been planning to slip her. She's safe now. Back with her friends. Trust me, it's not as if I found a quiet place, shifted, and decided to make her my supper. It was better this way. Human deaths are never easy to explain away. Not these days. Too many decent CSI teams around. Damn, those people have really screwed up some otherwise simple jobs." Theron strapped down his bag on the back of the bike. "Most of them aren't worth the time or effort, Buck. Maybe one day you'll accept that you're rare. That the majority of humanity isn't worth the time, effort, or even thought that my people would spare on a common flea."

"Or you'll accept that there is more to humanity than men like Lloyd and his kind." Buck shook his head as he raked one hand through his hair. "I know you don't have a high opinion of us, but there are times I don't think you have a decent opinion of anything other than your own reflection, Theron."

A rich laugh filled the air as Theron shook his head. "Ah, old friend. I'm not quite that bad. So I don't think much of your people; I'm not overly impressed with most of mine, either. Your kind are a mix; mine appear to be separated out into different types. The wolves are endless romantics, ever looking for their one true mate, yet have no problem with having the occasional lover on the side; they don't even hide that from their mate. The bears, they don't roam around on each other, but stay as family units. Then there are the eagles, hunters, ever looking for the next dream -- shit, my own people, find a willing partner, fuck them senseless, and leave. I don't think I've ever met a feline who has stayed with a partner for more than a few weeks. So tell me, just why would I have a high opinion of myself when I know only too well that I'll fuck the first female in heat who comes along, then move on to the next without ever looking back?"

Buck didn't speak for several long minutes, but when he did, his voice was soft, gentler than he'd ever heard the man speak before. "You hate yourself, then? I'd never thought of it that way. You're a strange one, Theron. I've never met a man like you, shifter or otherwise."

"Hate? No, I just accept what and who I am, nothing more."

"What you need, Theron, is a good woman. One who will rob you of your senses and teach you just what it is like to be in love.

The power, the denial, and the strength it can give you."

He growled, laughing and shaking his head at the same time. "You're wrong. So very wrong. The last thing I need in life is a good woman. I have neither time, nor the energy or inclination to form a lasting relationship with a woman, shifter or otherwise. You'll never understand it, Buck. It's not in my nature to be faithful or even interested in the same piece of female flesh for more than a few days."

Buck smiled, his eyes merry. "Ah, it will happen eventually."

"I doubt it, but for now I have a little hunting of my own to do. And yes, a woman. One in heat. She was in the bar before you called me back to deal with Lloyd." Theron's heart skipped a beat as he thought of the female he had seen and smelled, the desire that had coated her flesh. Ah, poor Buck, he would never be able to understand just what it was to be a feline shifter. The way the pleasures of the body called to him, demanded his attention. It would have appeared to be a form of love to those who did not know his kind. Yet it was little more than lust.

"Another one of your kind in heat?"

"What else would have pulled me from our quarry?"

Buck shrugged as he turned away and headed toward his own waiting car. "Good question. Perhaps one day the answer will be something more to my liking. You're a good man, Theron. No matter how carefully you deny that. And there's a woman out there, waiting for you."

"If there is, I pray we never meet," he called out at him. "I'll see you in a week's time. I'll need a few days rest after I catch up." And she would, no doubt, be glad enough to see the back of him after they had finished their sport.

Chapter Three

Emmie slipped out of the hotel room and closed the door carefully behind her. Brian still slept. The man had served his purpose, and he would sleep long through the night and into the following day by the way his soft snores had followed her out of the room. Only when she had reached the elevator did she breathe a sigh of relief.

She leaned against the metal wall as the doors closed and watched as the numbers changed on the panel. Brian hadn't been such a bad man; he'd been sweet and loving, grateful for the time that she had spent with him, but before he had passed out, he had muttered something about taking her home to meet his parents. He'd asked about dates, their future together, if they would buy a house on the edge of the city.

God.

Had he thought she was in love with him? That taking his virginity meant she wanted to spend the rest of her life with him?

Did people really do things like that?

Poor, sweet boy.

Not that it mattered. She wouldn't see him again. And in time, he'd come to view the evening they had spent together as nothing more than a pleasant memory. Or he'd rant, rave, and call her all the names under the sun. Either way, she wouldn't be there to hear it.

Her body throbbed from the hours she had spent with him, holding him against the bed, riding his cock until she had come again and again. Until his flesh had finally demanded that enough was enough; it could take no more. And now. Now she crept out of his room and his life like a thief in the night.

Heh, if I truly wanted to be a thief, at least I'd make a damn good cat burglar.

At least he hadn't woken up, not even when she'd spent a good twenty minutes in the shower cleaning off the last traces of the time they had spent together.

Emmie wrapped her arms about her body as she walked out of the hotel, quickly covering the short distance to the parking lot where she had left her car. The cramped confines of the city were already beginning to set her nerves on edge. The odd smells, the signs of too many people living in a small area, the low voices, shouts, the sounds of the cars even at this time of night, it was all too much for her. How any shifter could exist in a city was beyond her; did they learn to shut some of it out? If not, why didn't it drive them insane?

She slipped the key into the door lock then stopped, freezing in place.

Something tantalizing teased past her. A musky smell. Strong. Commanding. She turned, searching through the darkness for some sign of the owner. Her body tingled, skin tightened, her senses attuning to the scent even as her mind screamed a warning.

Shifter. Male. Shit, get out now!

Her hands shook as she opened the car door and dropped into the seat. The door locked at the same time that the engine gunned into life. The last thing she needed was a male shifter in her life. Dangerous. They were all dangerous. She couldn't take the chance of being cornered by one.

She was still shaking, even when she pulled out onto the interstate and left the city behind her. If there was one thing she needed to avoid it was contact with male feline shifters. She'd had the warnings drummed into her. Barefoot, pregnant, and abandoned to raise a child alone was not the way she wanted to spend the next couple of years. Not that her mom had regretted giving birth to Emmie, but the older woman had never hidden her resentment of the male shifter who had strolled into her life, turned it upside down, and then walked out again without even a word.

No, she wasn't about to let that happen to her.

Yet she could still smell him. Her body tingled afresh, nipples crinkling into firm, coral points beneath her dress. She groaned, shifting in the seat. She didn't have time for this, or the inclination. It didn't matter what he wanted from her, or even if he had no clue just where she was, she wasn't about to let him anywhere near her.

Drive. She had to keep driving.

Emmie glanced up into the rearview mirror searching for any sign that she was being followed. Whatever he was doing, he could stay the hell away from her. She wasn't going to end up making the same mistake her mom had made. Not if she had anything to do with it.

So, why did her body crave his touch? The touch of a male shifter. One she hadn't even seen. Aftereffects of her time with Brian, that had to be the answer. Nothing else made sense. Not when she knew just how dangerous his kind could be.

She sucked in her bottom lip and tried to focus on her driving, her gaze flickering up to the rearview mirror every thirty seconds. Nothing. No sign of being followed. Just the normal haze of lights that changed with the cars coming on and off the interstate, lights that vanished, or as good as, when she hit the exit for home.

Safe. He wouldn't have followed her out of the city. Realistically, she doubted he'd even been aware of her. Had he even seen her? No, she hadn't spotted him, just caught a touch of his scent. Damn it, all these years and the slightest smell of a male shifter was still enough to send her running for cover like a damn coward.

"Have to get a grip on this. The next one, I don't run from. I'm not going to spend the rest of my life running!"

Theron dismounted from the motorbike, resting his helmet on the seat. Following the car hadn't been easy; he'd barely made it to his bike in time to see her turn off onto the interstate, and then he'd struggled between chasing her down and giving her enough room to feel safe before he'd pulled off at the edge of town. She was here. Somewhere, in the town ahead. He hadn't needed to follow her into the town in order to know that she called this place home; her scent had been strong enough to tell him that. So she lived here, hiding amongst the small spread of humanity. But why?

Why that small town, of what, less than two thousand people? It couldn't offer her what she needed; she'd proven that much by the way she had paid a visit into the city last night. There weren't enough men to sate her needs here. Not without a price she would be unwilling to pay. And regardless of the way her body cried out to be sated, sexually, she would not risk her daily life by tumbling with the wrong man in such a small area.

No, so what kept her here?

Why follow her out of the city to begin with? It wasn't as if he couldn't track down another of their kind if he really wanted to, or find a willing human to sport with. Why go to all this trouble to follow a woman who had fled at the first sign of his existence?

Curious.

Her scent was strong enough that he knew she had been here for a year or more. Even from the outreaches, he could tell this was her home. He didn't even have to walk through the trees to know that much about her. There were other smells here, ones that he knew well, animals for the most part, some humans and another breed of shifters, the wolves, but the smell of the lupine pack was an old one at best.

How often did she step into the trees? More than once a week from the way her aroma lingered in the woods. He inhaled deeply, taking in every trace of her that still remained around the trees. Yes, she was still here, or a part of her was. Which meant, if she followed habit, she would return, and soon.

Moonlight stroked long silver fingers through the trees. Shadows offered hiding places for any shifter to use. He could see why she enjoyed spending time out here, and yes, he was assuming that she relished her time amongst the tall cottonwoods. The air was crisp and clean; the sounds of humanity were muted, little more than a low buzz in the distance even for his sharper hearing.

Tempting. It would be so very easy to shed his human form and run through the trees.

Well, why shouldn't he enjoy them? It was obviously safe for him to do so if she explored them in her feline form often enough that her scent marked this place as hers. With all the stress of work over the past few weeks -- no, months if he was going to be brutally honest about the situation -- he deserved a little time off to run free.

Theron walked farther into the woods until he found a place away from the road, where he would be protected from possible passersby.

Yes, he needed the freedom of the moment. He stripped off his clothing, setting them to one side on a stump, his boots quickly joining the clothing. He stretched, slowly, reaching up toward the sky, fingers curling as his back threatened to crack. He groaned, lowering his heels back to the floor, and summoned the change.

Pain rippled through his body, tearing into each and every nerve ending. He growled, not caring who heard him, or if anyone did; all that mattered was the change, shifting from human to animal.

Fur sprouted out, a thousand pinpricks of pain marking the growth of the dark covering that quickly transformed his body. He growled, teeth lengthening, his eyesight changing, becoming sharper; his sense of smell increased as his nails itched and grew into claws. The change happened so quickly, he couldn't keep track of each individual portion of it, but instead surrendered to the beast that now growled out a warning to the night sky.

She would be here.

And he would be waiting for her. Watching. Ready to see her

again. This time she would not be able to vanish into the darkness or the crowded city. Here he would be able to track her, confront her, and then...

Then what?

Theron's claws curled into the damp earth, his tail snapping quickly through the air. Clean. Crisp. Everything about this place was an anathema to the chemical-ridden city. No wonder she returned here, to the natural energy-charged circle of trees beyond the small town. Power. Natural power. It explained so much about why she chose this area as her home.

But what else was he missing?

He'd find out, soon enough, either before or after he slipped between her sweet thighs. If she didn't try and tear his throat out first. But not now. He didn't have the control he needed in order to face her. Dealing with Lloyd, the way the natural energy rippled through this place, and the power in her silent, pheromone-laden summons, would all combine to push him over the edge.

No. Tomorrow would be soon enough. He knew where she was now...

Chapter Four

"There's nothing wrong with being an alley cat." Emmie yawned and stretched out fully. Her hands clawed at the sky, back arched until she felt her joints pop, sending a delicious shiver through her body. With a lazy smile, she slumped down onto the long, brown couch and propped her feet up, curling her bare toes toward the ceiling. With the bar long behind her and no sign of the male shifter, she could finally relax. Sure, by the time Mags left for work, she'd want to shape shift and run out into the forest, but the urgency to find a male and fuck him senseless had faded into the background. "They come and go as they please. They aren't burdened with ties or commitments and refuse to permit other people's rules to place restrictions on their lives."

"Are you nuts? Of course there's something wrong with the idea of being a damn alley cat. Come on, you can't tell me that you like the idea of hanging around dark places, creeping through the shadows, and scratching a living out in parts of town that most people have the sense to avoid." Mags shook her head, sending a tumble of blonde hair across her shoulders, her blue eyes sparkled, and her full lips quirked in a smile. "I can't understand why you'd encourage them to hang around your yard."

"I wouldn't call it that. All I do is leave them a bit of tuna or chicken from time to time. It's not as if I leave a three-course dinner for them." Emmie flashed a grin and smoothed down her short yellow summer dress against her lithe, tanned legs. "Besides, I kinda like the company."

"So get your own cat instead of feeding any stray that wanders your way. Then you wouldn't have every tomcat in the neighborhood howling on your back step, or fighting for dominance with the others" Mags rolled her eyes.

"That would be too much responsibility for my taste. Once

you have a cat, you're owned by it, and they don't like it when you refuse to pay attention to them. Somehow the idea of cleaning up cat puke just because I refuse to give in to her demands doesn't appeal to me. And they don't fight, not that often, at least. They've learned if they want food from me they behave." Emmie shrugged. "At least this way I can enjoy their company when the mood suits me without tying myself down to one particular cat."

Mags finished off the cup of coffee and set it down on the table before she pushed to her feet. "You're as bad as the cats. You never stick anything out. No job lasts more than a couple of months with you, I've never seen you date the same man twice, and look at this place, you still have things in boxes after being here for two years. A normal human being would have at least unpacked most of the damn boxes by now. But not you; I'm beginning to think you'll have half your things still in boxes ten years from now. Don't you ever want a little bit of stability in your life?"

"Ah, Mags. If you knew me half as well as you think you do, you'd realize this is stable for me. I don't need the work; I just take on jobs when it amuses me." Emmie glanced up at the clock. "And speaking of jobs, if you don't hurry up, then you're going to be late, and I don't think your boss is the understanding sort"

Mags swore and dashed to her feet, grabbing her coat even as she spoke. "Shit, sorry. I lost track. Bill will dock my pay! I'll catch up with you later; call me!" She was out the door before Emmie even had the chance to reply.

Emmie lay there on the couch, her gaze fixed on the now-closed door for several long minutes before she swung her legs off and stood up, smoothing the slip dress down around her thighs People like Mags would never understand just why she chose to live this way, nor could she expect them to understand. But in the small town, Emmie had become known as something of an oddball. Oh, she heard the soft whispers when she walked past the older women who lived in the neighborhood.

Scars

What a waste. A good-looking young woman like that should have a steady man in her life.

Why would she want just one man, when there were so many to choose from? And how she acted tended to freak them out long term. They were used to being the ones who dropped the relationship and moved on, looking for the bigger, better deal. When a woman treated them like that, they didn't know how to handle it. Or, at least, the men she'd known so far hadn't.

Heat rippled through her core as she groaned and struggled to lock it down. There were no others of her kind in the area; if she wanted to sate the hunger that bubbled almost constantly in the pit of her being she would have to find a suitable human to dally with. And that did not appeal to her. Not this time at least.

Damn her blood. Every moon it was the same thing. Halfway through her cycle she'd come into heat and be left dealing with the consequences. She did not dare use one of the local men, not unless she had to, which meant that, either tonight or tomorrow, she would have to head out of town to a different city and find a man there.

There were just too many risks involved if she tried searching for a man closer to home.

Emmie shivered with the memory of her last companion. For a human, he hadn't been that bad. Just the type she preferred. Oh, they'd had fun -- she would be the first to admit that -- but there had still been something missing. She'd scratched a basic itch with the man, but nothing more. They were all the same in that respect, but what else did she expect?

A heart-stopping romance?

Something magical in bed with a stranger?

Passion that would leave her sobbing for his touch?

She didn't know and was quite content, at least for now, to pretend that she didn't care.

How does she pay for everything? She never holds down a job for longer than a few months.

She didn't need to work. She had enough money tucked away to see her through three lifetimes even if she decided to buy a brand-new car every year and wear nothing but designer clothes. But she'd learned not to flaunt it. Doing that would bring too many unwanted questions to her doorstep. Many assumed that when she went away to the cities for a few days each month that she had picked up a temp job there. And that assumption suited her purposes nicely.

Maybe she's one of those women who doesn't like men in that way?

In what way? Perhaps roasted and served on a bed of rice instead of in her bed? She couldn't help but laugh when she heard things like that. Oh, she knew what they really meant, but they couldn't have been more wrong. It wasn't that she didn't appreciate the female form, but they just didn't interest her in the same way men did.

Have you seen the way she walks? It's more like stalking. As if she's hunting something or someone.

Yes, she stalked, prowled, and slinked her way across the town, but what else did they expect? If they only knew the truth. But even if she did tell them, would they ever believe her? No, they'd call for a doctor and try to have her locked away in a padded cell for the rest of her life. There were times *she* barely accepted the truth, and she'd lived with it for as long as she could remember.

It was the same reason she welcomed the stray cats into her backyard and went as far as leaving food out for them.

She was one of them.

Emmie flicked the curtain away from the window for a heartbeat, checking outside. Nothing. Mags had dashed off to work in one of the local bars, and the rest of the neighborhood had given itself up to the night. Small patches of light from windows were the only sign that people actually lived in this quiet part of town, but the majority of her neighbors were elderly and were seldom out after nine.

Scars

It might have annoyed or even depressed another of her age range, but the peace and quiet suited Emmie nicely. And on nights like this, it meant she could slip out into her backyard to change before she began her nightly prowl of the town and the surrounding countryside. She turned and walked through her house, opening the back door so she could stand on the step and drink in the night.

The clean, crisp air carried with it the comforting smells and sounds of the town. She closed her eyes, taking it all in. A scent, one that would have set her teeth on edge if it had been fresh, one of a large cat, a shifter, drifted in on the evening breeze. But it could have been carried in several miles, and she shrugged the barely there smell off as something not to be concerned about. Not when there were other things going on far closer to home.

She turned her head, searching through the other noises and smells, tracing the evening's activity through her nose and ears. There, the noise from the bar half a mile away, the smell of a raccoon that had been foraging in her garbage can. Raised voices split the night as Aneta's drunken grandson from four houses away began to shout. Any plans to visit the city vanished as she listened to the argument. Would their fights ever end? Yes, and soon, if Emmie didn't do something about it.

Her jaw clenched as she focused on the two humans.

His anger, her fear -- the two combined, setting her teeth on edge, the hair on the back of her neck standing up. Her fingers curled, nails aching with the need to shift into claws.

Jamie. She could picture him now with his lank hair, dirty skin, and he would smell as though he hadn't bathed in a week. Yes, that was Jamie.

He needed to be taught a lesson before he did something more to Aneta than simply shout at her. The woman had to be in her eighties, and as far as Emmie knew, had done everything possible in order to keep her only living relative on the straight and narrow. But there were some souls that were born bad, at least as far as Emmie was concerned, and Jamie was one of them. Was he alone, or was David with him this time. She turned into the breeze, inhaling deeply. Nothing more than Aneta and Jamie. Good. That would make the situation easier to deal with.

Glass shattered, the sound sharp and dangerous. A scream rang out as she turned toward the source of the sound. Her skin itched. She needed to shed this form. Now.

Emmie closed her eyes and called for the beast that lurked within the shadows of her soul. The cat answered. Pain rippled across her body as she tore her clothing free, shedding the dress and panties moments before black fur pushed through her skin. She hissed, arching her back, nails shifting into claws, hands becoming paws, her senses changing as she surrendered to her feline nature.

She wanted to howl, to warn him she was coming, that those who took out their drunken rage on little old ladies in her town would pay the price, but she had to be careful. If she wanted to continue to protect the town, then being caught by a trapper or an overexcited hunter wasn't on her list of things to be done.

Emmie stretched out, flexing her claws out along the ground, her tail snapping back and forth inches above the earth. She sprang over the fence, her claws eating up the distance between her home and Aneta's.

"Just gimme the gawddamn money, woman! Now! He's waiting for me. You know that. He doesn't like to be kept waiting."

"Get out of my house, Jamie. Before I call the cops." Aneta's voice shook. "I don't care what you and David have planned. I'm not helping you out. Not this time. I want you out of my house and out of my life."

David. Emmie frowned, shit. That was the real problem behind Jamie; the one who silently pushed his drunken friend into foolish choices. He was sober, most of the time, unlike Jamie. But that only made him more dangerous. So whatever the idiot had planned, whatever the reason for hounding the woman who had protected him all these years, it had to do with David. He was a man who had tried to stick his fingers into every small, twisted deal within fifty miles of town. One of these days, Emmie knew she would have to deal with the problems that David had caused in the small town.

"Right, like you're gonna call those pigs on me? Even if you did, you'll not follow through. You'll not press charges, not against me. Who else have ya got? Some buddies down at the coffee shop? Stupid old bitches just like you. I could knock you down, and no one would even find you for a couple of days!" His words slurred in all the right places. Emmie eased her way around the edge of the house, blinking in the darkness. The smell hit her before she saw him. Alcohol. Raw and powerful. The local moonshine or a cheap knockoff whiskey; either way, it had left him mean and angry.

He stood just outside the back door; whatever had happened inside of the house, either Aneta had managed to get him outside, or he'd stumbled out there on his own. Good. That would make it easier.

"Get off my property, Jamie. And don't come back until you're sober and ready to apologize." Aneta's voice came from inside the house, a harsh double click ringing through the night. Heartache rang through every word the older woman uttered. "I don't want to have to use this, but I will. If you try to get back in, I'll shoot. You got that, boy?"

A shotgun?

Would Aneta use it?

If she did, it would solve one problem, but leave another in its place. Emmie doubted the older woman would ever forgive herself for pulling the trigger on her grandson.

"You're not scaring me, bitch!" Jamie hissed. "Try pulling that stunt on someone who doesn't know you. You don't have the guts to pull the trigger. You're too fucking weak! Don't make me bring David here! He won't have any patience with ya!"

"If he steps foot on my property, I'll shoot him. He's not welcome here, and it would be better for your friend if you made that perfectly clear." The older woman took a deep breath, her voice trembling slightly. "You never really knew me, Jamie, or you'd realize just what I am willing to do to protect me and mine. I don't understand you anymore. I raised you with better manners than this. I don't know what happened to the sweet boy I held in my arms."

"That little boy doesn't exist anymore. He grew up, became a man -- do you understand me?" Jamie stumbled forward, placing one foot on the back step. "He realized backing down to a frail, old bitch was a kid's way, not how a man acts. I'm not that stupid kid anymore. I'm not going to let you stand in my way."

Bastard. Everyone in town knew that Aneta had raised him. She'd given him a home when no one else would; he should have been treating the older woman with respect and care, not trying to bully her or frighten her. He didn't deserve to breathe the same air as the older woman. Her claws itched to bury themselves deep into the man's neck; she could almost taste his blood running down her throat and -- no. Emmie took a deep breath, focusing past the animal rage and hunger that threatened to take control. She wouldn't give in to the feral part of her nature; she ruled here, not the beast.

Human shifter, not enraged animal. Slowly the rage, the dark, bloodthirsty side of her being, accepted the reins of control from the human half of her soul.

Now. If she was going to do something, it had to be now. Emmie crouched down, her back legs tensing, tail snapping out across the ground in angry figure eights. Jamie tensed; from within the house, she heard Aneta take a step backward, and that was her signal to move.

Emmie launched herself through the darkness, across the back step, her front paws striking Jamie in the side. Hard enough to send them both to the ground. She darted away from his sprawled figure, turning quickly, reluctant to take her eyes off the downed man for more than a heartbeat.

He screamed, his eyes wide and wild as he rolled onto his back and stared directly into Emmie's face. He scrambled back, waving one hand in front of his face, trying to ward her off. "Shoo! G-get out of here! I'll hunt you down and pin your fuckin' hide to the wall!"

Emmie smiled and bared her teeth as she growled in the back of her throat, enjoying the sight of the brash man turning a deathly white. Good. He needed to be afraid after everything he had done to the old woman. What would he do if she closed her teeth on his throat?

"Gran'ma! God. Please, help me. There's something out here! Shoot it!"

"Help yourself! You're so drunk you can't even stand up straight. Why should I help you anymore?"

"No, there's something out here. Shit. Please. You gotta..."

"I don't have to do anything. You made your bed, lie in it. I'm done being pushed around by you. Get the hell off my property before the cops get here."

The back door slammed shut. A bolt locked into place. Aneta's panic-filled voice reached her ears. A phone call. Good. To the cops, by the sound of it, just as she had threatened, which meant Mike or one of his deputies would be on their way to collect the drunken Jamie within minutes; that was one of the beauties of living in a small town.

She had two minutes, maybe three, but that would still be enough time to put the fear of the cat into the quivering wreck of humanity before her. Emmie snarled, taking a step forward until she was close enough to touch him.

"D-don't!" He backed up, his shoulders hitting the chain-link fence. "God. Please. Just leave me alone! I've not done anything to you!"

Emmie rested one paw on the man's groin, extending her

claws slowly until the tips rested over his flaccid, jean-covered cock. It would have been so easy to roll him around the ground, bat him from one side of the yard to the other as a living toy, but this would work just as well. Terror flashed across the man's face, his lips moving, but the only sounds that reached her ears now were wordless whimpers. She shifted her weight, pressing down onto his cock just enough that her claws threatened to dig into his jeans.

The smell hit her instantly. Hot liquid soaked through his jeans, and she smirked, turning on her back paws before she bounded over the fence and vanished into the night. She darted out toward the trees, well away from the town in case someone spotted her tracks in the yard. Not that anyone with half a mind would believe the ravings of a drunken bully like Jamie, but better to play it safe than take even a small risk of leading someone back to her home.

It wasn't until she felt herself safe within the edge of the trees that Emmie finally stopped and turned, looking back at the town. Despite the lack of clothing, she shifted back into human form, keeping a wary eye out for any signs of someone following her into the wilds. The shift back into human form hurt, but nowhere near the waves of pain the transformation from human into panther did.

How would Jamie explain what he had seen? The idea of a panther patrolling the local area would be laughed at, especially with the lack of larger kills that they would associate with a big cat. Still, it paid to be careful and watch for any signs of hunters following her out from the edge of the town.

Nothing. Good. For now she remained safe. Not even the old scent she had caught on her back step of a shifter. Here she was safe. She'd remain safe. People like Jamie would never stop to think that the cat might also be a neighbor.

He lacked the imagination to see past the mundane and into the world of magic, shifters, and vampires that might exist along side of him.

Scars

She smiled, remembering the look on Jamie's face. Priceless. If that didn't keep him from bullying Aneta, then nothing would. Would he go back to his friend and try to convince him what he had seen? God, she would love to be a fly on the wall for that little meeting. No one, not even a shrink, would buy the story of a large cat playing tease the prey with a grown man. Not when there wasn't even a mark on him. Knowing Jamie, he'd keep silent rather than risk being laughed at.

She rolled out her shoulders and took a step farther back into the tree line.

"Now that is indeed a welcoming sight. Though not one I thought to see out here." A man's voice broke through the soft sounds of the forest, humor touching his rich timbre -- and something else as well. Something she had seldom heard directed at her. Lust.

Chapter Five

The hairs on the back of her neck stood up as she turned, quickly bringing both hands across her body in a show of human modesty. How in hell's name had anyone managed to creep up on her? Let alone a human male. A handsome, hungry, and completely naked human male standing in front of her. His grey green eyes sparkled as he folded his arms across his chest, making no attempt to hide himself from her gaze.

"See something you like?"

"No." Cocky too. Her jaw clenched as she shook her dark hair over her breasts. Damn him. He didn't even try to cover the fact he was shamelessly looking at her, taking in every inch of her nude form. Her breasts tingled, nipples crinkling into firm coral points, an unwanted warmth spread through her sex beneath the caress of his gaze. He had no right to look at her as if she were dinner and he a man who had not eaten in a week or longer. "What are you doing here?"

"A pity, then, and I could ask you the same thing as to what you are doing here" -- his full lips twitched into a sensual smile, the words purring from his lips -- "had I not seen just how you made your way here. I didn't know there was another shifter in the area. Normally I can pick up their scent, but not you. You're good -- well, most of the time, at least. Being caught like this, though, that's a cub's mistake. Careless."

"I'm no cub."

"I can see that." A wicked light glinted in his eyes. "And smell it. You're definitely full-grown in all respects."

She blinked, staring at him before it hit her. A smell she had so recently been introduced to. *Shit. How had he -- another shifter?* How had she missed the warning smell of his approach? Simple, she had traveled downwind, away from town, and now that had played against her. She knew this smell, not just as another shifter, but the one from the city. *Fuck.* He'd followed her here; that was the only explanation.

God. What was she supposed to do now?

Run!

No. That wasn't an option. She'd promised herself the very next time she faced off against a male shifter, she'd not run. She had to face the fear, meet it head-on, and then -- there would never be a reason to run from a male shifter again.

She stared at him, taking in his form and lack of clothing. At least being a shifter would explain why he stood there as naked as the day he came into the world. She swallowed hard, trying not to let his presence affect her, but there was something tempting about him. Taut muscles lay ribbed in a firm six-pack across his abdomen, moonlight played through the cover of the trees and glistened across his hairless chest, which narrowed into a lithe waist and long legs. And between them, oh, God, between them, something else beckoned her attention. Thick, heavy, and semihard, his cock rested between his legs, exposed to her gaze. "So you're like me, a shifter?"

"Yes." He took a step closer across the small clearing. A smug, knowing smile flashed across his lips. "I am, both in color and species. And from the smell of you, you're alone. No mate? Interesting. I would have thought a prime female like you would have been claimed long ago."

"There's no other shifter in the area that I know of; you're the first I've seen in over five years. That's if you are what you claim to be." Mate? What would she want with a mate? And claimed. Oh, no, that was not how she worked. The last thing she was going to permit was some male laying claim to her. "And you knew I didn't have a mate. Very few females of our kind have a mate. The males don't look for that. You fuck and go. That's how it is. That's how it's always been. You'd have known if I had anyone; besides, you followed me from the city. Don't deny it."

"True enough there. You wouldn't have been searching the bars for a playmate if you had a true mate at home." He gave a slight shrug. "Yes, I am like you, in all ways except one." He took a step forward, the moonlight playing over his taut form. "And right now, it's that one difference I'm interested in. You're in heat."

"And your point would be?" Every instinct screamed at her to take a step back, but this was her territory. "You saw me in the city. You know why I was there. What makes you think I need you at all?"

"Because you're still in heat. A female in heat needs a male, and as you've said, there are no other shifters around."

"If I need a male, I'll find a human. At least they don't try and do stupid things like claim me." She growled out the words, though her body had other ideas. Her nipples tingled, heat rippled across her inner walls. Her skin tightened across her body as if it had become one size too small for her body. She rolled back her shoulders, lifting her breasts up as she dropped her hands to her sides and shifted her weight, parting her legs softly. What was going on? She had never reacted this way to a male before. And she wanted nothing to do with him, no matter what her body thought.

"What? You'd pick a human over one of your kind?" He frowned, confusion flashing across his intense gaze, his cock thickening against his thigh.

"At least a human male normally tells me their name before they announce that they want to jump my bones."

"Theron."

"What?"

"My name is Theron Grave" He flashed a grin and offered a mocking, sweeping bow. "Are you going to return the favor and bless me with your name, gracious one?"

"Emmie Byron, and if you keep that nonsense up, you'll remember me as the woman who tore your nuts off and made them into a necklace." She bared her teeth at him, fingers flexing, her nails itching with the need to shift into claws. Serve him right if she did attack him. Maybe then he would think twice before assuming he was irresistible, though she doubted it.

"Ah, so I stumbled on a little hellcat who needs taming?" Theron took another step forward. "Good. I'm in the mood for a little rough-and-tumble."

Bastard!

"Taming?" She wanted to smack him into the middle of next week. What kind of name was Theron, anyway? Not American. It almost sounded Greek. Her gaze narrowed on him. With his dark hair and the shape of his nose, he might have almost passed for someone from the Mediterranean, but his eyes? They reminded her of something else. The sea? No, a storm-tossed sky; his eyes were almost the same color as the clouds before a tornado launched its devastation across the land.

Wild and dangerous, someone she would be better staying the hell away from. Except that would mean running away and she'd promised herself that wasn't going to happen again. She had to face him, face this fear, before it grew out of control.

"Yes, you need taming. You need bringing back into line, and that will take time spent with the right male. If only a very short time." The tip of his tongue slipped out from between his lips, tracing a slow line over his bottom lip. "You can't deny what you're feeling right now. I can see the heat playing through your body, taste it on the air. You're creaming. Just standing there, looking at me, your body is preparing itself for me."

She opened her mouth to protest, only to shut it again. Her body did feel warm. Her nipples ached for his touch; her inner walls rippled with the need to clench down on a cock. No. Not just *a* cock. His cock. Emmie shifted her weight and took a half step back from him. "I'm a grown woman, not some cub. I know what my body is doing. But it doesn't mean that I'm about to give in to its demands. I'm not some teenager on her first cycle -- you're not going to..."

"To what?" Theron advanced on her, closing the gap between them, grasping her upper arms. "To do this?" He leaned closer, claiming her lips fully.

Emmie groaned, her lips parting beneath his touch. His tongue slid into her mouth, stroking within. She tensed, instinct screaming at her to move away, to break the kiss, but her body had other ideas. She arched under his kiss, her tongue dancing with his; every inch of her body screamed at her to press closer to him, to be with him no matter what. But she knew the danger.

A male shifter. Arrogant, forceful, they wanted to take control of the women they were with. Emmie did not want that. She had spent her life being independent. Hunting. Killing only when she needed to. Finding ways to keep the beast under control. The animal instincts that had pushed at her control throughout her life. Yet, she had beaten them back, built levels of self-control in place. She had refused to let them destroy her. Now. Now all of that vanished under the pleasure of his kiss.

Spasms of hunger and need played a wicked path through her body as she surrendered to his kiss. Tingles of delight shimmered along her belly, they teased across her breasts, even across her buttocks, and still she wanted more. She groaned, closing her eyes as she felt his grip ease on her arms.

She reached up, wrapping her arms about his neck, her tongue dancing with his. Emmie pushed up onto her toes, her nipples scraping against his chest. A low moan of pleasure slipped free of their joined lips, his cock hardening further, throbbing against her legs. All it would have taken was one push, and she would have been on her back, thighs parted, hips lifted, waiting for him to thrust into her hungry core.

It would be so easy to surrender to her desires and welcome his touch. Even his scent spoke of lust, begging her to stay within his arms for a moment longer.

Reason screamed a warning in the back of her mind.

Her jaw clenched as she yanked her hands down from his neck

and thrust herself out of his grasp. "Get away from me!"

"You didn't seem to have a problem a moment ago, sweet one." He purred, but this time he didn't follow her across the clearing.

Her gaze lingered on his mouth, her lips tingling at the memory of his touch. Had they really just kissed, or had it been something more? "Well, let's just say I've seen the light."

"Given into your fear would be more honest." Theron let his gaze openly move back over her exposed breasts. "Why are you so afraid of being with one of your own kind?"

"I'm not." Her hands clenched into fists at her sides, shoulders tightening.

"Ah, and you like lying to yourself as well. Interesting."

"I'm not..."

"Emmie, lie to yourself all you want. But I can tell when a woman is interested in me. I can smell you, taste your desire on the air, and I'm not just going to walk away from a female shifter in heat, especially when she's buck naked and standing right in front of me."

Chapter Six

Heat flushed across her face and down her body as she brought her hands in front of her breasts and mound. Why was she suddenly ashamed of being nude? Because he was right.

Damn him!

Why was she so afraid of him? Nothing could happen between them unless she permitted it. From what her mother had told her, rape was unheard of amongst shifters, but that didn't stop a male shifter from trying to push things. Arrogant. They were all like this, from what she had been told and the rare few she could recall meeting.

Confident. Arrogant. Overbearing. The type of man who would always claim he knew best when it came to women, be they human or female shifters. If he thought a woman wanted them, he'd chase her down until she finally gave in to him, or knocked him off the face of the planet.

"If you take one more step toward me, then I'll..."

"Fight me? Good. I prefer a good scrap before I part a woman's thighs. You know how it works with our kind; are you willing to take that risk? If not, then shift and leave this place. I won't come after you. I've no need to try and take an unwilling woman like some human on a drinking binge. So make up your mind. Are you willing to risk losing the fight to me and then surrendering to my touch?" A feral grin claimed his lips, a dark, hungry light dancing within his storm-claimed eyes.

"You think I'm going to lose."

"Of course." That smug grin was the final straw.

Lose a fight? To this stuck-up pain in the ass? Not a chance in hell. "Yeah, I'm ready." Her words were little more than a low growl.

"Human form, cat, or halfway?" He stepped back, making sure

there was enough room between them so that neither could have an unfair advantage at the start of the fight.

Emmie faltered for a minute. She hadn't even thought that far. Human form, he'd win, hands down. Cat, and if she lost he'd take her in that form. Not something she wanted to experience. Halfway, she would have the advantage, strength, speed, and agility. "Halfway."

"I thought you'd say that."

Emmie bit back a snarl. Oh, she was going to enjoy bringing this one down to size. No wonder her mother told her to stay away from the males of their kind, if he was an example of how they behaved. A dozen retorts tried to break free, but she clamped her lips tight, keeping them locked away behind her gritted teeth.

"Are you going to shift, or just stand there, growling at the dirt?"

Arrogant son of a bitch!

Emmie closed her eyes and focused on the feline energy within. Slow. This had to be done slowly, or she would move fully into cat form and that would never do. *Nails first.* Pain lanced through her fingers as they lengthened, nails becoming claws. Fur peeked out of her skin, along her arms, and over her shoulders, itching at first, prickling into small, needlelike bursts of agony across her flesh A scant covering, but it was still enough to hide her body partially from his view. Her muscles changed shape under her tight skin, a strength in her legs and arms that she had rarely experienced before, her sense of hearing and smell increased tenfold. *Almost done.* God, it hurt though. Hurt more than a normal shift into full feline form. Her weight shifted onto the balls of her feet, her nails there now claws as well, as she focused the last of her change on her teeth.

Her incisors grew, teeth shifting in her mouth; fire danced across the bridge of her mouth until, at last, she felt the change flare through her tailbone, forcing the long, black-furred tail into life, and the shift came to its dramatic end.

Emmie opened her eyes and focused on Theron. Like her, he had changed into that dangerous cross between beast and man. Her breath caught in the back of her throat as she looked over every inch of his well-formed body. As a human, he had been beautiful, but as a shifter, he was magnificent. He stood easily five inches taller than she did, and black fur coated both his body and tail. He parted his lips, baring his changed teeth in a low, eager growl.

"Are you sure you wissssh to go through thisss?" His changed teeth made it hard to speak clearly, but she had understood him clearly enough.

"Yesss." She nodded, licking the tip of her tongue across one lengthened incisor. Now she could understand just how difficult it was to speak in this form, but she had managed it for the single word she had needed to utter.

"Good." He nodded, shifting his weight over the balls of his feet.

Her gaze narrowed, hands flexing, her claws itching to strike out. She'd show him. It wouldn't take long, either. He'd learn that she was not the sort of female to back down to some cocky bastard just because he walked into her hunting grounds.

He launched at her without warning, his shoulder aimed toward her stomach, but she was ready for him. With a low snarl, she darted left, rolling on the ground before she came back up onto her feet, turning to face him, her claws extended fully. It had been a low trick to try and pull; had he expected her to be taken down like an inexperienced cub?

Well, he would learn.

When he moved again, she lashed out with her left paw, her nails raking a dangerous path across his right shoulder and chest, her low growl filling the air. Blood beaded across his chest in five narrow furrows, his gaze narrowing, anger and pain flashing through his eyes, and she didn't bother to hide the smirk that now claimed her lips.

Scars

There. Maybe he would accept she was not the type of female to be pushed around and...

Theron turned swiftly, kicking out at her legs, swiping them out from under her. Emmie howled in shock and rolled, coming back up to her feet in a flash, her tail snapping out through the air. He reached for her, trying to yank her down to the ground, but she twisted out of his grasp and punched out toward his gut. If he could use human tactics in a fight, then so could she.

He backed away, rubbing at his stomach, his gaze narrowed fully.

Was she seeing things or had he nodded an approval at what she had done?

Theron took a step to the right, then another, shifting his weight. What did he think he was going to do? Emmie watched, keeping the distance between them, unwilling to let him get too close right now.

When he launched at her afresh, she couldn't move fast enough to avoid him. In a heartbeat, they were both on the floor, scrabbling for control. For a moment she gained the upper hand, her teeth scant inches from his neck as she tried to bite down into his flesh, then he shifted his weight, sending them both rolling over the ground.

Emmie struggled for control, but she was barely able to keep track of what was going on. She kicked out, raking her hind claws over his legs, only to then howl in pain when she felt his teeth sink into her right shoulder. She struggled under him, barely aware of the ground beneath her back. Fire lanced through her shoulder and down into her belly. She bucked, wriggling under him, desperate to throw him off, but his grip in her shoulder made it near impossible.

His cock brushed against her belly, thick, hard, and erect. Despite the pain and the fear that now threatened to gnaw its way into her belly, she couldn't ignore the erotic connection that was forming between them. The beast in her wanted this man, this male shifter; it needed him in a way she had never craved another living soul before.

This wasn't happening to her. It couldn't be. She didn't react to men like this. Especially not to one who had hurt her!

Heat rippled through her core, coating her inner walls, her breasts tingling beneath the thin coating of fur. Her nipples hardened, her breath burning in her lungs, and her instincts were now torn between fighting him and fucking him senseless.

She reached out, trying to claw at his face, but he caught both of her hands and pinned them to the ground, holding her there. His teeth released their grip on her shoulder, his gaze feral, blood coating his lips. Her blood. Helpless, she stared up at him, her lips parting in a soft protest, but there was nothing she could do.

"Yield," he growled above her.

No! Her pride screamed out in the back of her mind. She couldn't just surrender to him. It wasn't right. She'd never be able to live it down. Yet her body wanted him. Needed him. She was almost lost in the craving to feel his cock buried between her thighs, his balls slapping against her ass until she screamed out in delight. Moisture coated her entrance, her body shivered, her nipples throbbed, and still she couldn't bring herself to say the word.

"Do you yield, or mussst I bite again?" He snapped his teeth near her throat, his warm breath caressing her body.

Would he go that far? She tried to twist beneath him and felt his teeth close on her throat, but not bite down. The threat was all too clear. She froze, pressing herself back against the damp ground, her heart pounding so loudly in her chest that she knew he could hear it, or at least, feel her rapid pulse beneath his lips.

"Yield." She growled out the single word.

His rough tongue traced over her throat before he pulled back, a self-satisfied smirk claiming his lips. "Change. Human form. Now."

She bit back a dozen complaints and closed her eyes. He had

won. He had the right to demand she shift back out of this form, though his command had caught her off guard. She had been convinced he would not be able to wait if he won, and now he had proved her wrong. Again.

It hurt to shift back, but never quite as much as it did to assume nonhuman form. Still, her body answered sluggishly this time, reluctant to give up the strength she felt. But as she returned to human form, so did he.

Emmie frowned as she lay there, under him. Why had she taken the challenge of the fight? She hadn't known him. There was no way she could have known just what sort of fighting skills he had. Yet, she had charged into the fight like a cub, not stopping to think of the consequences fully.

And now she would pay the price.

Pheromones. It had to be those damn feline pheromones. Nothing else made sense. She just didn't take chances like this with males. *Men. Whatever!* There was something seriously wrong when she started thinking about Theron as a man, not a male shifter.

"You lost." Theron smiled. "Are you ready to pay the price?"

Her hips twitched, lifting up toward him, her body hungry for his touch. But her pride prevented her from speaking out. No, she would not give him the satisfaction of letting him know just how badly she wanted him. He was smug enough as it was.

"I see. Well, then, I make you this promise, stubborn Emmie. By the end of our time together, you will be crying out my name in delight."

"Like hell I will."

Theron just grinned.

Chapter Seven

Theron leaned down and nipped carefully at her throat, tracing the tip of his tongue over her pulse. Her heart skipped a beat, her eyes drifting closed under the light, sensual touch until she realized what she was doing and growled, her jaw clenching tight. Emmie tried to move, but he still had her wrists captured in his hands and held her against the ground. Anger flared through her being, then settled in her heart, simmering away.

He has no right!

But he did; she had given it to him. She had agreed to the fight and had accepted the consequences of losing. Now she had to pay the price. But it did not mean she had to pretend to enjoy it. No, she wasn't about to feed his ego and turn into a squirming, sex-starved female ready to do anything he wanted. No matter what desires now flooded through her body, she would remain in control of herself.

Like most males, he would be satisfied with her body, take what he wanted, and leave. They never stayed around. It wasn't in the nature of male shifters to linger after they had taken what they wanted. She had seen it with the alley cats. They screwed and then parted company. That would be the end of the matter, and unlike the smaller felines, she would not be left dealing with a baby at the end of it. She would not be left in the same position as her mother, to raise a child alone because of a wandering male shifter!

"You're so angry at the world, not just at me." Theron nibbled slowly on her throat. "Forget it. Just for now at least. Forget whatever has made you so angry at everything around you. Enjoy my touch. You want it. Your body craves it. So why fight it?"

Because she wasn't going to give some jumped-up tomcat the pleasure of making her think she actually wanted to be with him.

Scars

He was nothing more than a wandering male who wouldn't stay around, and she was determined not to let his touch affect her.

"Stubborn female." He scraped his teeth over her throat. "It's not going to work; you will eventually give me what we both want."

Yes, it would work and -- and what did he mean by "both want"? She didn't want him. She hated males like this one. Always on the prowl for a female in heat and never willing to take on the responsibility of what that time together might produce. Well, she wasn't about to end up pregnant by a damn prowling tomcat.

No, there were ways around that. And one of them had been implanted in her arm several months ago. So far, it had worked quite nicely. After all of her dalliances with human males, she had never shown a sign of becoming pregnant. She had even taken care to use a condom so the chances of her catching anything from her sport partners had been reduced.

He chuckled and shifted a little, easing down her body as he brought her arms down to rest at her sides, pinning them there. He nibbled slowly over the curves of her breasts. Jolts of pleasure surged into her nipples as she fought to stay still beneath him. Emmie closed her eyes, focusing within instead of what he was doing to her body. He wasn't there. He didn't exist. There was nothing he could do to her that would have any real effect on her.

Sooner or later he would come to realize that she was not going to react to his touch and -- oh!

He closed his lips around one ripe tip, suckling it into his mouth, his tongue flickering across the tight bud. A soft, undeniable rocking worked through her hips at his touch. Yet she could not deny the heat that continued to grow in her core, or the way her inner walls rippled in delight at his touch. She swallowed hard and clenched her fists, driving her nails into her palms. She didn't want to feel, to react to him; it wasn't right that Theron could trigger any form of pleasurable response from her body.

That didn't seem to matter to anyone other than the small

voice in the back of her mind. Heat spread slowly over her belly and between her thighs. Her sex throbbed, lower lips swelling with a slick, coated desire that she had no control over. Emmie inhaled deeply, tasting him on the air, his musk, her arousal; the two smells combined, threatening to wash away all other aromas in the small clearing.

The tips of his teeth scraped across her nipple as Theron pulled back from her coral tip. He let go of her hands and pressed his against the ground, his gaze meeting hers, his voice throaty. "Don't move unless I tell you to."

An order, with no room for disagreement. Fury bubbled into life as she stared into his eyes, then subsided. Like it or not, he had the right to do this. It was part of the price paid for losing the fight. One she would follow through with and then dismiss him and their time together from her mind once and for all.

So why did her body have other ideas?

Weak. She had become weak. His musk, the smell of his need that now coated his flesh and teased her desires higher with each passing moment. Yes. That had to be the cause. Nothing else. She had permitted the beast to rule her, instead of retaining human control over her body.

Theron edged slowly down her body until his head disappeared between her thighs. She growled under her breath, not wanting to react to him, but the soft sound carried out across the clearing. She tried not to notice the way his breath played across her mound, over her lower lips, or how it teased her delicate flesh.

Whatever he had planned, she would not let it affect her. What did he think he was doing down there, anyway? Staring at her? Looking for some sign that she was imperfect?

When he pushed her thighs farther apart and slowly nuzzled his way between them, she all but arched up from the ground.

"What --?"

"Lie down." He reached up and pressed his hands down

against her hips, holding her to the ground. Those two words rolled over her sex, her clit throbbed, and she bit down on her bottom lip, trying to regain control of her senses. She'd heard about men who were willing to do things like this, but had never met one who had been willing to do it.

Innocent and I'm letting him use it against me!

No, she wasn't innocent, just unlucky in her choice of lovers. Something she would be more careful about in future.

Theron purred against her sex, sending wave after wave of wicked vibrations through her core. Her inner walls clenched, spasms taking their toll on her being, until she pressed her heels into the ground. She groaned, fighting against the delight that he inflicted on her body. Why couldn't he just take what he wanted and leave; why did he have to torment her so?

And why was she fighting it?

Because -- because I have to.

No. She didn't.

His lips fastened around her clit, his tongue flickering over the trapped bud of heated flesh. Her jaw clenched, she struggled not to make a sound, to try and keep the signs of her arousal to a minimum, but she lacked the strength to fight what was happening to her. A low ripple of sheer delight washed through her body, crumbling any resistance that stood in its path. A low moan slipped from her lips, her hips lifted upward, buttocks tight as she writhed on the ground beneath his intimate caress.

Theron pressed one finger between her slick lower lips, parting them with a gentle touch. He lapped at her clit, suckling it carefully between his lips. Each touch threatened to send her higher as a delicious pressure built slowly within her body. He growled into her body even as he slipped his finger fully into her throbbing core.

Her heated walls clenched on his finger, her body hungry for more. Emmie shook her head, trapped by the waves of desire that now claimed her body. Pressure -- sweet, painful, delicious pressure -- washed a dangerous path through her body as he slowly worked his finger in and out of her sex.

Just when she thought he couldn't push her any further into the maelstrom of sensations that threatened to take control of her body, he found a way. The tip of his finger brushed against something hidden deep within her cream-coated core. Her inner walls tightened, her eyes snapped open wide, lips parting in a soft O. Just what was he doing to her? No one had ever touched her like that before, and she wasn't sure she liked it.

No, that wasn't true. She loved it, but fear niggled at the back of her mind. Each soft brush deep within her slick sex forced a new wave of pleasure-filled pressure through her body. She couldn't control what was happening to her; she felt wetter than she ever had before; her hips rolled in a wild dance; her breath burned in her lungs; and still he didn't stop.

His finger brushed deep within her body; his lips remained locked around her clit, his tongue stroking, teasing her higher with each passing minute. She groaned; thighs tight, heels digging into the ground, her hips lifted up for his intimate caress.

Emmie struggled to make sense of what was happening to her body, but her ability to think, to reason, fled under the onslaught of sensations that he subjected her to. Her skin tingled, small stabs of pain and ecstasy shot through her sex; with each touch to that tiny spot within, she sobbed out, afraid the dam would burst and leave her devoid of the shuddering bliss she now enjoyed.

She no longer cared what he thought of her.

Or what he wanted.

All that mattered was this moment and the pleasure that now controlled her body.

Then it was gone. Theron slipped his finger free of her core and pushed up onto his hands as he moved further along her body before he stared down into her hazy eyes. The tip of his cock teased over her swollen labia, tempting them apart, his voice a low growl. "You're mine."

His?

Theron thrust into her tight, wet sex, claiming her to the hilt. He growled, his gaze narrow, his hands pressed down into the dirt on either side of her head. He rolled his hips, stroking her deep within. She arched, reaching out for him, her nails digging into his arms.

Sweat beaded over her breasts. Her thighs tightened about his hips as she lifted her heels up and pressed them against his ass. Emmie whimpered; she couldn't take much more of this. Her body was no longer her own. Her nails bit fully into his arms, blood trickling down from the small wounds; her tight core rippled on his thick erection as he drove into her body, claiming it time and again, until she barely knew where he ended and she began.

Each thrust pushed her closer to the edge. Her body danced to a tune of passion and need that rocked through her being. Her jaw clenched, her hips rolled, slick heat coated her inner thighs as she felt herself being pushed toward the edge of sanity.

Now. She had to come now.

Theron stopped.

Her body ached as she opened her eyes fully and stared at him. Why wasn't he moving? She writhed under him, trying to get him to move again, but he didn't. Instead, he smiled down at her, watching every move she made.

"Wha-what are you doing?"

"Waiting."

"For what?" She swallowed hard, her inner walls shocked by soft spasms. She had to get him to move, to do something. If he stayed still much longer, she'd go insane.

"For you to beg me to fuck you." He leaned down, taking care not to move his hips, and pressed a gentle kiss against her lips.

Her lips parted beneath his kiss before his words fully registered. Emmie pulled back from his kiss, a growl forming at the back of her throat, only to falter and die. Her slick walls tightened about his cock; the hunger she felt would not ease. Instead it simmered, refusing to allow her body to ease down from the edge of bliss. Like a traitor all too willing to work for the other side, the soft spasms left her wriggling beneath him.

Say it. Say it and get it over with. God knows you want to.

But he'd win.

He already has won! He won the minute I said "Yield"!

She glared up at him, wanting to hate him, but the only one she was still angry with was herself. He hadn't done anything to hurt her. If anything, he had taken the time and effort to make sure she would enjoy it with him. What good would it do to deny what her body felt or how it reacted?

"Please." The word felt alien on her lips.

"Please what?" His gaze softened, a hunger in his eyes that matched how she felt.

"Fuck me." The words were little more than a whimper.

He moved almost before the words were out of her lips, thrusting deeply into her body, half lifting her up from the ground with each new claiming of her body. Tears slipped down her cheeks; her inner walls clamped down on his thick erection; her body willingly writhed beneath his.

Emmie lifted her hips, meeting each thrust into her core. She whimpered, her nails raking down his arms, the pressure in the pit of her being almost more than she could bear. What if she couldn't come back from this? If he pushed her so far into the depths of pleasure that she remained lost in the maelstrom he had introduced her to.

What if...

"Come for me. Now!"

His words unlocked the last of her control. Liquid heat coated her inner walls, wrapping about his cock as she screamed out, hips rolling, dancing beneath him in a wave of pleasure that knew no end. His cock throbbed deep within her core, pressing her wide, her body lost in the haze of sensation that flooded through her being. With a roar, Theron arched, crying out his own release as

Scars

her sex rocked with soft spasms around him.

Emmie trembled, her thighs aching; sweat coated her body from head to foot. She felt each root, every small stone and stick under her back, and yet she didn't care. Tears traced silently down her cheeks; her heart threatened to turn into a stone and plummet into the pit of her stomach. She didn't want to think about it, but she knew, oh, she knew that all too soon he would leave. He had taken what he wanted, enjoyed her body, and now there was nothing left to keep him here.

She knew this. She expected him to pull away from her body and just walk out of the clearing. So why did the idea of this man, this shifter, walking out of her life forever leave her feeling so damn empty?

Chapter Eight

Emmie rolled out her shoulders, then stretched upward until she felt a soft crack in her spine. Her skin felt sticky; she struggled against the growing urge to clean herself off, but she couldn't, not without walking down to the small stream a short distance from the clearing. For a moment she didn't move, weighing up the options, and then finally she accepted that unless she took the time to clean off, the need to wash would drive her insane.

He was still there. Even without turning to look at him, she could still feel the path of his gaze moving across her nude form.

Why was he still here?

He'd taken what he wanted, and yet Theron hadn't left; he hadn't even stepped away from the clearing. It just didn't make sense. Tomcats did not hang around. Shit, she'd been warned just what the males of her kind were like. Yet there he was, standing there, watching her every move.

Emmie stiffened as she walked past him to the edge of the stream and stepped into the cool water, cupping her hands as she shivered and washed off the drying signs of their shared passion.

"Is there something wrong?" His soft, seductive voice broke through the silence of the clearing. He followed her past the edge of the trees and settled down at the edge of the stream.

Emmie took a deep breath, then turned to face him, struggling to keep her gaze fixed on his face. "I'm just wondering why you're still here? You got what you wanted -- you got laid -- now why are you still here?"

"Ah, so you think all I wanted was sex?" Humor danced within his gaze; his full lips twitched into a dangerous smile.

"Yes, of course." Damn him, why did he have to make it so difficult?

"Interesting." He shook his head and looked away from her

as he pushed to his feet and walked into the stream, washing off in front. Tension played openly across his shoulders; his hands clenched for a moment, knuckles white, before he let out a low whistle and smoothed his hands out. Water dripped down his legs, tracing his lean muscles; the small, glistening droplets beckoned her gaze, and Emmie quickly realized she was staring at him. "Why do you assume I'd act like that?"

"Because that's what tomcats do. They screw and leave." She folded her arms under her breasts, no longer caring what she looked like. He'd already seen every inch of her body; modesty had no place between them now.

"And the fact that I'm part human, just like you, didn't occur to you?" His gaze lingered on her breasts before he forced himself to look at her face.

"Well, I -- I mean, well, obviously, but..."

"You expected me to be ruled by my animal side?"

"Yes."

"I'm not like that any more than you are." Theron took a step toward her. "Stop and think for a moment. If I just wanted sex from you, if I was the bastard you think I am, why would I still be here? You've been asking yourself why I stayed, watching me, looking for some sign that I was about to run out on you, yet I'm still here."

"For how long, though?" Her voice shook, a soft tremble working its way through her body. Her breasts tightened, her nipples tingled, and she brushed the lingering drops of water away from their full forms. Fine, she had been staring at him; he had the right to do the same with her.

"For as long as you want me around." Theron reached out, cupping her chin carefully. "I came here because of you. You called to me. I answered. How could I ignore your call for help?"

"Called to you? I didn't call out to anyone." Her jaw clenched.

"Are you so sure? If that wasn't the case, then why did you accept the challenge to fight instead of walking away? You had the right to just laugh in my face and leave the clearing. You know that. No male can force a female to fight; it goes against everything we are. We are not like them; rape is alien to us. But the fight, the bloodlust and drive to mate afterward -- you knew the risks; you knew the odds of you winning were slim to none, and yet you still did it. How can you tell me that was not your way of crying out to me?"

Emmie took a step away from him and the stream, turning her head away so she slipped free of his grasp on her chin. What was he talking about? She sucked in her bottom lip and turned away from him, shaking her hair over her breasts. Her heart pounded against her ribcage as she walked back toward the clearing.

Damn him! Didn't he know that she wasn't in the mood to deal with a man being difficult? Man? He wasn't really just a man. Theron was a male shifter, and she knew just how much trouble they could be. She had heard the stories, the warnings, time and again, from her mother. How her father hadn't even stayed around an hour after he'd finished his sport. That's what they were all like. So why couldn't he just turn around and leave so she could go back to her life?

Just because someone did that to Mom doesn't mean it's going to happen to me.

Emmie stopped in her tracks and stared at the trees as the thought played over and over again in the back of her mind. She wasn't her mom. History hadn't repeated itself. Theron was still here. But that didn't mean he would turn into the love of her life or that they were destined to be together until the end of their days.

How am I going to know if I never give him a chance?

"I know you're not ready to hear this, but I'm not leaving you. Not unless you tell me to get the hell out of your life and never look back." He spoke softly, his steps nearly silent as he followed her back into the clearing. "I can't even blame it on the pheromones, not anymore; if it were just a case of simple chemical reaction, the drive to mate, you're right, I'd have already left."

"Are you trying to tell me you're in love with me?" Emmie turned around and stared at him.

"No, shit, I'm not stupid. It's just -- there's something else there, and if I don't stop to find out what it is, then -- God, I'm not making any sense, am I?" Theron growled, his jaw set, muscles tight across his shoulders.

Neither of them were. Not if she wanted to be completely honest.

"And if I don't tell you to leave, then you'll do what? Expect to move in with me?" The minute she finished speaking, Emmie knew it had been the wrong thing to say.

"I'm a shifter, not an idiot!" Theron snapped. "I'm not expecting you to open up your house to a virtual stranger."

Emmie let out a long, slow breath from between her clenched teeth before she uttered two very difficult words. "I'm sorry."

"That wasn't easy for you to say."

"No," she admitted, ducking her head slightly. "This entire conversation would be a hell of a lot easier if we were both --well -- wearing something."

"After what we did together, now you're suddenly shy?"

"No, not shy, just -- just I'd prefer to take this conversation to a more civilized level. Tomorrow. Breakfast?"

"Where?"

"There's a diner on Main. Small place. Jo's. I'll be there around nine." Emmie shifted her weight slightly from one foot to the other. It didn't make sense; what was it about this damn man that left her feeling so awkward all of a sudden?

Whatever it was, she would deal with it in the morning. Dressed, and in a more comfortable setting, she would face it and him with a fresh meal in her stomach.

Would it change anything between them?

Hell, for all she knew, he would never turn up the following morning, and she'd be left to enjoy a breakfast on her own without having to look him in the eyes again.

Chapter Nine

Theron watched as she shifted back into feline form and stalked away through the trees, vanishing from his line of sight. God, he'd never expected things to work out this well, or this complicated, all rolled into one. Emmie was not the type of woman he could or would walk away from. No matter what his instincts screamed at him to do.

His body throbbed at the memory of what they had shared together, his soul demanded he hunt her down, clamp his teeth into the back of her neck, and pin her to the ground until she lifted her hips, willing and wet for him again. A scene they could replay a dozen times over, not just for the length of this cycle, but for weeks, months to come.

But that would mean staying with her. Accepting there was something between them and that -- that he could never do.

He waited a moment longer, watching, listening for signs that she would return, before he turned and sprinted back through the forest. It didn't take him long to return to the spot where he had left his clothing, and he pulled them back on without a moment's thought.

It wasn't until he had pulled his crash helmet on and mounted his motorbike that he realized he had no idea what he was supposed to do with his time until tomorrow morning. He didn't know the town or the people in it; shit, he didn't even know if there was a motel or hotel in the area. Not that he would have a real problem with spending the night sleeping rough, but it wouldn't exactly put him in a good position for the following day.

He'd need a shower and something clean to change into. Well, the new clothing wasn't a problem, he had enough of that in the bags tied onto the back of his motorbike, but he'd still need a place to sleep and clean off. Just as long as she wasn't expecting him to turn up in anything more than jeans and a clean T-shirt.

Theron kicked out the stand and gunned the bike, turning back onto the road. There would be something in easy traveling distance. There had to be, even if it turned out to be an edge of the road mom-and-pop place, it would still mean clean, hot water and a semiclean bed.

Well, it was worth a try.

Twenty minutes later, he turned off the road and into a decent-sized parking lot. The Motel 6 wasn't the cream of the crop, but he'd learned from experience that they could be trusted to be clean, with decent beds and a shower, and that he'd be left alone, which at the end of the day, was all he needed from a motel. Sure, it was nice to relax in a hot tub now and then, or pick out a place that came with all the extras like a steam room, restaurant and bar, but they were luxuries he could live without.

Only when he had closed the door on his motel room and tossed the bags onto his bed, did he begin to replay the events amongst the trees over and over again in his mind. Just what was he doing by staying here? He had tasted her, taken her, been taken, and now he should, if he had any senses left, be on the road and back to the city. Or wherever Buck had settled himself down. Anywhere but here and certainly not planning on meeting her the following morning.

That was just -- well -- too human for his tastes.

Emmie was cute, he'd agree to that. No, more than cute; there was something outright amazing about her. But to hang around, even agree to meet her for breakfast, shit, that was too much like a relationship as far as he was concerned. So just what was he doing here?

The connection he had felt with her amongst the trees. No, it wasn't that.

Sex?

Sure, it had started out that way; he'd been drawn to her by the smell of her need, the pheromones that had tugged him toward her the same way they would have drawn any other male shifter. Fuck, they even affected human males in a limited way. He'd seen how a in-heat female shifter could walk into a crowded bar and capture the attention of every man in the place. Most shrugged it off; they'd look away from her and return to the drinks, not understanding why heat would surge through their bodies, or why the only thing on their minds for the rest of the night would be sex, the need to be laid. An intense desire to fuck their brains out with any willing soul that crossed their path was still a mild reaction compared to the way the scent of a female in heat affected a male shifter.

And it was something he knew well; he'd been lost in the arms of a female shifter before. When they called to you, when they claimed you, if only for a few hours, it was a pleasure finer than the sweetest wine, a delight that no living being could walk away from, and he had struggled not to surrender himself completely to her touch.

But with Emmie, it had been different. He didn't know how to explain it. His heart, his soul had cried out for more. So much more than he knew sanity would permit to exist between them.

He growled and set his helmet on the dressing table, rolling his shoulders out before he stripped down and headed for the shower. Pheromones -- it had to be nothing more than the concentrated pheromones that saturated the air around her. He'd breathed in too many of them, and he was still wrapped up in the sexual desires that she had triggered.

A good hot shower, scrub down, and it would work. He'd be able to push aside the control she still had over his body. She was no doubt laughing about him even now. Amused by the way he had agreed to meet her. Would she even be there in the morning? Somehow he doubted it.

At best, she would be hiding across the road, watching for him to turn up and make a fool of himself. Well, he wasn't going to be there. He'd find his own vantage point and watch, wait for her to finally give up and make an appearance in the town. But he wasn't about to walk into the diner and be laughed at.

He growled, furious at himself for allowing the desire he had known could be triggered by a she cat in heat to then take control of him so deeply. No, it wouldn't happen again. He wouldn't permit it Theron turned the water on full blast and stepped in when he could see the steam curl upward into the air. He knew better than this; he knew better than many just how strong and dangerous the pull of a female shifter could be. So, why had he allowed it to strike him this deeply?

Theron turned his face into the stream of hot water and closed his eyes, allowing it to pelt against his face.

Emmie with her compelling eyes. The soft sway of her hips and the low moans that had filled the air in such a seductive manner. The way she had clung to him, her body hot and needy beneath his, sweat coating her body, her nipples scraping over his chest, and her nails...

Heat surged through his cock as it thickened against his thigh. His balls tightened as they pressed against his body. God, this was not helping any. Just what sort of pull did she have over his body? He'd been through encounters with female shifters before; they'd never affected him this deeply.

But the others hadn't been Emmie with her blazing spirit and need to defy him. They had lacked her passion, her hunger. Their bodies hadn't melded to his in the same way and...

He closed his eyes, trying to think of something else. Anything. Lloyd. Yeah, think about Lloyd and the others like him who hung out in the bars -- the same bar he'd seen Emmie. God. She'd moved, writhed, welcomed him into her body and then been willing to enjoy more. Would it be so wrong to see her again?

His balls tightened.

"Leave me alone," he growled into the water.

His cock twitched.

"And you can stop that as well. She's just a piece of tail! A nice piece of tail -- hot, sexy, willing -- oh, fuck it." He turned, leaned his head against the glass door of the shower, and slid one hand down between his thighs. He groaned, wrapping his hand about his cock, sliding it slowly over the thickening shaft.

God. She'd been so good. Her sex tight, wet, welcoming. He could have stayed within her forever. Maybe he should have? At least then he wouldn't be in the shower, jacking himself off.

Her perfume, the natural mix of sweat, desire, and her own sweetness; he could taste it, smell it still, and yet he knew she wasn't here. Emmie hadn't followed him to the hotel; she'd be in her own bed by now or laughing with a friend. Maybe even with another man...

He growled, fury building without warning. She didn't belong to someone else, not now. They belonged together; the way she fit around his body was something he couldn't deny, but it was more than that, something so much more.

His hand tightened about his cock, stroking it, teasing his own body, his mind all too willing to provide him with images of Emmie. The way she had moved, the soft sounds she had made, the low growls, even the feel of her nails digging into his body. His, she belonged to him; never again would he let another man, shifter or otherwise, take her, touch her, slide his cock into her tight, slick heat.

The water drummed against his back, sliding down his ass, teasing between his thighs as the water tickled and pulled at his balls. No, not water -- her touch, her tongue and lips, stroking his balls, licking at his body, yes -- oh, God, yes. He'd show her, teach her just what it felt like to be with someone who needed her, not just for one day or a few nights, but something more, something stronger, lasting. His cock throbbed in his hand, pressure building up in the pit of his stomach, pressing up from the base of his shaft. Waves of delight surged through his body, pushing him further, higher than he wanted to right now. He'd wanted to hold onto the moment, the dream of her body, the play of the shower, but now

-- now he had no choice.

He growled, tipping back his head, his knees weak as his cock pulsed in his hand. Lights danced before his eyes, colors, blazing like the sun as his knees gave out, and he dropped down on the floor of the shower, his release coating his hand for a brief moment before the hot water cleaned him off.

His. She belonged to him and always would.

Even if she refused to accept it just yet.

Chapter Ten

What the hell had she been doing last night? Rolling around on the ground with a stranger like that? God, had she gone completely mad? She'd tumbled through the woods, had sex with a shifter, and what? Then agreed to meet him for breakfast, as if they were a human couple exploring the option of a second date? There hadn't even been a first date. Insane! More than insane. She didn't have to go; she could stay here, hidden away -- he didn't know where she was.

Like that would help?

He'd only have to walk through the town for a few minutes before he'd pick up her scent. If he hadn't already traced her through to her front door before they even met in the woods.

He had no right to do this to her! He'd walked into her life and turned it upside down. So now what was she supposed to do? Just hang around in case he wanted to see her again? What if he wasn't even going to show up? If this was some sort of cruel trick... She knew, only too well, that shifters could be cruel, thoughtless; her mom had warned her all about that. This was how they acted. What had she been told to watch for? The jokes, the barbed words, and the knowing looks as they walked past; yes, she'd heard all the stories. Just how the males of her kind acted. If she did turn up, it would leave her wide open for his barbs. Maybe he'd called his friends, and they'd all home in on her now. She'd be passed around like some little prize, and with her body in full hormonal swing, she wouldn't be able to fight them. Not fully.

Well, she wasn't going to let him treat her like this. There had to be a way of bringing her reactions back under control. She just had to focus. Focus and not let the animal side of her nature win.

Emmie glared at the mirror and rested her hands on the edge of the sink. All of her good intentions about staying away from male shifters had been destroyed by one night of passion in Theron's arms. She groaned and lowered her head, refusing to look at her reflection any longer.

All they had shared had been sex. Sure, it had been mind-blowing, out-of-this-world sex that had left her sated in a way no one had ever managed before. But it wasn't as though he'd asked her to marry him. Or mate. Or whatever it was shifters did.

Come to think of it, she didn't know that much about her own kind, except for what little her mom had told her. The other shifters she had come into contact with? They had been a mixed bunch at best, ranging from werewolves through to those who assumed bird form, but feline shifters had been few and far between.

Theron was the first adult feline shifter she had seen in over ten years.

"And what did I go and do? Jump into the sack with him." She groaned and turned on the faucet, letting the cold water run for several long minutes before she scooped it up by the handful and splashed it on her face. Well, hanging around the house was not going to improve things. She had arranged to meet him and had to go through with the meeting, or she would never get him out of her system.

That's all she needed to do. She could meet him in broad daylight, convince herself that he was nothing special, then tell him to leave. He had said if she told him to leave then he would do so.

At least, she thought he had said something along those lines. Any time she tried to replay the conversation, her mind immediately shifted to other things instead. The way his body had touched hers, the way she'd arched beneath him, enjoyed every touch, the feel of his lips, his hands, his hair sliding over her flesh...

Emmie snatched up the hairbrush and pulled it through her dark mane, the sharp tugs of pain enough to bring her thoughts back into focus. A meal, polite conversation, and it would be over.

Scars

No one could be as compelling in daylight as he had appeared to be under the moonlight. It just didn't work that way.

By the time she had tied back her hair into a loose ponytail and pulled on her boots, Emmie had almost calmed down. She locked the door and slung her black leather satchel over her shoulders before she headed out. The short yellow summer dress swished over her thighs, the breeze playing with her hair, teasing long lengths out of the ponytail as she headed toward Main Street.

Jamie's voice stopped her in her tracks.

"Well, well, if it isn't the town bitch." He stepped out from the end of the street, already smelling of sour, cheap whiskey. "Wasn't expecting to see you today. But I'm not gonna turn away the offer."

"It's a bit early for you to be out and about, isn't it?" Emmie kept her voice cool and low, refusing to take a step back from the man. He'd changed his clothes from the night before, and his face and lower arms bore the signs of his run-in with the cat. The smell that hit her let her know that he hadn't been drinking, so the smell had to be coming from his body processing the booze out from the night before.

"They just let me out." He grunted and jerked his head back toward Main Street. "Must have known you were wandering the streets looking for me. What's up? Couldn't keep your thoughts away from me? Need to get a taste of me before I'm snatched off the market?"

"Out?" She wasn't going to rise to the bait. Not this time. She had bigger fish to fry than a drunk with delusions of grandeur.

"Jail." Jamie shrugged.

"Ah, you got in trouble again, didn't you? Drink too much?" It wouldn't have been wise to let him know she'd been aware of just what had happened the previous night. Her gaze narrowed slightly; he hadn't been wearing those clothes when he had been carted off, so she doubted that he had come straight from the jail. Unless Aneta had taken him the clean clothing? It would have been just like the older woman to try and offer him some level of comfort, despite how he had treated her the night before. Still, she couldn't fault the woman; Jamie, for all his faults, was her only living relative now.

"I can hold my liquor, bitch. Don't you go saying I can't!"

Sure he could. Just as long as he wasn't around anyone else, and the cops were on hand to haul him away at the right moment. "Fine, so if you can hold it, why did you end up in a cell for the night?"

"Nosy slut, aren't ya?" Jamie took a step toward her, his dark gaze narrowing on her face. "Or maybe you got a reason to ask about me? Something else you wanna know? Like how I am in the sack? Come on, then, ask away. Got nothing to hide there. Come on, you've wanted me since the first minute you saw me. Don't think I can't tell when a woman wants me. Yeah, I've seen how you look at me. All that hunger simmering beneath the posh bitch you pretend to be."

"I wouldn't be interested in you sexually, not if you were the last man on the planet." *Or the universe, for that matter* What was it with men like Jamie? You talked to them, so much as breathed in their direction, and they instantly assumed you wanted to get into their pants?

"You can be honest with me, Emmie-girl. Let it loose. Stop lying to yourself. We both known you've wanted me, ever since you arrived in this godforsaken hellhole; no point in hiding it. There's no one else around to hear you. So tell me the truth. You want a piece of ol' Jim-boy Well, I can arrange that. We can go back to your place, and we'll..."

"Touch me and I'll call the cops." *That's if I don't rip your hands off and eat them in front of you.* Her stomach lurched. The very thought of touching him sexually left her feeling sick. "You're still drunk, and I'm not in the mood to deal with your pathetic ass right now. Get out of my sight before I give Mike a call."

Scars

Jamie's jaw clenched, his lips pressed into a tight, thin line as he took a step back. "You're too stuck up for your own good, girl. Don't know a good thing when you see it. I could make your life in this town mighty unpleasant if you want to be a bitch, so best you think about that."

"Leave her be, Jamie." A new voice broke through the tension.

Her gaze narrowed on the newcomer as she took in every inch of his face. From his cold eyes to the narrow scar that traced the left side of his jaw. "David." She nodded slightly.

"Aw, come on, man. Just having a bit of fun with her," Jamie whined, his weight shifting from one foot to the next. "You know she needs bringing back down to earth. Or my bed. Flat on her back, legs spread. Let's just relax, kick back, get laid and stoned."

"Not with her. I've got other things in mind for today." David Stone shook his head, his shoulder-length hair caught in a ponytail. His lips twitched into a cool smile. "Besides, she's too fucking good for you."

"Did you just diss me?" Jamie turned instantly on the other man.

"Too fuckin' right. Come on, man, are you blind? She's way out of your reach. Now fuck off. I'll meet you in five." David glared at his companion, waiting until Jamie grumbled under his breath, then turned and walked away. Then he changed; in a heartbeat, he changed and took a step closer to Emmie. "You're too good for him; he wouldn't know what to do with a woman like you. But not me. I know how to treat you. You and me, we've got business to take care of when I get some free time."

The hair on the back of her neck stood up. "And just what business do you think we have together?"

"You'll find out. You're mine, Em' baby. You just don't know it yet. I've watched you for a long time. Once this little bit of business is over and done with, you and I are going to get to know each other very well indeed." He leaned closer, his breath caressing her face in a way that left her skin crawling.

"I'm no more yours than I am Jamie's. So you can drop the macho act. It doesn't impress me. It never has." *Men.* What was it about them that they had to try and lay claim to a woman in order to prove something to the world? "I don't belong to any man, and that isn't about to change any time soon." *If ever.*

"You are, you just don't know it yet." David leaned forward, stopping only when she pressed one hand firmly against his chest. His gaze flickered down to the hand against his chest, laughing as he shook his head, his eyes dancing with a cruel humor. "Later, lover."

Emmie shook her head as she watched David turn around and walk away. Just who did he think he was? Since when did the town bully have any authority or ability to make her life difficult? Talk about having an inflated ego. He'd been watching her? Waiting for something to happen between them? Just what in hell's name were the men in this town drinking?

Well, she'd have to bring him back into line after this whole mess with Theron was sorted out. Maybe she just needed to drop something in the water supply that would knock the men back on their asses?

With a low chuckle, Emmie pushed all thoughts of the drunken Jamie or his friend out of her mind as she walked the short distance to Main Street. One of the good things about living in a small town was that almost everything remained in walking distance, which made her life easier.

"Fuckhead, what are you doing hanging around here?" David called out, the sober one. The more dangerous of the two. "I told you we had things to do."

"She pissed me off."

"Save it and use it for later; got it, man? But you leave her alone. She's mine. I don't want you anywhere near her." David shoved one hand hard against Jamie's back. "Come on, we've got shit to do."

Scars

"Yours? Like hell she is! I've had my eyes on that slut since she moved into town. If you think I'm going to let someone else get to her first, then…"

Something clicked, metal, cold. Not a gun, though. A blade. "You'll do as you're fuckin' told. Get it? If you go anywhere near her -- anywhere -- without my permission, I'll cut you so deep you'll never get over it."

"What the fuck!" Jamie took a step back, his shoulders tense, hands clenching into fists. "Put that thing away. You can't threaten me like that, not over a bitch. She's just a woman. A slut. Plenty more of them out there. What's gotten into you, man?"

"Keep your dirty hands away from her, got it?" David growled, pressing closer with the blade. "I'll slice you into a thousand tiny pieces if you ever lay a finger on her again."

"Sure, man, whatever. She's just a piece of tail. I'm not going -- all right, she's yours."

"You go after her, and I'll find out. You try to touch her, and I'll start slicing." For a moment neither man moved, and then the lock blade vanished back into the man's pocket. "Just you remember that"

"Yeah. Got it."

Theron growled as he stepped out from the shadows, watching as the men walked away from him down the street. One stumbled, not drunk, but tired. Bone tired. Why? Stale alcohol -- he'd been drinking the night before. But what else? There was something else that lingered around the man. Not Emmie, not a woman at all, but something else. The smell of stale urine, grime, confinement. Jail. The man had spent the night in jail. Interesting. So whatever he was, the man was also a problem child, the type of idiot who ended up in a cell overnight. The drunk tank?

Follow them both and find out? No, he was running out of time. Emmie, if she had turned up, wouldn't be impressed by having to wait for him. This was going to be hard enough as it was.

Just what was it about the woman?

If he had been human, he'd have laughed and claimed it was something ridiculous like love at first sight, but -- no. Oh, no. He wasn't even going there with that word. He couldn't possibly be in love with a woman, shifter or not. It didn't happen. Not to him. Not to feline shifters. They screwed and moved on with their lives. Love just wasn't part of the equation. Sure the wolves managed to get themselves trapped with all that nonsense, but cats knew better. Dogs were stupid anyway, any cat knew that.

His stomach knotted. Every time he thought about Emmie, his emotions were torn in two. The desire to see her again, coupled with the need to fuck her and leave, to get her out of his system, yet the idea of never seeing her again after that left him sick to his stomach.

God. He was never going to live this down.

Chapter Eleven

The heels of Emmie's knee-high black boots rang out on the sidewalk, and she tipped up her chin, a confident smile settling into place as she walked down the street. Oh, she knew the looks they shot her way. She didn't fit into the small town image of how a woman was supposed to dress. Not that she had any idea just what that image entailed now.

Emmie glanced at her slender strap watch before she pushed open the door and stepped inside. The diner hadn't changed in years, from what Mags had told her about the place. Several tables had been shoved together at the far end of the long, narrow room, with chairs scattered around it. Three men, all in their sixties, had claimed the table, which was now scattered with empty coffee mugs and newspapers. All three of the men looked up as she claimed an empty booth close to the door, but not one of them spoke to her or even nodded in her direction.

No, instead, they did what many had done before them and shifted the focus of their conversation to Emmie. She should have been used to it by now, but it still caught her off guard.

"She's an odd one." The eldest at the table, a man with little more than a few stray silver white hairs on his otherwise bald head, grunted as he reached for his coffee mug. "Thought she'd have hooked up with one of the local boys by now, but she keeps them at arm's length."

A wry smile touched her lips as she looked up, waiting for the waitress to approach the table. She knew, all too well, that the men at the table had no way of knowing that she could hear every word they said as clearly as if she had been sitting there with them.

"Quit your whining, Ted. Maybe she has a reason, or she's one of those girls who likes to take her time before she hooks up with someone. More power to her, I say. Too many of her generation like to jump from one bad marriage to the next." Alvin folded down the paper and set it back on the table.

"Coffee?" The middle-aged waitress in sensible shoes inquired.

"Yes, please. I have someone joining me shortly." *If he shows up.*

"'Kay, I'll be back in a few with your coffee." She shuffled away from the booth without another word.

"Since when did you care what women her age do? Besides, you're just pissed off that she turned your boy down."

"Who, Nick? Harv, you're smoking something there. Nick would have eaten that young woman alive," Ted grumbled and leaned back in his chair.

"More like she would have eaten him; don't go thinking that just because she's a pretty slip of a thing she can't look after herself." Alvin spoke quietly. "There's something dangerous about that one. I pity the fool who tries to get in her way. The entire town knows Jamie has the hots for her, but he'd be an idiot to try and force something on her. She'd kill him without so much as blinking."

"Now I know you're insane. That girl? A stiff breeze would blow her away! She's not the type to carry a gun or even a knife, so I don't know why you'd think she could defend herself?" Ted openly laughed, but the conversation ended as the door opened.

The hairs on the back of her neck stood up as Theron walked into the diner. Whatever interest she'd had in the conversation died in that minute. Her stomach knotted, sweat covered the palms of her hands, and she quickly rubbed them dry on her dress.

An all-too-confident and smug smile flashed across Theron's face as he slid across the booth on the opposite side of the table. "I wasn't sure you'd actually turn up."

"Funny, I had the same thoughts about you. But, for future reference, I'm no coward. I made the arrangements to meet you;

why would I back out?"

"Because you didn't want to see me again." He gave a slight shrug. "No, that's not quite true. You did, you were just afraid of your own reactions when and if we met again."

"As I just told you, I'm no coward." Why did it irk her that he had such a low opinion of her character?

"I don't know you, remember. One night, not even that -- it's not long enough to form a firm judgment of a person." He leaned back against the padded bench seat, his gaze never leaving her face. "You're an odd one. And intriguing. I've never met a woman quite like you before."

"And you're just annoying, arrogant, and I'll be glad to see the back of you," she snapped without thinking.

"So, tell me to leave, and I will." Theron's gaze locked with hers. "That's all you have to do."

Sure. He'd leave. Just like that? Who was he trying to fool? Still, it would be interesting to see the look on his face when she told him to get the hell out of Dodge and never look back. Emmie let the tip of her tongue slip out between her lips, holding it there for five long seconds. So, if she wanted to be rid of him, why hadn't she told him to leave already? Come on, it wasn't that hard to say. All she had to do was open her mouth and say it.

"Coffee?" The waitress set the tall, white mug on the table in front of Emmie, her question aimed at Theron.

"Yes, thanks." Theron nodded, breaking eye contact with Emmie.

"Anything else?"

"Menus?" Theron flashed a suggestive grin. "Emmie here might know what you have on offer, but I don't."

"Erm, sorry. Yes, I'll be right back." The waitress hurried away.

Theron turned his attention back to Emmie. "I think I've left her a little flustered."

"Considering you're the hottest thing to have walked into the diner in the past few years, I'd say yes." Heat flushed across her face the moment she realized what she'd said. *Fuck, why did I have to say that; now he's going to become even more arrogant, if that's even possible.*

"Ah, so you finally admit that I look hot? That's at least a start."

"Bastard."

"Yes, I am. I have no idea who my father is." He didn't even blink as he spoke. "So your point would be what, exactly?"

Okay, that she hadn't been expecting. "You're impossible."

"Thank you, I try."

Fine, this wasn't turning out the way she'd hoped. "Are you going to tell me just what brought you into town?"

"You did, of course."

"Sorry about that." The waitress placed two menus on the table, along with Theron's coffee. Her arrival forced a pause into the conversation as the woman shifted her weight from one foot to the other. "I'll be back in a few minutes. Unless there is anything else you need right now?"

"No, we're good. Thanks." Theron dismissed the woman with a quick wave of his hand and a warm smile. The waitress let her gaze trail over Theron, taking in every inch of his body, lingering on the broad expanse of his back, before she slipped away from the booth with an added sway in her hips.

Emmie waited long enough for the other woman to be out of hearing range before she leaned across the table and hissed at him. "Drop the bullshit. I didn't call out for you, and I'm not buying it. This town isn't on the main highway; no one comes here without a good reason, which is why I like it here."

"I had some business nearby. After that was complete, I shifted and caught your scent on the wind. It was easy to tell that you were in heat, but I wasn't certain if there were some other male shifters around." Theron took a sip of the coffee, grimaced, and reached for the sugar. "That was two days ago now. I'm surprised you didn't pick up my scent when you went on your patrol the other night. Not that it matters now, but if we hadn't bumped into each other last night, I would have spent today trying to put myself in your way."

"Why?" Had that been the scent she had caught on the wind? No. Whatever she'd smelled, it hadn't been his scent. The one that had taunted her, however briefly, with its presence, had been older. A lot older.

"At first, I wanted to do that because I knew you were in heat. You know how compelling that is. How it pulls at us."

"At first?" She bristled, her hands clenching into fists on the table. "Well, you got what you wanted and…"

"That changed, last night." He glanced toward her hands. "If you're going to try and hit me you might want to wait until after breakfast. I don't think they'd appreciate two alley cats going at it in the middle of the diner."

Emmie grabbed the menu, a low growl forming at the back of her throat. "And who says we'd get into a fight right here and now?"

"You're tempted, though. I can see it. You want to reach out across the table and wipe the smirk from my face. It won't do any good, though. You'd still be trying to figure out just why I'm still here." Theron glanced at the menu, then looked back at her. "I'm not that good at this socializing thing, and small talk isn't a skill I've acquired over the years, so I'm well aware that I'm pissing you off with every fifth word."

"Every second."

"Shit, that bad?" Theron grinned. "Well, I guess I'll have to work on that if you're going to accept me hanging around."

"You've still not…"

"Did you need any more time? Or are you both ready to order?" The waitress slipped back to the side of the table, her smile focused on Theron.

"I'll have the steak and eggs, rare and over easy, hash browns, and wheat toast." Emmie glanced up at the woman as she handed back the plastic-covered menu.

"I'll have the same." Theron nodded slightly and waited until the waitress had left before he spoke again. "Yes, I know I've not explained why I stayed after we finished our -- after last night." He shifted a little on the bench and looked away from her, twin points of heat burning across his face.

"So, are you going to explain, or are we just going to sit here playing guessing games?"

"I like you." He didn't meet her eyes. "Yeah, I know, that sounds like some lame schoolboy crush. Shit, I don't know how else to explain it. I enjoyed last night; it felt right, but more than that, the thought of walking away from you after we -- it felt wrong. As though I'd be leaving a part of myself behind. I know I'm not making much sense here, but I'm asking you to trust me on this. When the time came to walk away, I just couldn't." He took a slow breath, tapping one finger against the side of his coffee mug. "I spent most of last night thinking about this, and all I could come up with was I felt right being with you. Complete. As if you were the answer to a question."

"You're right, that sounds lame." Emmie struggled not to laugh right in his face.

"Emmie!"

"Well, it does. I don't believe in all that love-at-first-sight shit. That's for fairytales and kids, not shifters." Did he think she was nuts? Or just stupid that she would fall for the lines he was spinning? God, she'd heard better excuses from three-year-olds after they'd been caught with their hand in the cookie jar.

"I don't think I mentioned love."

"No, you didn't, but a crush kinda implies that. And you're too old to have crushes on people; that's for kids."

"Right, sure. You're telling me you've never seen someone in a movie or a picture and had the instant hots for them?" Theron's brow creased in a frown, his voice a low whisper.

"That's different. That's nothing more than a fantasy. Grown men and women don't have crushes on real people."

Scars

"Emmie, be serious here for a minute. Do you think I like this? I'm not some eighteen-year-old kid falling in love with his first bedmate. Shit. If I could walk away I would. Believe me I would. And since when do adults stop having crushes? I bet if you asked your hum-- err, other friends, they'd tell you it's a very common thing to experience."

"Right, so much for that *I have a human side too* crap you were trying to pull on me last night." Male shifters. She wasn't going to fall for his lines, no matter how cute he was. "You know what's really sad? For a moment last night, I almost believed you. Thanks. I should of known better than to even hope for more from the likes of you." If she hadn't already put in the order for her breakfast, then she'd be out the door.

"This isn't going quite the way I had planned." He groaned and rested his head in his hands. "Funny, I had this all worked out before I walked into the diner, and now I'm babbling like an idiot."

"No shit, Sherlock." Last night he'd been smooth, confident, he'd known exactly what he was doing. Now, in the light of day, he'd turned out to be -- to be what? Nervous? Okay, so he was still hot, cute, and oh-so-very-fuckable, but that didn't change the fact he was a shifter and wasn't to be trusted.

"Fine. I screwed up. So, will you give me a chance to prove to you that there's more to me than a man looking for a quick lay?"

Whatever she thought about last night, *quick* didn't enter into it. "Why should I bother?"

"Maybe for the chance to be proven right?"

Is that how he views me? As someone who wants the chance to laugh in his face at being proven right? Emmie looked away from him, pretending to be distracted by the return of the waitress with their meal. His words shouldn't have affected her. What he thought about her wasn't important. Yet that question hurt. No, not the question, but the assumption behind it.

But why did she really care what he thought of her?

"Three days. I'm giving you three days."

"That's all I'll need."

Chapter Twelve

What the hell was he going to do in the span of three days that would help her change her mind about him? And why did it matter if she cared about him in the first place? He wasn't planning on hanging around, was he? Fuck. Yeah, he was. Despite everything the very loud and annoying voice was screaming at the back of his mind, he wanted to stay with her, near her, and not just for three days. This was ridiculous. But now he'd made the deal with her, he couldn't just back out. Not without having to swallow his pride even further than he already had.

Theron groaned and lowered his head into his hands as he rested his elbows on the table in the diner. Emmie had walked out after her agreement to give him three days to prove that there was a real reason behind his decision to stay. One that would make sense.

Now, all he had to do was come up with that reason and explain it to himself.

God, I'm fucked. Completely, utterly, and royally screwed, and I've done it to myself. He couldn't even blame her. He should have realized that a woman who could, without saying a word, compel him to leave the city and follow her out into the boondocks, would be a danger to him. Maybe he should just follow her out there, go to her house, fuck her brains out again, then leave!

Sure, he could do that. Just as long as he didn't mind breaking his own word, giving into his fears, and retreating into the darkness like a coward in the night.

"You look bothered there, son. Something I can help with?" One of the older men had walked over from the large table where they had sat, gathered over their coffee and papers. "Young Emmie giving you a hard time there?" Without waiting for an answer, the man slid into the booth, taking up the same space

Emmie had so recently vacated.

Theron stared at the man. "Sorry -- erm. I wasn't expecting to -- did I do something wrong?" Had he invited the man over and forgotten that he'd done so?

"Ah, city-born aren't you? Not used to how we do things over here." The man nodded and waved over to the waitress. "You'll get used to us if you're going to stay around to spend some time with Emmie. Smart girl that one, strongwilled too. Not many catch her attention. In fact I think you're the first man I've seen her have more than a five-minute conversation with."

Well, that was something. "She keeps to herself?"

"For the most part, when it comes to men at least. Guess there's something different about you that's caught her eye, then. Good on ya, boy. But from the look on your face, this is turning out to be more than you were ready to deal with."

"Understatement of the century," Theron grumbled as he took a good look at the older man. "Who are you again?"

"Harvey. Me and the boys have lived here most of our lives; there's nothing that goes on in this town that we don't know about. Take your Emmie, for instance, she vanishes off to the city once or twice a month, stays overnight there. Think she has some business she checks in on as she's never short of cash."

Business? That was one way of putting it, though he doubted that she ever charged the men she took into her bed. So where did her money come from? That was something else he'd have to find out about her. It wasn't as though he was hurting for funds, either, but would she have a problem with what he did for a living? Tracking down rogue shifters or the troublemaker humans for well-paying clients wasn't exactly the type of business he could brag about to most, not even amongst their own people. Still, it paid a decent living.

Even if it wasn't entirely legal.

All right, it wasn't legal at all. He tried to find ways of dealing with issues that would not come back to bite him in the ass later in life, but sometimes the problems he dealt with ended up dead. Problems whose bodies were buried under a pile of garbage, or burned, or disposed of in some way that would not bring attention to the preternatural creatures that also called Earth home. It had become harder over the past few years; the further the humans' abilities with science grew, the better they became at tracking microscopic clues, the more difficult his work became.

Sooner or later their abilities to use science to find the answers would outclass the skills of the preternatural beings that did their best to keep their lives hidden and away from the prying eyes of so-called normal human beings. But, until then, he would continue to be one of the few, overworked problem-solvers of their hidden society.

"Well, whatever it is that draws her to the city, she seems to prefer living here during the rest of the month." Theron pushed his empty mug toward the waitress when she refilled Harvey's. "So there must be something that keeps her here. Does she have any family?"

"Not that we know of. She arrived here a couple of years ago, lives on the edge of town, but I don't recall ever seeing anyone come to visit her who might have been a family member. Best person to ask would be Mags. She's often around Emmie's place. Good friends, they are. Mags works down at the bar, on the corner of the block."

Theron nodded, he'd seen the bar when he'd worked his way through town in order to find the diner. "I'll keep that in mind if I need to find out a little more about her."

"So, what's got you so upset about Emmie? She obviously didn't tell you to piss off completely. Which means you got one step closer to her than anyone managed to do, something that might piss off a few people here."

"Like who?"

"Jamie is one you need to watch for. Local drunk and bully boy. He's not too pleased with Emmie ignoring his attentions. And

David. Mike won't care, so you don't have to worry about pissing off law enforcement. But David and Jamie are the two you have to watch for. Troublemakers, both of them, and they have an interest in Emmie. One that's none too healthy in my opinion."

Jamie and David, had those been the names of the men who had put themselves in Emmie's way earlier in the day? Interesting. "Does Jamie have lank hair and a taste for cheap whiskey? Torn jeans? Tanned?"

"Sounds like Jamie-boy. He has a grandmother who lives just a few doors down from Emmie, so they're always bumping into each other in town. Seems he's had an interest in her since she moved in. But he's not her type. Not that any of us are entirely sure what her type really is, seeing as she's never been seen with a date, or a man for more than a few minutes, until this morning, that is."

A smug smile claimed his lips for a brief moment, until he managed to get his ego under control. Considering the way the woman had him confused and ready to act completely out of character, being seen in her company wasn't the best of situations. He tried not to groan. What had happened to the strong-willed, confident man he knew himself to be on a normal day?

He didn't belong here. He wasn't the sort of man who needed a woman in his life. He'd never be able to look other felines in the eye if they found out he'd fallen in love. No, he'd stay the three days, get her out of his system, screw her senseless, and then leave. That would be enough time to deal with whatever it was she had done to him.

Wouldn't it?

He didn't know anymore. And it was infuriating. He'd have laughed himself silly if this had been happening to someone else, but being caught up in the middle of this wasn't something he had ever planned on having to live through. Women. They were a source of pleasure, pain, and endless problems.

"You look kinda lost there."

"I should just get the hell of outta town and never look back."

"But?"

"I just can't," Theron admitted, before he realized he'd even spoken again.

"You're kinda hooked on her, aren't you, boy?" Harvey leaned closer across the table. "I've seen that look before. You've got it bad. And it's bugging the snot out of ya. Well, now, we'll have to see what we can do about that. 'Tain't no good to have a grown man so wrapped around a woman that he's not making sense, even to himself."

"Women just don't have this..." He stopped and looked at the man. What in hell's name was he doing spilling his guts to the old fool? Had being around Emmie turned him into a woman? This was worse than he'd thought. "Never mind. I'll get this sorted myself. Forget I said anything."

Harvey opened his mouth to protest, a merry light dancing within his eyes, then something made him stop, and the older man just nodded. He reached out and patted Theron's arm. "Sure, kid, whatever you say. Just remember, being a man doesn't mean you have to work things out on your own or shut down your ability to feel. You're a human being, with all that entails."

Sure, if only things were that easy.

A siren's wail broke through the low conversation in the diner, and the roar of a car hurrying past the front of the building as it rattled windows and drew the attention of everyone within the room.

"What in hell's name? Young Mike must really be bored to be running through the middle of town like that. Knew they shouldn't have got him that new car. All those bells and whistles on it. Damn stupid, if you ask me," Harvey grumbled and picked up his coffee and wandered back to the large table.

No, whatever Harvey thought was going on, it didn't fit in with why a cop would barrel through the middle of a small, quiet town. He didn't like where this might be leading, but he couldn't sit still in the diner waiting to find out just what had happened. Theron swallowed the remains of his coffee, set some bills down on the table, and headed for the door.

If he was going to stay in town for the next few days, he needed to find out just what was going on.

Chapter Thirteen

Emmie slammed the door shut behind her, rattling the only picture she had bothered to hang up on the wall. She reached out, catching it moments before it hit the floor, and growled as she put it back in place. Just what the hell did he think he was doing? Three days? What did he plan on doing on the space of three days that would change her opinion of him?

If that wasn't bad enough, then dealing with David and Jamie only made matters worse. What was it with men lately? Was she walking around with a CLAIM ME NOW sign posted on her back? Whatever it was that was going on, she didn't like it, and it could stop. Right now. If not sooner.

The long wail of a siren broke through her thoughts, and she almost pulled the front door open to see what was going on, but when the car stopped close by, Emmie shrugged and put it down to new problems between Jamie and Aneta. If it wasn't one thing, then it certainly was another. She'd stepped into things last night; the cops were already there, so there was no need for her to become involved again today. Maybe this time they'd lock the jerk up and throw away the key.

Good. At least it would keep him off her back. She'd still have to deal with David, but it would be easier without his pet drunk hanging around.

Emmie turned back to look around her small home. What she needed to do was catch up with some of the work in the house. So she didn't like it entirely clean and tidy, but neither did she want to live in a pigpen. A little healthy clutter was a good thing. Mold growing on plates wasn't.

She ran her fingers through her hair. At least she wouldn't feel ashamed if he turned up on her doorstep.

Sure, right, she wanted him so badly she'd care just what he thought of her housekeeping. Since when had it ever mattered to her just what someone thought about her home, or the way she kept it? God, what if her mom had been right? That being with a male shifter changed everything? That they turned you into a little housecat.

Oh, no, like hell *that* was ever going to happen. She growled and smacked one cushion off the sofa, so it bounced across the floor. There, that looked better. With a smug smile, Emmie stalked out of the living room and pulled coffee cups out, only to find herself once again focusing on cleaning the kitchen instead of messing things up.

An hour later, she slumped down onto the couch and pulled a cushion over her face. This wasn't like her. Every inch of her bathroom had been scrubbed, her bedroom tidied up, even clean sheets put on the bed. Was she sick? It was his fault. It had to be. She wouldn't have wasted the time and energy doing all this housework if it hadn't been for him. Now she lay on the couch, shaking, her hands raw from scrubbing things down. She couldn't decide if she needed to be furious or proud of the work she had done.

Emmie had barely had a chance to take three deep breaths when someone pounded on the door.

"Emmie? Are you in there?" Mags's voice filtered past the closed door, forcing her to roll off the couch and stumble toward the door. Panic touched each new word as Mags pounded on the door again. "Emmie, it's important. Come on, please! Let me in!"

She tugged the door open. "What's going on?"

Mags forced her way inside and slammed the door shut behind her. "Haven't you heard the cars out there? The siren! It's Aneta; she's been taken to the ER. They're not sure if she'll make it through the night. God. It's awful. Someone beat her to a pulp. Not just that, but she's marked up as well. Like some big cat got to her. Her face is all sliced up. There are claw marks on her body, at least that's what Mike told me when I tried to get in to see what was going on."

"What?" Her heart sank. No, the only way that could have happened is if Theron had -- but why? Why would he do something like that? It didn't make sense? He'd just got through telling her he wanted to prove there was something there between them? What had he done!

Why had he done it?

No. Hold on. There'd been that other smell. Another shifter. Sure the scent had been an old one, but what if he'd come into town whilst she'd been busy with Theron in the diner. Fuck. She should have known better than to...

"A big cat. At least that's the first rumor. She was slashed up. Hard to tell. There are some nasty marks down her face. I don't know what to think. There isn't a big cat in the area, is there? I mean, you hear rumors from the hunters, the tracks they've seen the past few years, but no one's ever seen the cat. Maybe it got into her house or something?"

No, that wasn't quite true. One person had seen a large cat. But would the cops have believed the ravings of a piss-soaked drunk? Even if they had, why would they think a cat large enough to attack a human being would wander into Aneta's house? Even then, she hadn't done anything to Aneta; she'd never have attacked the woman.

But she didn't know if Theron, or another shifter, would be so careful.

"Where are they taking her? Not the local clinic, surely?" Emmie grabbed her jacket and purse.

"Pelican Mills has a small ER. So she's been taken there." Mags openly shook, her face pale, sweat beading across her brow. "I just -- Aneta has always been here, you know? She's been one of the few people in town everyone could rely on. Shit, no one even blames her for the way Jamie acts up. We know just how much work she put into raising the idiot, and she tried her best. I just can't imagine -- they said that her face -- the animal had clawed her face."

Animal. It couldn't have been a shifter. It didn't matter how little she thought of males of her kind; they weren't stupid. Not in that sense. No shifter went after people without a good reason. She'd gone further than most would by scaring Jamie, but to attack a helpless old woman? It just didn't make sense.

Even if she did want to blame Theron as a way of chasing him out of town.

"Erm, where are you going? You can't expect that they'll let you into the ER -- she's going to be pretty badly shaken up, if she even makes it. They wouldn't even tell me how bad it was, and I've known her all of my life. I -- I just..."

"No, I'm going to the house, see if I can spot any signs of that cat." Cat. Shifter. Whoever was behind the attack, she needed to know. This was her town. She couldn't just sit back and let this happen to someone like Aneta; it wasn't right.

"But you can't. What if it comes back? What are you going to do? Scream at it to go away? Are you nuts?"

"I don't..." Emmie faltered. She couldn't tell Mags that she didn't care, or that she wasn't afraid of facing off against a big cat; that would have raised too many questions. Not something she was quite ready to deal with. Still, there had to be a way, an option that would allow her to take a better look at Aneta's house. If there were any answers to be had, it would be there. "You're right. Sorry. I wasn't thinking."

"That's not like you. Normally you're so careful, it's scary."

If only she knew. "I don't like the idea of just sitting around waiting for news."

"I don't like it, either, but what other choice do we have?" Mags slumped down into the large recliner and kicked her feet up. "At least we can wait together, right?"

Emmie's shoulders tensed, her hands tightening on the bag she was still holding, before she forced a smile onto her face and tossed the bag down. She couldn't kick Mags out, and with her friend here, slipping out to try and find out what was going on just wasn't in the cards. "Fine, but if we're going to wait, then we can do that with coffee."

"Sorry, sir. I can't let you enter." The fresh-faced police officer raised his hand and tried to ignore the fact that it shook. "Unless you live on this street, we're having to restrict access. Ongoing investigation. Nothing I can do about it."

Okay, that was a new one on him. He peered around the edge of the officer, who barely looked old enough to be out of high school. He could see Emmie's car in the drive of one of the houses, but the second police car had been parked in the driveway of a house five doors away from Emmie's. Something to do with the siren he had heard? Well, it made sense that the local cops wouldn't have turned on the siren without a good reason. "So, whatever is going on involves the entire street?"

"Well, no, but Mike said I should -- I mean, Sheriff Banyon -- said I should keep people out of the street until they catch it."

"It?" His heart missed a beat.

"The animal that attacked Aneta. Big beast, they think. After what it did to Aneta, I wouldn't want to meet it face-to-face." The blond-haired deputy nodded and pushed his hat back with one finger as he shifted his weight over the balls of his feet. "We're looking for it before it can hurt someone else. Don't need it attacking someone else or killing them. Animal like that could kill a kid before we could stop it."

"Animal? What sort of animal? Did anyone have a description of it?"

"Big cat, they're saying. Her grandson said he saw it leave. Like a streak of black fur with claws and teeth. They think maybe it escaped from one of the private collections around here. So they're looking into it. Makes sense. No human could have marked the old woman up like that. Nasty shit."

Private collections? Big cat? No, if there had been a wild, or even half-tame, large feline in the area, either he or Emmie would have picked up on it. Another shifter? He took a deeper breath, tasting the aromas on the air, but the only scents he picked up were those belonging to himself and Emmie. The rest were human-based or small animals. There was nothing in the air that smelled like another shifter or even a normal large cat. Except for -- no, that one was too old to be a threat.

Then what, or who, had been behind the attack? The cop was wrong on one thing. There were weapons, human weapons, that could mimic the slashes of a claw. Well, he couldn't blame the cop for not knowing. Unless he had an interest in martial arts weapons or had studied them for a previous case, he was unlikely to know.

"Who is this Aneta?"

"You're new around here, aren't you?" The young man took a step back and looked at him. "Thought so. What brings you here? Why did you want access to this street?"

"Emmie -- we met in the city on her last trip there." Not entirely the truth, but it was close enough that the deputy was unlikely to hear the slight hitch in his voice. "Aneta is...?"

"A good woman, someone who doesn't deserve to be hurt. She's lived here most of her life, if not all. Certainly as long as I've been alive. She's the type of woman who would give you the shirt off her back. Just tears me up that she could be hurt like this." The younger man clammed up quickly and shook his head before he shifted onto a different track. "Sorry, sir. But I really can't let you enter the street. I'm sure Emmie will find a way to contact you when she's ready to. Betting she's in shock. Most of the town will be. Best if you head back to wherever you're staying."

Theron's hands clenched. He didn't like the idea of turning around and walking away. Not if there was something or someone dangerous in the area. But just what else was he meant to do? Knock the deputy senseless?

Tempting as the thought might have been, Theron nodded his thanks to the younger man, turned, and walked back down the road. There were other ways of reaching Emmie and prying into the situation. And they were ones that the deputy and his friends would not be expecting.

Coffee hadn't helped. Three hours later and she was still batting ideas back and forth with Mags over what would happen. Finally Mags's cell phone had rung, and the news had been passed down through the small-town communication chain.

"She's going to make it. Her face is marked up, but the rest of the injuries are bruises and one cracked rib. There weren't any real marks to her body from claws. And they're not even sure what caused them. They're calling in a specialist from the city to take a look at the injuries, because they're like nothing the doctors there have ever seen before. They're going to keep her in for two days to make sure she's all right and give the police a chance to investigate, but she's going to be okay." Mags closed her phone and slid it back into the pocket of her jeans.

Emmie glanced at the clock. Damn it, she couldn't just sit here all day holding her friend's hand. Not when she needed to find out just what had been going on at Aneta's. She couldn't exactly claim she needed to call it a night -- it was what? Noon? Little after that? All right, maybe this would work instead. "Mags, I hate to do this to you, but I didn't sleep well last night, and I should..."

"God, I'm sorry. I've sat here, babbling away without thinking about you. You have to be exhausted. I know you normally don't like visitors for the first few days after you've been to the city. Not sure what you get up to there, and I didn't give you an evening to yourself -- sorry about last night. I just -- Well, I kinda forgot that it was your night to shut the world out. Now look at me. I've been taking up your entire day."

"There's nothing to be sorry about, okay? I just need to grab a bath and get some sleep before I end up collapsing for a few hours. Then, maybe, we'll know more about what happened to Aneta? You look like you could do with a rest yourself." *Come on, little fishy, take the bait. You need some down time for yourself.*

"A bath. Sounds like a good idea. Might have one myself. I'll be back later. Tonight? After we've both had a rest. Maybe by then Mike will let us into Aneta's house. She can't be allowed to return home with the place in a mess, and you know men, they'll have trampled all over the place. It'll need cleaning when we can get inside. She won't like that it's been left in a mess. Would you mind helping me when we can get access?"

"Sure."

That the police and whatever investigators they would have called in would have taken care not to damage evidence was not something she was about to correct Mags on. Though there was always a chance that in such a small town the niceties of scene of crime protocols would either have been ignored or were unheard of. She doubted, in all honesty, that the sheriff and his two deputies had ever dealt with anything worse than drunken Jamie and the occasional speeding driver.

Unfair. They have their share of problems here as well. True enough. As with any rural area there were issues with drugs, meth labs, and other problems, but even with those taken into account, the town and surrounding area were relatively problem free.

"Tonight will be fine. Just go and get yourself something to eat, clean up, and we can meet up later." That's if she had finished tracking down just what, or who, had attacked Aneta.

Mags hugged her friend tight, then darted through the door without another word, leaving Emmie alone with her own thoughts.

Just what had attacked Aneta? There were only two big cats in the area, and both of them were shifters. She hadn't attacked the older woman, and despite the fact that a part of her wanted to believe that Theron would be behind the attack, she knew all too well that he wouldn't have done that. No, not without good cause, and she could think of no reason why he would have assaulted Aneta.

So, there had to be another option.

But who or what?

She was missing something. She had to be. A piece of the pie, the evidence, and in her distracted state, she wasn't able to think things through clearly.

Staying in the house wasn't going to provide any answers, and it was still daylight which would have made risking the shift to cat form dangerous enough even without the added presence of the police now combing the area for clues.

Or, at least, she presumed that's what they were doing. She hadn't even had a chance to look outside since she had been told just what was going on. And now that she opened her door and stepped outside into the driveway, she could see just how things were being handled. At the far end of the road sat the second of the three patrol cars that the small town boasted. Another, even now, pulled out from in front of Aneta's house. So whatever initial investigation had been put into place was now over.

Unless Mike assumed that no one would be foolish enough to try and enter Aneta's house?

God alone knew what was going through the man's mind.

At least she's alive.

Her gaze narrowed as she watched Mike pull out of the street, but still left behind the second car at one end of road. There was little need to block off the other end, as the road quickly vanished into little more than a track that led to a farm held by Mike's family for at least the last three generations.

The farm dogs would alert the family if a car tried to leave via the back farm roads. Not something that would, under cover of darkness, present a problem to her. But in broad daylight, with the deputy sitting at one end of the street in his car and God knew who else now wandering around, she did not dare shift into feline form and attempt to investigate matters herself.

Not yet, at least.

Waiting was something cats could do very well, when the need arose. But it didn't mean that she had to enjoy it.

Just as long as Theron kept his distance. She had to be able to focus on the problems. On whatever, or whoever, had attacked Aneta. Not on some guy who made her crave sex. Her body tightened at the memory of his touch. Maybe she needed that shower after all? Time where she could relax, replay their time together, and then...

No. Fuck no. I'm not giving him that level of power over me. Especially when he isn't even in the damn room!

Chapter Fourteen

What the hell am I doing wasting my time on this? No client. No complaint from a shifter, yet here he was, out in the woods, looking for some sign of a large cat, or an explanation as to just what was going on. It made no sense; he knew full well there wouldn't be any signs of such an animal. *I have better things I could be doing, work that would at least pay the bills, and what am I doing? Skulking around here in the hopes that it will impress some woman…*

No, not just *some woman* Emmie.

Right, she's still just some woman. A decent fuck. Pretty woman. But at the end of the day, she's just one of a dozen I've run into in the past year. Why the hell would I want to waste my time hanging around like this?

Because she was worth it? Because even whilst he had been searching through the forest, he had been unable to get her out of his mind. Every time he turned his attention to something else, he still saw her, remembered how she had writhed under him, the way her eyes had widened, the softness of her lips, and the way she had managed to crawl under his skin.

"New breed, that's what this is. She's some new breed of shifter with a chemical agent that makes her addictive. Yeah, that makes sense. Not," Theron muttered as he walked toward the edge of the trees.

Fine. So maybe I'm actually in love.

This wasn't happening!

Theron growled, his hands clenching into tight fists, knuckles white, as he stared out from the trees toward the line of houses. He was not some weak-willed human male who fell in love just because he'd fucked a woman. It didn't work that way, not with him. Or his kind. It just -- it was the only thing that made sense.

There had to be a way to…

So maybe it wouldn't be so bad if only he could…

If anyone else found out about this, he would be the laughingstock of the shifter community. So, the only real answer would mean never telling Emmie and never seeing her again. Except -- the very thought of walking away from her left him sick to his stomach.

Come on, there has to be a way. And I've known this since, well, this morning. So, I wasn't going to say the L word, but it's out there now, and once the source of a problem is discovered, it should be easier to deal with.

Right, and just how was he supposed to deal with being in love? He wasn't equipped to handle something like this.

At least Emmie didn't know, and he wasn't about to tell her. Maybe he could convince her that the reason he wanted to stay around was to see if she had children? His children? That he wanted to be a part of their lives?

It might work, but it was a long shot.

Hey, I'm supposed to be a damn professional, and I'm here arguing with myself over a bloody woman instead of doing my job.

A job he wasn't being paid for, but the mental jolt was enough to set him back on track. Buck would have his hide for this.

Theron crouched down at the edge of the tree line, searching for some sign that there had been anything other than two shifters and human beings out here. He traced his fingers over the outline of one paw print. A dog. Big one. German shepherd? It could have been one of the local farm dogs, but he didn't imagine that farm dogs were left to roam wild.

Old track though, at least a week or more, as the scent had become faint. So if the dog hadn't been one of the farm dogs, then where had it come from? A wolf? One of the canine shifters? Were there any in the area?

Theron shook his head and pushed to his feet. It hadn't been a dog that had been named as the old woman's attacker, so this wasn't getting him anywhere, either. Fuck it. This wasn't the best way to track. His senses were cut in half in human form. He needed to give up his human form and find out just what was going on. But even as Theron was about to pull at his clothing and shift into feline form, his gaze narrowed on a figure walking out, away from the houses, toward the trees.

Male, by the way he walked. Striding, little or no sway in the figure's hips. Dark jeans, and the breeze carried with it the smell of whiskey. A smell he'd had the pleasure of running into earlier on the day. The drunk. What was he doing out here? He wasn't heading toward the trees No, the man continued along the line of houses, searching for something, until he reached the chain-link fence that surrounded the back of one house.

The man stopped and looked around, before he rested his hand on the top of one fence pole, using it as a vaulting point as he jumped over the fence and into the yard. Just what in hell's name did the man think he was doing? He obviously didn't live there, and with the police presence in the area, he had to be drunk again.

Theron stepped back farther into the trees, seeking the comfort of the shadows as he watched the man walk around the edge of the houses, only to be stopped by a woman.

No. Not just a woman.

His Emmie.

"What the hell do you think you're doing, creeping round my house like this?" Emmie yanked open the back door and walked out into the yard, her gaze narrowed on Jamie. "I thought your little friend told you to stay the hell away from me."

"Come looking for you, of course. Time you and I had a word. Some things we need to sort out between us. And David doesn't need to know about this. Got it? I don't want you running telling tales on me." Jamie swayed slightly as he spoke. "Best you start treating me good, or we're gonna have a real problem."

"Ah, so you think I'm just going to lie down and let you get whatever it is you want. Shit, are you insane, Jamie, or just so drunk again that you don't even realize that climbing into someone else's yard with the cops close by is stupid even by your standards? God, you're a moron." Emmie rested her hands on her hips, staring him down. If the idiot thought she was just going to back down, he had another thing coming. Sure, changing into her cat form would have been an ideal way of frightening the fool away, but changing in broad daylight brought other dangers with it, and she couldn't risk being seen by a more sober set of eyes.

Whiskey. She could smell it on him -- and something else. A smell she knew well. Blood. Stale. Dried. She frowned, searching for some signs on his hands and face. Nothing. No cuts. No marks on his clothing that suggested he'd been in a fight. So where was the smell coming from. It was faint as well, so he hadn't bathed in the blood.

The hair on the back of her neck lifted, her skin taut, as her stomach tightened.

Sure, if he'd been in Aneta's house after she had been attacked, that would be a reasonable explanation as to why he smelled of blood. But there was another, darker reason, as to why she would be able to pick up on that scent, and it was one that sat ill at ease with her and didn't make sense as she'd been told that the woman had been attacked by an animal.

"You need a good lesson, bitch." Jamie took a wobbling step forward, and she had to wonder how the man had managed to make it over her fence without falling flat on his face.

"What you need is a strong cup of coffee and a cold shower. Go on, get out of my sight before I scream for the cops. Just what you need right now, isn't it? Another night in jail. Only this time it wouldn't be because your grandma called them. Ever thought of that? She drops the charges, or lets you off with a warning. Not me. I'd have them throw the book at you. I wouldn't even have to tell your good buddy about this. You'd end up in prison. Not just the local lock shop. The pen. Assault. And I bet you're armed too, illegally, of course. So you'd go down for threatening a woman with a weapon, or whatever the correct phrasing would be. That would look really good on your rap sheet, wouldn't it?"

The color drained from his face as Jamie took a step back, his hands tightening into fists at his side. "You wouldn't dare. They'd never believe you, even if you tried. I'd tell them you invited me over and -- and ..."

"And what? Everyone around here knows I don't have a boyfriend, Jamie. They'd never accept any half-baked lie of yours claiming that you and I had something going. Shit, they know I've turned you down. Want to try again?" Emmie struggled not to laugh in his face. Sober, the man wasn't too smart, but drunk, he came close to being a complete moron. "Or are you going to back the fuck down and crawl out of here."

Jamie stood there, his hands clenching and unclenching at his sides. "You're -- I've always known you belonged to me. Ever since you moved in to this godforsaken shit hole."

"Gee, I must've missed the time-warp sign where it let me know men here had a right to wander up to a woman, grab her by the hair, club her over the head, and drag her back to their cave."

"But I..."

"Get out. Now. Before I get the cops in here," Emmie growled. "And you know I'll do it. I don't care if you spend the rest of your life behind bars. I don't have a soft spot for you like Aneta does. I'll laugh if they lock you up."

"Emmie, please..." His bottom lip trembled.

God, drunks were pathetic. "I said, get out."

"You can't do this to me. I -- I love you."

It took every ounce of self-control Emmie possessed not to roll her eyes and laugh in his face. After all of the work Aneta had put into the man, all those years of care and love, and this is what he had decided to do with his life? Spend it as a hopeless, violent drunk. "No, Jamie. You don't. The only thing you love is the booze.

Maybe if you stopped drinking for a few days, you'd realize just how big a fool you're making of yourself and how fucked up your life is."

Jamie didn't speak, not for several long minutes. Instead he stood there, shaking violently, before he finally turned around and stumbled out of the yard, clambering over the fence to then vanish from sight.

Only then did Emmie let out a long, slow breath, one she hadn't even been aware that she'd been holding onto. She couldn't just stand there and wait for the next blow to fall, or the new problem to arrive in her backyard. Even if she couldn't risk shifting into cat form, she had to find out just what was going on.

Standing out here, she'd become all too well aware of just how quiet it now was. No police, no dogs, nothing searching through the trees or the surrounding area for some trace of whatever had been responsible for the attack on Aneta. She didn't even know, for certain, if Mags had been right. If there had been an animal-like attack on the older woman, then there would have been a search party out for the animal. Yet she hadn't seen, nor heard, any sign of such.

Had Mags been wrong?

It would explain a lot, but then why had Mags been so convinced that there had been an animal involved in the attack. It wasn't something she'd have said unless she had either seen the results herself, or had been told of them by someone she trusted. So just why had no one let loose the dogs to track down the animal responsible for the assault?

A change in the breeze brought something else into focus.

Theron. He was out there. Watching her.

His scent tormented her. It threatened to wrap itself about her body, heart, and soul. She growled, under her breath. Her nipples crinkled beneath her dress. Heat rippled through her core, liquid need coated her inner walls, and without thinking, she took a step toward the chain-link fence.

Scars

No.

She froze, her hands clenched into fists, nails digging into her palms. *No.* She wouldn't answer the call of her body. Not this time. She would rule her body; she would not let her body rule her choices. It didn't matter that her needs demanded her attention. Not until she was certain that he was innocent of the attack on Aneta would she allow him to touch her again.

But it would have been so very easy to give in to the desires that bubbled into life. He knew how to caress her, how to make her body soar, and she wanted to feel that again. To taste the ecstasy. She belonged in his arms, touching him, being touched, the feel of his lips against hers, the way he had stroked her body, teased her senses…

She took a deep breath, shaking as she tried to focus away from what they had shared the night before. It didn't help that her inner walls rippled with hunger, or that her skin tightened, nipples tingled, or heart raced. She couldn't give in to this, not even when her heart and soul both demanded that she vault over the back of the fence and chase him down. Chase him and claim him.

And then what? Be with him for a few hours before he finally moves on? What would be the point? Other than mind-blowing sex?

Am I saying that isn't enough of a reason? God knows he left me sated in a way no other man has managed. Would spending one more night with him really be such a bad idea? Just as long as I remember that he's going to leave after we've finished?

Emmie turned and walked back into the house, her mind in turmoil. She had to get to the bottom of this before the oddities of the situation drove her insane.

Chapter Fifteen

Theron had barely covered half of the distance to the house when Jamie had re-appeared on the right side of the fence. Relief washed through him as he witnessed the drunken sot stumble away from Emmie's house; but even with Jamie now out of the way, and his sharp sense of hearing able to pick up the sound of Emmie's path back into the house and the sound of the door being closed, he still wasn't convinced that she was safe. Even with Jamie out of the way, there still remained the mystery of just what had been behind the attack on the other woman.

Jamie and his friend, David. They both left him wanting to shift into cat form and scare the shit out of them. Do something, anything that would keep them away from Emmie. They didn't deserve to be anywhere near her. His hands clenched, the muscles knotting across his shoulders. He couldn't do anything to keep them away from her. And by rights, unless they attacked her, there was nothing he had the right to do. She hadn't asked him for his help. She wasn't in real danger. Nothing that would put her in a danger that she lacked the ability to protect herself from.

Never before had Theron felt so lost or helpless. He didn't know where to start. What path to take. He couldn't find any sign of other big cats except the two shifters he knew were in the area. He hadn't attacked the woman, and he doubted that Emmie had, though he would be the first to admit he didn't know the woman.

Could Emmie be behind the attack?

No. That made no sense.

The only reason a shifter attacked a human, other than to protect themselves, or their people, would be for a criminal act. Insanity? She hadn't shown any signs of madness or the rage that he had come to associate with those rare shifters who sought out humans as prey.

Could he have misjudged her that easily?

Theron ran his fingers through his hair and tried to look normal as he turned and walked back toward town. His motorbike would still be parked on the edge of town, and it wouldn't take him long to drive back to the motel. Maybe there, away from the constant reminder of her alluring scent, he would be able to think clearly and work out just what was going on.

His path took him past the back of Aneta's house, the same direction Jamie had walked. In a larger city, he wouldn't have been able to do this, walk so close to the scene of a crime, but out here they lacked the manpower. Or they were out trying to track down the animal they thought was responsible for the attack. No, he'd have seen some sign of them out in the forest. He hadn't even heard dogs. Just what was going on out here?

What was he missing?

Small towns didn't mean lack of intelligence or the inability to understand procedure. It just meant fewer people and perhaps a lack of some of the niceties that the larger cities had. No individual CSI unit to call on and they had smaller pools of resources and manpower to use in situations like this, but there was still something missing here.

Theron stopped at the edge of the yard that marked the house where Aneta lived. The more he thought about it, the more he knew he was missing something in all of this. He peered through the chain-link fence, searching. Had anyone, other than Jamie, even been in the backyard? If not, why not?

He inhaled slowly, tasting the scents on the air. Jamie. Aneta, perhaps? He hadn't met the woman, so couldn't be certain that he was picking up on her scent. But who else had traipsed through the yard? David? He knew that man's smell. He'd been here and recently. And one other. Another man. One he hadn't met yet. There was something familiar about the trail, and he was close. Still close enough to be a problem.

"What are you doing out here?" A new voice broke through his thoughts. One that belonged to the smell he had been picking up. "Do I know you?"

"Just taking a walk, and no, I don't believe we've met, Sheriff." He turned to face the newcomer. Uniform. That's what he had been smelling. The starch that had been used on the man's uniform. He had to have been in it all day, and yet it looked as though it had just come out of the closet. Theron had never seen creases that sharp on a set of pants before, or a shirt. Ex-military?

Even then, this was going a little far.

He took a deep breath. There was something else, something that set his teeth on edge.

"Your name?" The man's voice was cold, distant, as he took in every inch of Theron's body. Not in a sexual way. No, instead Theron knew just what the man was looking for. Weapons.

"Theron Grave."

"Odd name. Greek? Never mind, doesn't matter." The sheriff grunted, shaking his head. "And what's brought you to town? When did you arrive?"

"Emmie." He nodded toward the back of Emmie's house. Although he wanted to tell the man to go to hell, he knew, only too well, that wasn't the way to deal with members of law enforcement. "We met in the city. I came down to see her again. I booked into the Motel 6 on the edge of town last night."

"Emmie, huh? Never met one of her men before. You're not quite what I expected to see." The man took a step back and looked over him again. "Not what I expected at all."

The hair on the back of Theron's neck stood up. Did this one know that Emmie sought out men every month to sate her needs? No, Emmie struck him as the careful type. She wouldn't have done something that could alert those in town to her true nature. It just wasn't like her or any shifter that he had known. Still, he pushed, trying to find out a little more. "Ah, and just what did you expect?"

"Something a little more -- well -- wild." The man shrugged. "Not that it matters what Emmie gets up to or with whom. Not as though she's family or anything like that. Anyway, I'm Mike Banyon, town sheriff." He held out his hand for a friendly shake, but there was nothing warm or welcoming in the man's eyes. "Good to meet you."

Theron took Mike's hand, gripping it firmly. "Good to meet you too. I heard there's been a bit of trouble here?"

"Nothing I can't handle." Neither man broke the grip they had on the other. "We've already got the matter in hand. I'm sure we'll have the culprit under lock and key before much longer."

Lock and key? Not something you normally applied to an animal. "Ah, I was told this was an animal attack."

"Sorry." Mike pulled his hand back quickly, shifting his weight from one foot to the other. "How long do you plan on being in town? A few days?"

The warning signs became full-blown "Danger, Will Robinson!" announcements in the back of his mind. He'd never met a member of law enforcement who acted like this before. It couldn't just be because this was a small town. That didn't make sense. So just what in hell's name was going on?

He inhaled slowly, tasting the man's scent fully. There. Something he recognized. Masked carefully. But how? And why? God, of course. Why hadn't he realized it sooner?

"I asked you a question," Mike pressed.

"Not sure yet. But do you mind if I ask you a question in return?" *How the hell did he learn to mask this? And where is he getting the aftershave from, or whatever it is he's calling it?* Theron relaxed, the tension easing from his shoulders as he looked the man directly in the eyes.

Mike nodded sharply.

"How many others know you're a werewolf, Sheriff Banyon?"

The color drained from Mike's face. "How the hell..."

"Did I know? Not easy, but I make my living out of tracking shifters down. I've never met one able to disguise his scent as well as you, though. Nice little trick. Not one others have seen past before, or you'd have denied it. I doubt you thought anyone else would ever figure it out."

For several long minutes, Mike didn't speak as he eased his weight from one foot to the other. "I'd prefer it if you didn't tell Emmie, or anyone else for that matter."

"Ashamed?"

"No, I just don't want what I am to be used to compromise my ability to do my work." Mike looked him straight in the eye. "I'm a cop first, shifter second. Look, if I ever have to arrest a shifter, I don't want them blackmailing me and trying to get me to drop the charges."

Interesting. Would a shifter try to blackmail his way out of trouble? Why wouldn't they? Just because they had the ability to shift shape didn't mean they were born with a better sense of morals. But there was something else that suddenly hit Theron, and he felt his gaze narrowing. "Then you know that the one responsible for the attack on the old woman is neither a shifter, nor a large cat." Theron nodded toward the back of Aneta's house.

"Yes. Unfortunately, until the test results come back, I've nothing more to go on than instincts that will never stand up in court."

And that was a situation he understood all too well. "So what will you do now?"

"Do what any cop does -- follow the evidence. As for you" -- Mike nodded toward Emmie's house -- "it might be best if you keep her occupied so she doesn't get in the way of things. Emmie's a good woman, but she's not the type to sit meekly out of the way when the shit hits the fan."

"What makes you think she'd get in the way?"

"I saw Jamie try and push things with her. She's not the type to just let him get away with that. Right now she'll be stewing, pacing in her house, and muttering to herself. Sooner or later, she'll explode and go after him, or try to do something stupid like track down those responsible for Aneta's injuries. I can't have that.

Scars

If you want to keep her out of trouble, then I suggest you go and keep her occupied. I'm sure a big, strong cat can figure out a way to distract her."

Emmie paced through the small house, muttering under her breath. Just what was it with men recently? Was she wearing a sign that stated, hey, I'm available, even if I'm not, so come claim me?

Well, it wasn't going to work that way. If those men thought she was just going to roll over for the first one who walked into her life, they had another thing coming. It wasn't going to work that way. No, she had plans, and they didn't involve a man. Not even if he could make her body sing.

A sharp knock on the door pulled her out of her thoughts. She growled and turned, stalking her way to the door. Before she even touched it, the smell hit her. His scent. What the fuck was he doing here? Her shoulders tensed, knuckles white as she closed her hand on the door and yanked it open. Anger flickered and lost its hold on her body. Her nipples crinkled, body tightening even before she looked into his eyes. She wanted him. Even as she looked at him, she wanted him. Why couldn't she just smack him in the jaw and be done with him?

"What the hell are you doing here?" She glared at him, trying to look as angry as she wanted to feel.

"I would have thought that was obvious. I came to see you." Theron leaned against the doorframe and stared down at her.

She blinked, only now realizing that he was a good three inches taller when in human form than she was. How had she missed that last night? Her inner walls rippled, heat coating them, as she stared at him. Just what was it about this man? She was at the tail end of her cycle; he shouldn't have the ability to affect her this way. So what the hell was going on with her? "Well, I'm not in the mood for visitors."

"Oh, you could have fooled me." He took a step into the house, his voice a low growl. "In fact, I'm convinced that you want me in your house and inside your body."

Her hand clenched, before Emmie was even aware of what she was doing, her hand was flying out toward his face. "You arrogant son of a bitch!"

He caught her wrist before her hand could strike and pushed farther into the house, kicking the door closed behind him. "Yes, I am. But you already knew that."

"Funny, for a short while, in the diner, I thought I glimpsed a human side." Emmie growled and tried to yank her wrist back out of his grasp. "Remember, you offered to give me three days."

"Yes, I did. I never said I'd leave you alone for those three days." He let go of her wrist and leaned against the now-closed door. "But if you really want me to leave, just say the word. I'll turn around and walk out of the door without so much as tasting your sweet body. No tender touches across your back, no firm hand cupping your ass, nothing more than a smile, a nod, and I'll walk out of the house."

She opened her mouth, knowing she wanted to tell him to get the hell out of her house and never come back. But somewhere between her mind and her lips, the words lost their path, and instead of a cold, taut demand, a low whimper slipped free instead. No, she couldn't give in to this. Not when she had other things she could be doing, he was just -- just a...

Just the most handsome, sensual, strong man she had ever known. Her body throbbed with the need for his touch. She belonged with him. Under him. On top of him. Any way she could get him. Her lips ached for the feel of his kiss. But her mind screamed the warning, to stay away, keep back from him, not let him touch her. He -- he was just a male shifter. He was someone who would only ever bring her heartbreak, and she knew better than to let him in.

"You want me to stay, don't you?" He leaned closer, his breath teasing across her lips with the promise of so much more to come.

Scars

"You're angry at yourself, even at the world around you, for how your body craves my touch. But you can't help how you feel, either."

"Just -- please. I need time." The words slipped out as little more than a whimper. God. She had to take control of the situation. Before it was too late. "This isn't happening between us. I won't let it. I don't need…"

"No, what you need is my touch. You can deny it all you want. God knows, I've tried justifying it to myself. I don't want to need you, either. It's humiliating. Shifters don't act like this. But this is happening. We can either give in to and enjoy it, or suffer in silence, alone, our bodies aching for each other." Theron let his gaze slowly work over her body, lingering across her breasts even as her nipples tightened and pressed against the soft material. "You think I'm an arrogant bastard. Right now you'd be correct. You can't understand why you'd want to be with me anymore than I understand why I'm drawn to you. But why don't we just enjoy what we're feeling and find out the reasons later."

Tell him to get out. Now. Before it's too late. Simple words to say, but why didn't it work. Why couldn't she just look him in the eye and tell him to leave? *Because I want him. I need him. I can't get him out of my system.*

Fine. They could figure out the reasons behind this later. He'd already made it clear that whatever it was that was affecting them both had him as uncomfortable with the situation as she was.

"Close the door." Emmie took a step back from him, her gaze never leaving his face as she fumbled with her dress, pulling it off. Without a word, she dropped it to the floor and stood there in nothing more than a pair of panties and her pride. "Well, are you going to stand there all day, or do something about this?"

Theron let out a long, low growl, his eyes alight, his gaze narrowed on her near-naked form. "You have a way with words, my little kitty."

"Call me that again, and I'll cut your damn balls off." Her hands clenched, nails lengthening without effort. "I'm not yours, and don't ever call me kitty again. My name is Emmie. Remember that. I don't care if you scream it out, but that's the only name you'll ever call me. Got it!"

His face cracked with a wicked grin as he took a step toward her. "Oh, I think you'll be the one doing the screaming, Emmie."

Oddly enough, she didn't doubt that. "Not if all you do is stand there trying to come up with something witty to say."

Theron pulled at his clothing, a low purr filling the air as he stalked slowly toward her, dropping his shirt and jeans along the way. Her heart skipped a beat. No underwear. Commando. God. What was it about this man? He could have her shivering, ready for sex, just by looking at her. It just -- just wasn't fair.

And neither of them were blond, so that didn't count.

His cock throbbed, thickening between his thighs, his body taut as he closed the gap between them, his hands claiming her upper arms. "You're mine. If only for a few hours, Emmie. Mine and no one else's. I'll make you forget those humans. I'll spoil you for them."

She had no doubt he was about to do just that. Her body tingled, and all he was doing was holding her by the arms. *All right, so he was naked and holding her, but it wasn't as though he was -- Oh.* He lowered his head, lips touching her skin as he nibbled softly along the line of her shoulder. Teasing her flesh with the tip of his tongue, he felt her skin tightened beneath his touch.

Emmie arched under his caress. Her eyes drifted closed, her body alive, craving so much more than a simple kiss, a shiver running through her body as heat rippled through her being and into her sex. Men shouldn't have the ability to do this to her, to leave her wanting everything and nothing at the same time. Her nipples throbbed; she wanted to feel his skin brushing over them, or his hair loose teasing her flesh.

She needed him.

More than she had ever needed a living soul before.

Scars

Her thighs clenched, a soft rocking claimed her hips. She wasn't going to just stand there, waiting for him to press her against the floor, or the wall, or bend her over the couch...

Fuck. That sounded like a good idea.

Emmie pulled away from him, smiling as he growled. His eyes glowed, body tight; his lips parted, baring his teeth.

"Wait there. Just wait." She backed away, trying to think straight. God, she needed him. Now. Waiting just wasn't an option. Not this time. Second time around they could take it slow, but right now all she wanted was his cock buried deep within her body.

"Why."

"Because it will be worth the wait." Emmie turned her back on him and walked over to the table she very rarely used. Her hips swayed with each step, her hair loose over her shoulders, teasing her flesh with featherlight touches. His gaze traced her body; he wasn't even touching her, and she could feel his presence, the way her skin craved him, needed him. Her inner walls tightened. She needed to feel him press deep within her body, to claim her, bury his thick cock between her walls, and it would be enough. Just enough to keep her going through the next few hours, enough to calm her body down so she could think again.

Emmie pressed her hands against the smooth wood of the table. Would she ever be able to eat a meal off it again? Come to think of it, had she ever used it for that before?

"God!" Theron hissed as she leaned over the table and looked back at him through a mane of dark hair.

"Fuck me." She purred at him, wriggling her ass slowly, lifting up her hips. "Pull down my panties and just fuck me. You want to. I know you do."

He took a step closer, tracing the tip of his finger across her panty-covered ass. "Pull them down? No, not fully. Not when I can do this instead." He tugged them slowly down over the curve of her ass cheeks, leaving them at the bottom of her buttocks, a tight band of cloth that served to bind her legs together. "Such a sexy little beast you are."

She growled, pressing her hands against the wood as she tried to lift up from the wood. No. She wasn't a beast!

But I am. I've always been one.

He pressed down against her back, forcing her back onto the wood with one hand, even as he teased his fingertips along her buttocks. Her hips rolled, a low whimper forming at the back of her throat. Here. She belonged here, with him, his touch bringing her body to life. Her inner walls cream-coated, panties damp, and her thighs taut as she lifted her bottom up into his touch.

"You like that, don't you." One hand remained pressed down against her back, his grip firm as he held her against the table. "Yes, I can see you do. Hungry for more. You can't understand why I want to tease you, why I need to see you squirm. But you will. In time, you will."

Emmie whimpered, her nails scraping against the wood. "Please. Just…"

"No. Not yet." He leaned down, nibbling slowly along her back as he traced his fingertips over her buttocks. "Not yet, Emmie."

Why. God, why did he want to tease her? Hadn't it been enough to see her walk over to the table, bend over, and tell him to fuck her? Most men would have been within her by now. But not Theron. What was he doing?

Proving he was the dominant one between them?

Could it be that simple?

At the end of the day, it didn't matter. Just as long as he eventually plunged his cock into her willing body.

Chapter Sixteen

It would have been so very easy to rip her panties from her body, part her thighs, and plunge into her damp, tight core. He could almost feel it, the way her cream-coated walls would clamp around his cock, the pulsing desire that would ripple through her body, and yet -- yet he couldn't. Not yet.

Come on. Why wait? She needs it. Wants it.

She wasn't his. Not yet. That's why. When he claimed her, he wanted to know that he owned her. Body, mind, and soul. That she cried out his name because it was the only one that she knew. The only man she would ever accept again.

Do I want to go that far? Do I need to claim her as mine to that level? Do I have to mark her soul for all eternity?

Yes. Hell, yes. She belonged to him. She had since the first moment he had caught her scent. He just had to find a way of showing her that, teaching her that within his arms she would be safe. Not just now, but until the end of their days.

His breath caught in the back of his throat as he moved through the room, his gaze fixing on her backside. Slowly he leaned forward, tugging down her panties, her plea to be fucked still echoing in his ears. His cock pulsed, heat claimed his being, and yet he knew he couldn't give in to the desires that threatened to consume him. Not if he wanted to stand a chance at claiming her.

She arched half up off the table, but with one of his hands pressed against the small of her back, Emmie was quickly pinned back down on the wood. Her body writhed under his light touch, responding as if he had stroked her with a thousand touches instead of barely a handful. How could he be this lucky? To find a woman so warm, willing, and sensual. Yet strong, powerful, with enough courage to face him down, to stand against him in the forest, to strip herself off in the middle of her living room and set down a challenge for him, then submit, in a small fashion, to his touch.

"Please," she whimpered, her hips rolling, pressed against the edge of the table. "You're teasing me. Don't."

"Yes."

"Don't, please don't."

"Why?" He leaned down, pressing his lips against the back of her neck. Emmie shivered under his light touch. A low moan slipped free, her breasts pressed fully to the wood, nipples hard, her thighs trying to part, but her panties holding them together.

"I need you." Emmie twisted, looking up at him. "God, please. Just fuck me. Now."

His cock jumped, his balls tight, pressed against his groin. It would have been so very easy to strip off her panties and thrust into her tight, willing sex. But it wasn't time. No, it wasn't time. "Patience, Emmie. Please."

But who was the one who really had to be patient? Emmie or the man who now traced his fingers over her sweet curves.

He growled. Her body arched. The smell of her arousal filled the air. Each low moan or whimper only served to tease him. He wanted her. His cock craved the feel of her slick walls, but his mind screamed, "*No!*" Wait. Be patient. Tease her a little more. He lifted up his hand, watching how her buttocks lifted up, waiting for the next gentle touch of his fingers.

A wicked grin claimed his lips as he cracked his hand down against her backside. Her head lifted up from the table, a low O formed on her lips as she cried out in shock and pain. Her body jerked with the blow, a soft cry filling the air as his hand stung. He spanked her. For the first time in his life he'd spanked a grown woman. She groaned and lowered her head back down on the table, heat radiated out from the red spot on her bottom. His cock jerked. The memory of the sound replayed through his mind, and his cock liked it.

Scars

His hand tightened. What would it be like to spank her, fully, to tease soft yelps into life from her sweet lips? She'd enjoy it. They both would. That much he knew without asking.

No, not this time.

Not this time, but maybe next? If there were other times together. Yes, there would be, days or nights when he could explore what it was like to have her whimpering and squirming from the feeling of his hand cracking down against her ass. She hadn't complained. Or begged, or snarled for him to stop. Instead he could see she half lifted her ass up toward him, silently wanting to feel his touch again.

Her pink, swollen lips peeked out at him between her thighs. Slick heat beckoned his touch. She groaned, hips rolling as she looked back at him, her eyes wide. "Please, Theron, please. Don't make me wait any longer. I can't stand it. I need you. I need to feel you inside me."

It would have been so very easy. His cock throbbed. All he had to do was walk behind her and press his cock between her thighs, and he'd feel it. Her hungry, damp walls wrapped about his body. He licked slowly down her spine, tasting her. She groaned, wriggling beneath his touch, her thighs straining as she tried to force them apart, only to find her panties still bound them together.

Right now she was sweet, helpless, and almost innocent, at least in the momentary fantasy that forced its way into the forefront of his mind.

"Such a naughty kitty, aren't you? Panties down around your thighs, ass up in the air." He growled against the curve of her spine. "Maybe I should spank you again. No -- no, not this time. But another. I can just imagine how pink your skin will turn under my touch."

Emmie caught her lip between her teeth as she looked at him through a mane of dark hair. Heat flushed across her cheeks, her eyes wide, shocked, that deer-in-the-headlights look, something he had never expected to see on her face.

"Yes, another time, kitten."

She growled instantly at that name, arching up, trying to fight her way off the table, but he could still smell it. Her arousal. Her need. She wasn't fighting his touch, just the name he had called her.

"Pretty little kitten."

She growled afresh, her fingers shifting, nails lengthening back into claws. The points dug into the wood, her body changing as she snarled her fury at him, then whimpered, shifting back into full human form. "Arrogant bastard!"

"Yes, I am."

"I told you not to call me that." She groaned, her eyes closing for a brief moment. "Are you going to tease me all night or actually do something here?" She squirmed against the table. "You're just -- just trying to anger me, frustrate me. You've no intention of fucking me. So let me go, and I'll go find a human to..."

Anger and hunger raged into life at her words. No. She wasn't going to find some human to fuck around with. She belonged to him. Totally to him. He'd show her. Have her. Take her. Claim her. She was his. His mate!

He moved behind her, grasping her hips with both hands, the head of his cock sliding between her thighs. With a low growl, he rolled his hips, sliding deep within her sex, claiming her to the hilt as she cried out in joy, her slick, tight walls clenching around his erection, holding him deep within her. His balls slapped against her body, heat and pressure building up in the pit of his being. His fingers dug into her hips, holding her close, rocking her against the table. Each thrust scraped the table a little farther along the floor. He knew, even without looking, that the edge of the table now jarred a line against her body, a deep set of bruises that would be there the following day.

Neither of them cared.

Slick sounds filled the air as she rocked back against him,

welcoming each thrust into her body. His cock throbbed, thighs shook, sweat dripped down from his face and chest onto his back as she clawed against the table. She lifted her head up, hair falling across her face, catching in her full lips as she groaned, welcoming him with each thrust into her body.

He couldn't hold back. Pressure built. Pain and pleasure mixed as her body tightened on his cock. He couldn't stop this. He didn't want to. He growled, lifting his head, screaming out his delight to the world as his seed filled her being. Claiming her. Owning her.

She sobbed out, arching on the table, her core rippling, liquid desire mingling with his release, her hips still rolling, responding to his presence. He hadn't even realized she'd been close. Yet it felt right. So very right that they had come together.

This is where he belonged, buried deep in her body, her scent, the hunger that rocked through them both, filling the air. He'd waited so very long to feel this way, never knowing what he was missing, or why sex with others felt empty, leaving him wanting something he had no name for.

Now it had a name.

She had a name.

Emmie.

Chapter Seventeen

"Theron?" Emmie pressed against the table, his weight pinned her to the smooth, polished wood. Helpless. She hadn't wanted to disturb him. She'd never felt so right with a man still buried in her body. Instead she'd normally tell them to move the moment it was over. But with him, it felt right. His body, hers, they meshed completely. But now she needed to move, to clean up, perhaps -- perhaps even share that time with him?

"Am I too heavy for you?" he whispered against her ear, sending a soft shiver of delight through her body. "Do you need me to move yet?"

"A little too heavy. But it's not painful. Not yet." The edge of the table dug into her hips. She'd feel that later, but the bruise would be gone by the following morning. At least that was something about being a shifter; the ability to heal quickly was one of the few blessings of her people. "I need to clean up. A shower. Just so I don't feel so sticky."

Theron shifted his weight, his cock pressing against her inner walls before he pulled back from her and took a step away from the table. "A shower sounds like a good idea to me right now." His voice shook, the certainty fading as he held out one hand to her, offering her a steadying point.

What had happened? They'd both enjoyed what they had shared, but there was something going on with him now. A look in his eyes that she hadn't seen before -- no, not entirely true, she'd seen something like it when they'd spoken in the diner earlier in the day. "One you'd like to share?"

"Sure," he nodded.

Emmie looked at him, watching him closely. Her body throbbing, nipples still tingled, craving his touch. It would have been so very easy to be with him again, to feel his touch stroke its way across her body, teasing her into life again. But they couldn't. Not now. She needed time, so did he, to figure out just what was going on between them.

Why wasn't he walking out? It didn't make any sense to her.

Twice now they'd fucked each other senseless. By shifter standards that was once too often. So what the hell was going on?

"I'm as confused as you are, Emmie." He reached out, stroking his fingers across the line of her jaw. "I know how it works. Shit, I've always just walked away after -- well, yeah. And now. Now I can't leave. The thought of walking out on you is sickening to me. I can't do it."

"But that -- it's not how it works with cats. We both know that."

"Yeah, tell me about it," he grumbled, shaking his head. "I'm not sure what's going on. I wish I had an answer for you, but I don't. I just don't. God. It's weird. I need you. Want you. I have to be with you. It's like I have no control over this. Something's happening to me. You're all I can think of. All I want -- and I'm sounding like a fuckin' madman." He groaned and turned away from her, sitting down hard on the couch, naked as the day he'd been born.

"That's because you are one." She tried to let a hint of humor slip into her voice, but it didn't work. Theron flinched and glared at her.

"Thanks a lot," he grumbled, though a light danced within his eyes.

"Sorry, I'm just not sure what else to say." Emmie took a deep breath. She wanted answers, needed them, but her body wanted something else as well. A shower, clean clothing, and maybe some food. There were other things as well, the way -- even after the way he had taken her -- the way his body had buried into hers, she still wanted him. She needed him again, his cock claiming her core, rocking into her, taking her deeper by the moment, just as he had on the table.

No. This wasn't going to happen again. Not right now. They had things they needed to discuss. Or they did once they were cleaned up and thinking straight. "I need that shower. You can either wait for me to finish in the bathroom, or join me." *Join me, touch me, be with me again. God. I don't understand this. I belong to you. With you.*

For a moment he didn't move, his gaze locked on her face. His lips parted in a soft, hungry smile as he slowly pushed to his feet. His gaze slowly moved down from her face, lingering over her breasts, then down, carefully down her body, her taut stomach, to the soft down between her thighs, before he moved his gaze back up to her face. His eyes all but glowed, his lips parting softly before he spoke. "Yes, I think I'll join you, Emmie."

Heat surged through her core at his words. A dozen unseen fingers brushed over her breasts. Her nipples crinkled afresh into hardened pips on her breasts. A shower. Just a shower. If she kept focused on that, then they'd be safe. It wouldn't turn into anything more between them. She didn't need it to become anything more.

Did she?

She swallowed hard and turned, leading him through the house. Her bare feet made little sound on the floor. Her panties were lost behind her on the rug. Her inner thighs were slick with the pleasure they had so recently shared. But she had to clean herself off. It wasn't like her to enjoy being sticky. She'd never liked being sticky.

He followed close behind her, reaching out once to trace his fingertips down her back, over her buttocks. She tried not to whimper, not to press back against his light caress. No, she had to ignore it. Shut it out. Just focus on being clean. That would help. She had to clean off.

"Nice place you have here." He leaned close as she bent over the tub and turned the water on. "Pretty. But you've not been here long, have you?"

Scars

"What makes you say that?"

"You've still got unpacked boxes around the house." He leaned down, pressing his lips against the curve of her spine.

Emmie shivered, her breath catching in the back of her throat. She didn't have time to go through this again with him.

Why not? It's not as though I have an appointment to be somewhere else today.

Because -- well, there were other things she had to do. Besides, Mags would be knocking on the door later on. And she still wanted to find out just what was going on with Aneta, who had attacked her and why. Had Theron had something to do with that? No, if nothing else, the time line didn't fit. He'd been at the diner with her, and being a newcomer to town, he'd be the first potential human suspect. Well, maybe not the first, but pretty close to it. So, no, despite her initial feelings that it could have been him, her common sense had firmly knocked that idea on the head.

"I haven't seen the need to unpack them all." The words sounded lame, even to her own ears. Just why wouldn't she unpack? "I moved around a lot as a kid; I guess I'm just used to leaving some stuff in boxes in case I have to move again."

"So, are you planning on leaving, moving somewhere else?" He rested his hands on her waist as she stood up. "I would have thought this town suited you, except for one thing. The need to vanish into the city every month."

Her skin tingled beneath his touch, her racing heart pounding against her rib cage. Every inch of her body felt drawn tight, waiting for his caress, for something more than simply being held. But it didn't make sense. She'd already been with him; her body had been sated, so why did she now crave his touch again?

"Does it really matter if I am or not?" She tried to edge away from him. Water hit the tub, steam curling upward into the air, filling the bathroom. "Did you want to wait for the shower?" She half wanted him to say yes, that he'd wait for her to finish in the shower before taking one himself, but his gaze lit up.

"No, I don't see a reason to wait, do you? Not when we can share and enjoy the moment together."

Her throat closed, little more than a low whimper slipping from her lips. Emmie swallowed hard and turned, setting out clean towels before she stepped into the shower, trembling under the caress of the hot water. The shower curtain flipped a second time as he followed her into the tub and stepped close behind her.

"Cats don't like water. Strange, isn't it, that feline shifters seem to enjoy it? It doesn't really make sense, does it?"

"It's our human side." She tried to force her voice to sound normal, but it wasn't working. "That's the only thing that fits." Maybe it was their human sides that even now forced them together? Sure, her pheromones, the call of her body in heat, had been the initial trigger to pull them together, but keeping him here? That had to be a human need, not a feline one.

"Then it's a human pleasure I've come to enjoy a great deal in the past few moments." He leaned closer, his hands skimming their way along her thighs before they came to settle on her waist. "One I could come to love, in the right circumstances."

A long shiver rocked a teasing path through her body, her eyes closing, thick lashes brushing the upper curves of her cheeks. Small droplets of water caught on her lashes, danced across her face, even as larger drops beaded across her breasts, tugging a sensual path down over her taut skin.

She leaned back against him, a soft jolt claiming her hips as she felt the outline of his thick erection press between her buttocks. She groaned, trying not to press back onto him, though her core ached for the feel of his cock deep within her again. What had he done to her? She'd never been this hungry for sex before now, not unless she was fully in heat, and she hadn't been touched for a good month. But this wasn't the case this time. Her body had been sated not fifteen minutes ago.

Was this love?

Scars

Or just overpowering lust?

Does it matter? Just go with the flow!

Why not, it had worked so far.

"I've never met anyone like you, Emmie. I should be running a mile. Finding a way to keep you away from me. You're dangerous to me. So why am I not halfway out of the door already?"

"You mean with me chasing you away, my hands on a shotgun? I wish I had an answer for you. For both of us. Shit, you're everything I was warned about. You're the boogeyman. The shadow in the night that should send me screaming or hiding under the bedclothes. Theron, you're the man that I was warned would walk into my life and turn it upside down without a thought." She groaned, wishing she could take back the words, but it was too late.

"Ah, so have I turned the world upside down for you?" He leaned down, nipping softly along her shoulder before he scraped his teeth over the back of her neck. "Well, now. Are you going to answer? Tell me, then, have I truly walked into your life and left you wondering which way to turn? I think I should know the answer to that one."

"Yes."

"Yes, I should know. Or yes, I have?" He chuckled, nuzzling into her hair, his fingers tracing slow patterns along her sides.

Shivers ran down her spine, into her core, teasing her senses as she tried to focus and reach for the soap. Her fingers closed on the bottle of shower gel, her lips parting for a moment before she found the strength to reply to him. "You've turned everything upside down."

"Good." He reached out and took the bottle from her hand. "Let me do that."

"What?" She gulped as the bottle slipped from her grasp.

"I want to wash you down." He took a step back from her, a low chuckle in his voice.

Emmie turned to face him, the water now pounding against

her back as she looked at him. Her nipples tightened, beads of water falling from their ripe points, tugging at her sensitive flesh. His eyes gleamed, a wicked smile danced across his face as he looked at her. Heat burned a path through her intimate flesh, a low moan threatening to erupt into life as she swallowed it and forced what she hoped sounded like normal speech from her lips. "I thought we were just going to get cleaned off? Wasn't that the plan?"

"Who said I had anything more in mind?" He poured a generous handful of soap into the palm of his hand and set the bottle down before rubbing them together.

"You mean apart from the look in your eyes, the way you're acting like the evil overlord who just captured the helpless maiden -- or is that the wicked lord? Though you're missing the long moustache to twirl there. Then again, it could just be the fact you're rock hard despite what we just did out in the living room." Emmie tried not to laugh. "You're not fooling me, Theron."

"Ah, and you'd have no interest in doing anything else other than showering?"

"Well, I didn't quite say that." She chuckled, giving into the mirth that bubbled through her. Laughing with another shifter, enjoying simple, human pleasures such as sharing a shower with him, she'd never thought that she'd be able to do things like this with a male of her kind, and yet here she was. With him. Naked in the shower.

God, help me. I want his touch again.

"Then close your eyes and just enjoy it." His voice was little more than a whisper.

The small voice inside protested that she was just delaying the inevitable. That despite everything he'd said, he'd leave soon enough, and she'd never see him again. He'd be gone, and there'd be nothing between them. She'd wake up tomorrow morning, and he'd have vanished for good. But until then, she could relax and enjoy their time together.

Scars

Just one day together. One more night. Pleasure. Forget the pain that would follow, just focus on the pleasure. That's all she had to do.

She closed her eyes, her hands loose at her sides as she waited for his touch. For several long minutes nothing happened and then she whimpered. His hands brushed over her breasts, smoothing the soap over her taut, tingling skin. Emmie struggled to stay still as his hands slicked a path across her belly and down to the soft curls between her thighs. With a soft nudge, he parted her legs and slipped one soap-covered hand between.

Emmie groaned, her hips rolling under the light touch. Pressure built in the pit of her being, the soft caress only serving to tease her senses. Her hands clenched instantly. She couldn't give in to this. Not if she wanted to keep control of her thoughts and be able to walk out of the shower without her knees giving out.

Her breath caught in the back of her throat. Her nails threatened to dig into the palms of her hands as she stood there, trembling. A thousand drumming pellets of water massaged her back. Her body screamed for something more, only to arch as his fingers slipped between her lower lips, parting them gently as he massaged the soap into her tender flesh. She groaned.

Her thighs parted a little more, his finger playing over her clit, teasing her body. Small jolts of pleasure rippled through her being. She couldn't let this take over, but all she wanted to do was stand there and let him play his intimate game across her sensitive flesh.

"You like this, don't you?" he whispered through the spray of water. Her thighs quivered, heat burning out of control between her thighs. "You're trembling. I can feel it."

"Yes." How could she deny it? Her body throbbed with a hunger she had no control over.

"A pity I have to move on to other parts of your body," he purred and slipped his fingers free, tracing them over her belly and across her hips. With a low murmur, he traced his hands upward until he cupped her breasts in both hands. "You're beautiful. I've never met a woman like you before, Emmie. You're everything I've ever wanted. Ever dreamed of in a woman and more."

God, she needed him. But this wasn't fair. She wasn't about to let him get away with this. Not when he had done everything possible in the shower so far to leave her whimpering, panting for more. Her nipples throbbed under his touch. Her skin tight across her breasts. She couldn't let him take control this way. Not in her own house and not in her own shower. It just -- just wasn't fair. His thumbs circled her nipples, taunting them, stroking them slowly. Her heart pounded, her throat tightened, slick heat coated her inner walls, but she couldn't let this continue. She reached out, tracing her fingernails over his chest. "Please, I can't believe you're doing this to me."

"Doing what? I'm just washing you down." He flashed a wicked smile. "I'm totally innocent."

If that was all he was doing, then she needed to find just what more from him would be. "I don't think so."

"Are you accusing me of doing something, Emmie? I thought I was just doing you a favor. A nice, gentle shower. Nothing bad about that is there? In fact, I thought you were enjoying it. You certainly looked like you were enjoying it."

"Accusing you of something? No. I know what you're doing. And turnabout is fair play." She smiled and reached for the shower gel. "Or are you chicken? Yes, that's what it is -- you're afraid of what I might do to you?"

"Ah, now, that I'd never be. What's there to fear?" He smiled, arching one eyebrow as a low chuckle spilled free. "Sure, feel free. But it will only make matters worse for you. I can see it in your eyes now. Just how much control do you think you still have left?"

Not much. Bastard. He knew exactly what he had been doing to her. Well, it was her turn. Emmie poured a little shower gel into the palms of her hands and stepped away from the shower. "Step into the water, Theron. It's my turn."

He edged around her, his slick body brushing against her flesh. Tingles of delight surged through her body, and it took everything she had not to reach out to him and beg him to fuck her, right there, in the shower, and toss aside any ideas of teaching him a lesson. His cock throbbed openly in front of her, thick and erect, taunting her with the idea of his body sliding deep into her. Her inner walls rippled; slick heat coated her being. It would have been so very easy to accept him there, to clasp her legs about his hips and enjoy every moment of it.

"Something the matter, Emmie? I thought you were going to return the favor?" He stood with his back to her now, his firm buttocks so close to her fingers, a wicked grin flashed over his shoulder. "And right now you're just standing there, staring at me."

Arrogant son of a bitch!

Emmie reached out, cupping his buttocks with both hands, tracing the line of his bottom with her fingers, a smile claiming her lips. His bottom clenched, a low growl almost lost in the haze of steam and water that rolled over his naked flesh. She chuckled and started to massage the soap into his buttocks. His muscles tensed beneath her touch as she kneaded his firm body, watching his shoulders tense, his hands clenching into fists.

"So you like that?" She leaned in close, her breasts brushing over his back, her nipples teasing his back. His muscles rippled beneath her touch, a low groan almost swallowed by the sound of the shower. "Yes, I think you do."

"How could I not?" he growled, pressing back into her touch. "You're a wicked woman."

"Yes, I am." Odd, it took work to tease him. Normally she had no problem doing this with other men. Why was it so damn hard with Theron? "And I'm going to show you just how wicked I can be."

"Promises, promises." He pulled back away from her touch for a brief moment before a low shudder ran through his hips. "You can keep your hands just on my back."

"Oh, no, I don't think so." She chuckled and reached around with one hand, cupping his heavy sac. "Not when you took such care to explore every inch of my body."

"I wou-wouldn't say I went that far." He lifted onto his toes under her carefully cupping fingers. "But you're going to make it very difficult for me -- me to focus on the shower."

"And you didn't do the same to me?" Emmie teased one finger along his throbbing cock. Power. That's what this was. Power. He'd given it to her with one simple turn of his naked body in the shower. And she planned on using it to the full extent of her abilities. At least this way he'd never assume she was unwilling to give as good as she received.

"I'm not sure I went that far." He almost laughed, his balls tightening under her soft touch.

"Oh, I know you did." She grasped the base of his cock, her breasts pressed tight against his back as she slowly began to stroke his thick erection. "You made very sure I was clean in one particular spot, it's only fair that I do the same in return, don't you think?"

"Think? That just became an optional extra." He growled, thrusting into her touch. "God, if you keep this up, I'll not be able to..."

"To what?"

"Control myself."

"Then I'd best be very careful, don't you think?" She slowly stroked his cock with each word, grinding her hips against his back, all too well aware that each soft shiver only served to tease her further. But at least she now set the pace. She had control, and she wasn't about to give that up. "So I'll wash this very gently and make sure I don't miss a single spot."

His breath hitched as she reached down between his thighs carefully, stroking down the length of his cock, between his toned limbs as she lowered herself to her knees behind him. Her lips pressed against his ass, a gentle, soft kiss. He groaned, pressing his hands against the slick tiles as he tried to control himself. "You're asking for trouble, woman."

"Am I?" She looked up at him, blinking as the water hit her face. His balls were full, even after their sport out in the living room; she could see just how needy his body now was. "I thought I was just being nice." She nuzzled between his legs, the temptation to reach up and play with his balls with her lips and tongue, almost too much to resist. Only the knowledge that she'd taste soap prevented her from following through with her wicked impulse.

"No, you went beyond that."

Chapter Eighteen

Just how he had managed to keep his body from exploding under her touch he'd never know. Theron replayed every touch that had been used on his trembling body before he'd finally said enough and clambered out of the shower, tugging a towel around his waist. Now he leaned against the counter, watching Emmie as she dried herself off, her eyes all but glowing from the hunger he knew now raged through her body.

Oh, he'd given her good reason to torment him, after the way he had treated her under the spray of warm water. Still, he wasn't going to complain. Sure, his cock throbbed, his balls ached, but he wasn't going to sit back and just let his body continue to growl with the need to slide his cock into her body. No, before the hour was through, he'd have her pinned to the bed and show her just what it meant to be with him.

He'd take her. Touch her. Make love to her. Again and again and again. As many times as it took until she accepted that they were meant to be together. He'd show her just what it meant to be with him. All that mind-blowing sex. He could show her that as many times as needed, if that was the only way of convincing Emmie that he wasn't about to walk out on her.

He was lucky. He just had to find a way to accept what his body was telling him. That they belonged together. That despite everything he had been taught about his people, no matter how he had lived before he met Emmie, he had to accept that this woman was the answer to the loneliness inside. The emptiness he had refused to admit existed until he had met this woman, this beautiful creature who had walked into his life without a care for how she would turn his world upside down.

"Did you need something to eat?" Emmie wrapped a dry towel about her body, tucking it into place over the lush curves of her breasts. "You look famished."

"The only thing I want to eat is you," he growled, his hands clenching tight at his sides. "And you look delicious to me."

She blanched, blinking as she looked at him. "You're -- you're bad."

"Yes, I've never denied otherwise." He flashed a feral grin her way. "But I'm also honest. I'm hungry, and you're lunch."

"Or maybe you are." She took a step toward him, one hand fastening on the towel he'd wrapped loosely about his waist. Without another word, she tugged the towel away from his body and dropped it onto the floor.

"Just what did you have in mind?"

Emmie lowered slowly to her knees, her soft gaze playing over his nude form. His heart missed a beat; the sight of her soft, delectable lips so close to his cock was almost too much to take. His cock throbbed, aching to slide deep into her mouth, to know what it was like to be that intimate with her. He'd tasted those lips, he knew what they felt like beneath his, and now -- now he wanted more.

He lost sight of those sweet lips as they wrapped around the head of his cock, and he shuddered, closing his eyes. Her tongue gently swept across the tip of his erection, teasing the soft, sensitive skin with a tender lap as her lips held him in a velvet grip. He tried not to groan, a low roll playing through his hips, the urge to thrust fully into her mouth almost more than he had the ability to control. He leaned back against the counter, grasping the edges, his knuckles turning white with the strength of his grip.

There was nothing quite like the feel of a woman's mouth on a man's cock. No matter what a man said, how he tried to deny it, what every man wanted was the feel of his lover's mouth on his cock. Kissing him. Tasting him. Exploring him until he screamed, groaned, and filled her mouth.

She cupped his balls, massaging the sac with gentle fingers, one finger pressing behind it to find that small, semi-hidden spot. He groaned, half rising onto his toes with the fresh wave of pleasure-filled pressure that claimed him. Theron groaned, trying to shake off the tension that now took control of his body, yet every touch of her skilled tongue only pushed him further into the abyss of pleasure.

Any self-control he had left vanished as she sucked him fully into her mouth, her tongue wrapping itself about his erection, tormenting him with each passing moment. He struggled to regain himself, to find a way to prevent his body from betraying him by releasing into her mouth, but Theron knew he was fighting a losing battle. Shivers ran through his body, pain and pleasure merged under the cruel bittersweet caress of her tongue, he let go of the edge of the counter and tangled his fingers into her hair.

She whimpered, the soft sound vibrating through his cock. Her fingers stroked behind his balls, pressing into that spot, each touch pushing him a little higher. His hips rolled, his cock sliding in and out of her sweet mouth until he thought he could stand it no longer. He tried not to give in to his instincts to do nothing more than fuck her mouth, to take her hard and deep, but the effort strained his already scant control.

Without warning, she pulled back from his cock and pushed slowly to her feet. "Follow me."

Could he walk?

His gaze played over her body, still semicovered by the towel. Oh, yes, he could follow her, even if it took the last of his energy resources to do so. His legs shook, thighs complaining, but he wasn't about to be left behind, not when Emmie offered so much of herself. He pushed up from the edge of the counter, barely aware of the line that had been left by the hard surface. Damn, if things continued this way, he was going to need another shower, and this time he'd have to make sure he took it alone.

Maybe.

Emmie dropped the towel at the entrance to her bedroom and looked back over her shoulder at him. Her dark eyes shining, her wet hair hanging down her back in long, midnight strands, small streams of water made their way over her taut ass and down her thighs. One small trickle vanished between the curves of her ass cheeks, leaving him envious of the path it was taking.

"Maybe you should rest a little bit before we do anything else." She didn't turn around; instead she continued to look at him over her shoulder. Her lips parted, a small shake of her head lifted her damp hair away from her back, only to send it slapping down against her damp flesh with a soft smack.

"I don't think so." The words were little more than a low growl, pressure throbbing a dangerous path through his cock. "I'll rest later, with you in my arms. Or when I'm dead."

"And if I have other plans?"

"Change them."

"I'll think about it."

Enough of this. Do it. Now. Before she teases anymore and I end up coming on myself like a teenager caught in the throes of a wet dream.

Theron moved forward, capturing her, wrapping his arms about her waist as he carried her to the bed and lowered her onto the soft covers. With one hand, he captured her wrists, and pinned them to the bed above her head. "Don't move."

"Why?"

"Because I'll spank you if you do." He was in charge here. Not her. Not this time.

"Is that a threat?" Her dark eyes sparkled, the tip of her tongue dancing out from between her lips, wetting the soft, seductive curves.

"A promise."

"Maybe I'll be good, then." She crossed her wrists as he let go of them, a hint of mischief twitching across her lips.

He almost chuckled, until he turned his attention to her body. Her breasts beckoned him. He cupped her full mounds, thumbing her nipples before he began to knead her firm breasts. A low whimper filled the air, his cock brushing between her thighs as he shifted his weight and lowered his lips to claim one ripe bud. A soft rocking pressed through her hips, her thighs parting a little farther, her heat so close to the head of his cock that he struggled not to thrust deep within her body. No. He had to make this last this time. She'd call for him. Beg for his touch. Cry out for him to take her before he gave into the desire that burned through his body and let his cock finally slide deep within her clenching core.

He lapped at the trapped nipple, rolling it between his lips before he slowly kissed his way down her body, the soft bedding dragged at his cock, adding to his heightened pleasures. Theron groaned between clenched teeth before he forced himself between her thighs, his breath caressing her lower lips as he watched her sex open up before him.

Emmie's swollen, pink lips glistened with her arousal. The scent filled his nostrils, her soft whimpers urging him on, pleading without words for his touch between her thighs. He'd told her in the bathroom the only thing he wanted to eat was her, and now he planned on showing her just how serious he had been about that.

Theron pressed his hands on her inner thighs, sliding his fingers closer to her sex before he parted her fully to his view. He'd never seen a more beautiful sight than the one he looked on now. He edged closer, tracing the tip of his tongue between her lower lips, teasing it across her slick sex before he lapped, slowly over the glistening bud of her clit. She whimpered, her hips lifting up, thighs straining to part a little more. Heat, sensual heat, caressed his face, her taste filling his mouth. The sweetest of honey and wine combined, intoxicating him.

His lips closed around her clit, suckling it gently, tasting every delicious drop of her sex as she groaned, arching beneath his intimate caress. He smiled, lapping across her clit, teasing between her soft lips, tempting her further, higher than before. Her soft groans filling the air, her delight borne on low, sensual whimpers. So close, so very close. She'd not be able to hold on much longer, not with the way her sweet liquid heat coated her inner walls.

"Theron. Please!"

He lifted up from between her thighs, blowing lightly over her glistening sex. "Yes?"

"Fuck me, please. God, I can't wait any longer."

That was what he'd been waiting to hear. He shifted up onto his hands and eased his way back up along her quivering body. Emmie whimpered, her lips parted, eyes glazed, soft tremors playing through her being as she tried to look at him with unfocused eyes.

The head of his cock slipped over her slick lower lips, taunting her with his presence. She writhed, trying to capture him with her body, but he held back a moment longer, just enough to position himself where he could see every wonderful sensation dance across her features.

"Please," she whimpered, her lips barely moving.

He thrust forward, his cock sliding into her slick core, filling her, claiming her. She groaned beneath him, her eyes wide. Her inner walls clamped on his thick erection, holding him deep within her body. He rolled his hips, teasing her core, taking everything she had to offer him and more.

Pleasure rocked through his body. Pressure built in the base of his cock, his balls tightened, pulling close to his body. Her core rippled, her body welcoming him, squeezing on his erection, her soft whimpers merging with his low groans of hunger and need. Sweat dripped from his body, onto hers, her nipples scraping his chest, her breath coming in long, low gasps.

He tried to hold back, to keep some level of control over himself. But his body had other ideas. And it didn't help when her body tightened around him, squeezing, massaging his cock with a velvet grip. He growled down at her, the slick sounds of their shared passion almost too much to take. Pressure, unlike anything he had experienced before, threatened to push in pain-pleasure shards through his body.

Theron looked down into her eyes; her body writhed beneath his; his cock throbbed; her inner walls clenched him like a velvet-wrapped hand. He couldn't hold on, not one moment longer. He had to -- had to come. To fill her. Own her.

"Come for me," he growled down at her. "Come for me now!"

Emmie's eyes widened She locked her thighs around his hips, her body arching, rocking beneath him as she finally moved her arms and wrapped them about his neck. Light flashed across her eyes, a low cry slipping free; heat claimed her inner walls as she sobbed in delight.

Theron growled, letting out the beast for a moment, his snarl echoing through the room as he let go of his control...

Chapter Nineteen

Emmie stretched out slowly on the bed, relishing every move, each click of her joints; the delicious play of pain and oh, God, yes, pleasure that rolled through her muscles only served to bring a soft sigh of delight into life. Just how long had she been asleep in the bed after they had played?

Did it really matter? She'd needed the rest. They both had.

She rolled onto her stomach and glanced over at his still-sleeping form. His dark hair fell about his shoulders, the sheet tangled around his waist as he slumbered. The stress had vanished from his face, the tension gone from his shoulders. For a moment, she could almost picture him as an innocent. That was until her body clenched and reminded her of just what they had done and where.

After the woods, her living room, the shower, and finally the bedroom, the last thing he could be described as was an innocent.

Emmie slipped out of the bed, her bare feet touching the floor, the only real sign of her movement away from the soft mattress being the heat that swiftly vanished from the sheets. She glanced back at the man on the bed and then hurried away to the bathroom. This time, at least, her shower would not be interrupted by the sensual, teasing touches of the man who still slept in her bed.

Hot water sprayed across her body within a moment of stepping into the shower. His scent. It had coated her body until the water washed her clean. Regret seeped through her being at the loss of his invisible marking on her flesh, but she disliked being sticky or smelling dry sweat on her body, and how she had fallen asleep without cleaning off she'd never know.

He hadn't left. It was daylight, they'd slept the entire night through, according to the clock she'd caught a glimpse of on the dressing table. Unusual for her -- normally she slept lightly, but within his arms she'd been safe, able to drop into a deep sleep, one she had been reluctant to leave. Daylight and he was still here. With her. Sleeping in her bed.

Despite all her fears, her concerns, he hadn't left her alone in the house after they had finished. Twice now they'd met, twice made love -- well, three times if she wanted to count properly -- and yet he was still here.

Had her mom been mistaken about male shifters?

No, that didn't make sense. Her mom had been adamant that males of their kind only wanted one thing, and then they would leave. He'd even said he was confused by how he was reacting. Maybe he'd leave when he woke up?

Or was he different somehow? Theron had made it all too clear that this need to stay with her was as alien to him as it was to her. So what had caused it? What drew him to be with her? The pheromones had eased, the pull of those potent natural chemicals had faded into little more than a subtle perfume, and yet he was still drawn to her.

Emmie closed her eyes and let the water play across her face. No matter what it was that continued to pull him to her, she had no power over it. Sooner or later he would shake free of its hold, and then he would be gone. That was the nature of a male feline shifter. They had neither the need nor the will to stay with the females of their kind. It didn't matter that she wanted him, or needed him; before much longer he would walk out of her life to never return.

But what was to stop her from enjoying the time they did have together? If she knew, without a shadow of a doubt, that he would eventually leave, then why couldn't she relax and enjoy his touch, the feel of his lips, his fingers, his skin against hers? He fed her desires, brought her to release time and again; her body craved and welcomed his touch, and he wanted her.

Her heart skipped a beat, a soft rush of heat rippled through her being afresh, though tiny compared to what she had felt the night before. It wasn't time to play again, but if she wasn't careful that hunger would rage out of control until she crawled back into the bed and sought out his company. How would he take that? Being woken by the feel of a mouth wrapped about his cock?

No. Not this time. She needed a little longer to recover. And some food in her stomach, not to mention catching up with...

Shit. Mags. She'd promised to call her, hadn't she? Then there was Aneta, she still hadn't checked up on the older woman. God. What had she been thinking?

She hadn't. Thought hadn't entered the equation. Not this time. Just raw, sensual need, and now she had things she had to do. Food. Clean clothing. Phone calls. Not necessarily in that order. She couldn't just hang around in her bedroom waiting for Theron to wake up. Or slide over his body, tease his cock into life, and ride it until...

No. Not only no, but hell, no. There'd been enough sex for now.

Thirty minutes later, with a fresh pot of coffee on, clean clothes, and a plate of scrambled eggs in front of her, Emmie almost felt human again. He still hadn't appeared from the bedroom, and fortunately she'd had clean clothes in the laundry room, so hadn't had to nip into the bedroom and risk disturbing him. Sooner or later he'd wake up, and she had a good idea that the smell of the coffee and eggs would tempt him out of bed.

She'd barely had time to eat three forkfuls before he made an appearance, dressed in little more than a sheet around his waist.

"Something smells good. Is there any left?"

"I can scramble some eggs up for you, and there's plenty of coffee." Her mom would be turning in her grave. Here she was playing domestic bliss with a -- a damn tomcat! That just didn't happen. Well, a lot of things that weren't supposed to happen had been merrily occurring in the past few days -- so by now her mom would not just be turning, but doing a madcap seventies-style disco dance.

"Thanks." Theron settled down at the table, his storm-cloud gaze tracing over her face. "You have to admit, this is..."

"Odd?"

"Yeah." He reached for the coffee mug as she set it down on the table. "In ways I never thought possible."

"Do you think someone, well, cursed us?"

"It could be, though I've worked with witches before so I should have been able to pick up on the spell if there was one being used."

"Oh." There went that idea. Damn, and it had been such a good one as well. At least with a curse, there would have been someone else to blame for the entire mess. "Fine. Rule that option out."

"I've been wrong before, though, so it's something I could look into. I found out last night that things aren't always what they first appear to be."

Emmie cracked four eggs into the pan and whisked them up, even as she glanced over her shoulder at him. "How so?"

"The sheriff."

"Mike? What about him?" God. What else had gone wrong. *Don't tell me, there's a warrant out for loverboy? Just what I need right now. Not.*

"He's a werewolf."

Emmie almost dropped the pan. "But -- that's impossible. I'd have smelled him. He can't be..."

"Well, he is. He has something a witch put together for him that helps mask his scent." Theron yawned and gulped down a full mug of coffee before he blinked and stared at her. "Shit, don't repeat that. He asked me not to say anything." He groaned and lowered his head to the table with a muffled thump. "God, did you fuck my brains out?"

"Hmm, if I did, I'll have to remember to do it again -- if I ever need information out of you, that is." A wicked smile claimed her lips as she turned her attention back to the eggs.

"Cruel. You're just plain cruel."

"Yes, but I do it so well."

Theron chuckled and slid the now empty mug across the table. "How long are those eggs going to be?"

"You could always come and cook them yourself," she muttered, shaking her head as she grabbed a clean plate and dumped the scrambled eggs onto it. "Men -- always being picky about something."

"Huh? I just asked about the eggs?"

Emmie set his breakfast down and returned to her own. "Sure, eggs now; next time it'll be your laundry or something like that. Men. You're helpless most of the time." She flashed a smile to take the sting out of her words and shoveled down the rest of her breakfast.

"Sure, and women can't even change a tire without calling for roadside assistance or breaking three nails." Theron gave as good as he was getting.

"Arrogant bastard."

"Helpless floozy."

"Socks dropped everywhere."

"You wouldn't know what a fan belt was if it swore at you."

"Do you even know what a washing machine looks like?"

"I don't need to. That's one of the few things women are good at."

"Yeah, well, the only thing a man is good for is snoring."

"Well, you -- oh, God." Theron leaned back in the chair, laughing until tears spilled down his face.

Emmie quickly joined him, and the kitchen filled with their laughter. "You're bad. But that was fun. Haven't had a decent bitch session in months."

"Ah, is that what we were doing?" Theron looked back at her and winked. "Damn. Okay, this feels weird."

"Never been around a woman long enough to chat with her?"

"Not after we'd fu -- err, finished business, no." Heat flushed across his face, and he pushed back from the table. "So what do we do now?"

"About?"

"This. Us."

"Ah, there's an 'us'?" Her stomach knotted.

"There certainly appears to be, at least for now." He turned around but didn't look her in the eyes.

"Well, I have things I need to do today. Mags. Aneta."

"The woman who was attacked? I'm pretty sure that was a human thing. Mike wasn't acting as though he thought it was a shifter attack or even large cat. No hunting teams out there, not even dogs, or there weren't yesterday."

Relief washed through her body. Mike was good people, even if she didn't like the man personally. "I had thought, for a moment, that you'd..."

"Yes, I know. I wondered the same about you." His lips twitched into a full smile. "At least we both know we were thinking along the same lines. Sorry about that, though. I just couldn't think of what else -- who else -- would be behind the attack."

"Same here."

Silence settled over the kitchen, except for the soft pops of her coffee pot. Odd, had anyone else even suggested they'd suspected her of being behind the attack on Aneta she'd have torn their throat out. If not with claws, at least with her words. Yet, from him, she could take it.

"We're still back at the same problem. What do we do next?" Theron leaned against the kitchen counter, his gaze finally seeking out her face.

"We find out just who it was that did attack her." Emmie spoke softly, thinking each word through before granting it life. "If we don't, we'll always wonder just what we missed, if we were wrong about each other, or if another shifter managed to sneak in under our noses. It's one thing to believe the person you've just had mind-blowing sex with is innocent; it's another to know it."

Theron nodded and rubbed his fingertips over his jaw. "Razor?"

"Only the pretty pink kind."

He winced and headed for the bathroom, only to stop and look back at her, flashing a grin. "It was mind-blowing, wasn't it?"

Chapter Twenty

He needed a shower, a shave, clean clothing. But the thought of leaving Emmie, even for a short time, disturbed him. With fresh water splashed onto his face, he then looked into the mirror and frowned. Like it or not, he needed to leave for a short while. Emmie would understand. She wouldn't appreciate him walking around her house in a shirt he had worn for a day already. The sensitive noses of their kind would play against her in that respect.

And he needed a shave, before the itching began and only added to his growing nerves. Using a pink razor offended his sense of -- well -- it was just wrong. Besides, he had no idea if the razors they made for women would work on his face without tearing it up. He snatched one up off the counter and peered at it.

A thin strip of some sort of moisturizing material glared back at him. He sniffed it and shuddered. It smelled girlie, perfume and sweetness. The razor was dropped back onto the counter, and he stalked off in search of his clothing. Where had he left his jeans?

Theron stumbled over his jeans and shirt in the middle of the living room, along with his shoes. God, he was lucky she hadn't thrown them at him.

He caught a glance of the table and remembered just what she had looked like, bent across the smooth, polished wood. The way her bottom had lifted up for his touch, her soft whimpers and pleas.

His cock hardened, throbbing into life.

"God, not right now, okay?"

It twitched defiantly.

"Stop it," he muttered, pulling on his jeans. For some odd reason his body refused to listen to him.

"Talking to yourself?" Emmie slipped into the room, her bare feet making little sound.

"Erm, yeah. Look, I have to head to the motel."

The color drained from her face. "Ah. I see. Well, I expected this would come sooner or later."

"No, it's not like that. Just. No clean clothing. No razor. No deodorant. I'm going to stink your place out unless I borrow things from you, and no offence meant, vanilla-scented deodorant just isn't my thing."

The tension eased from her face as Emmie chuckled and shook her head. "Fair point. All right, that will give me time to catch up on a few things. Did you want me to wait here or meet you somewhere?"

"Here. If we're going to check this out, this whole situation with Aneta, then I need you around to fill me in on how things work around here." He watched her, taking in every inch of her sweetly curved form. His cock throbbed again, pressing against his jeans. Damn it. They'd fucked each other senseless the previous night, and now his body was ready for round three. Or was it four?

He had to be raw and just not feeling it yet. But he would. Another hour or so, after the jeans had rubbed at his cock and balls, oh, yeah, he'd feel it.

"Okay, how long will you need?" She didn't move, but even from here he could see that her nipples had hardened. A soft quiver in her voice spoke of something else, a hunger, perhaps? And not for seconds of her scrambled eggs.

"A few hours at most." He couldn't see it taking him that long, but at least this way he had a margin for error. "I should catch up with my business partners, let them know where I am, what I'm doing, all that good stuff."

"Business?" A frown creased her otherwise perfect brow.

"I'll explain when I get back. But at least you know I'm not a freeloader." He flashed a grin and pulled on his shirt. "I work for a living. Harder than some, not as hard as others."

"I never thought you were a freeloader."

He glanced at her; the line of her jaw said otherwise. Fine.

That was something they could deal with later. It would be easy enough to prove to Emmie that he had his own resources and didn't need whatever source of income she had access to. He couldn't blame her. There were enough men, shifters and otherwise, who used women for anything they could get, but the only thing he'd ever used them for had been sex. And she'd done her own share of using men for exactly the same thing.

Theron walked back through the living room and pulled her into his arms, his lips claiming hers. A soft shiver ran through her body, nipples hard beneath her clothing. Her gaze softened, breath catching in the back of her throat as she looked up into his eyes.

"I'm just expecting everything to go wrong, that's all."

He cupped her chin and smiled. "I'll be back. Trust me. I'm not going to just walk out of your life."

Emmie watched the door for three long minutes after Theron had walked out of the house. Her heart pounded against her chest, sweat beaded across her brow, her hands clenched tight as she watched, waited, and listened as he walked away from her house. What if he'd lied and had no intention of coming back?

He'd have said. He wasn't the type of man to look her in the eyes and lie like that. It just wasn't how most shifters handled things. Especially not feline. Oh, it wasn't as though there weren't bad apples amongst their own kind; there were, but Theron? He wasn't one of them.

So why was she still so uneasy about all of this?

Maybe it's not him; it could be all of this with Aneta.

Shit. Mags! She still hadn't checked in. God. They were lucky that Mags hadn't pounded on the door, or come in the back way and discovered them both. She'd never have lived that one down.

Twenty minutes later she was still on the phone trying to explain things to Mags, who had, apparently, seen Theron walk into her home.

"He's just a friend." She spoke calmly into the phone. *Sure. One she'd fucked. Repeatedly. And would do so again just as soon as they both had the chance.*

"One who stayed with you overnight? I'm not buying it. And I want the details. All of them." Mags all but yelled through the phone, laughing openly. "I'm on my way over. Put the coffee on!"

Before Emmie had the chance to tell her to wait, the phone went dead at the other end. She groaned and set the phone down, shaking as she waited for the pounding on the door that hit minutes later. She was never going to live this one down. She'd spent so long keeping her distance from men in the town and now this? Mags would keep on at her until she found out every delicious detail and then hang on for more.

"Emmie?"

"The door's open." Locking it wouldn't have helped. Not with Mags. She'd have stood there, pounding on the door and yelling until Emmie had given up and opened it.

Mags walked in, barely letting the door slam shut behind her before she started. "So, who is he? Where is he? And..."

"Wait. Please. One thing at a time. Just give me a few minutes." Emmie looked up at her friend, praying for the strength to see the conversation through. The last thing she'd wanted, or needed, was to end up facing her friend over this. "He's a good man. So you don't have to worry about me."

"And?"

"And what?"

"God, Emmie. Details, please. He's a hunk. I've seen that much for myself. I'd jump him myself, given half the chance. Well, he's off limits now he's with you. So spill. I want the details, every single one. What's he like. Does he leave you singing?"

"You wanted a coffee didn't you?" Time. She needed time to put her thoughts in order, even if she could only grab a couple of minutes. Or a distraction.

Right. Distract Mags from something she wants? Not

happening.

"Sure, but don't think you're going to avoid this conversation. It is happening. Even if I have to sit on you to get you to tell me every delicious, intimate moment. He's left you smiling. And I'm not going to be able to experience his delights myself, so the least you could do is share with me. Come on, Emmie. You can't hide him, not any longer. I saw him leave and so did that David Stone. It will be all over town before lunchtime. You know how it works around here."

Oh, yes, she knew all too well.

This was not going to be easy.

Theron glanced back at Emmie's front door before he headed, on foot, back toward Main Street, where he'd left his motorbike. At least he wouldn't have to walk back to the motel. With luck he'd be able to change, shave, and be on his way back to Emmie's within the hour, ninety minutes at most. The fresh air would help clear his head before he took the trip back to the motel.

Still. He'd be gone an hour, two at most, and it was too long to be parted from her.

He picked up the pace into a fast walk. That didn't work. Not quick enough. He frowned and broke into a sprint.

Emmie Byron. Lover. Shifter. Woman. And something more. His mate. If he only had the courage to take that step with her. To defy everything he had been taught about being a feline shifter and ask her to spend the rest of her life with him. He had to find the courage. Somewhere. Somehow.

Marriage.

Wasn't that just for humans?

He'd find a way of wording it, something that didn't sound quite so strange. He just had to put some thought into it.

A shiver walked down his spine, and he turned, looking behind him.

Nothing. Just a few kids playing in a yard.

Scars

Fine, now he was letting the shadows get to him. He needed another coffee, and time away from Emmie in order to put his thoughts in order. At least then he might stop jumping at shadows.

"Just sweetener this time." Mags followed her into the kitchen. "And start by telling me where you met him. Where he was. Are there any more like him at home?"

"My last trip into the city." All right, so it wasn't the entire truth. They'd come close to meeting each other then, but she couldn't exactly tell Mags that she'd run at the scent of him. "We met, briefly, there."

"Ah, and from that he followed you home? Well, now, that's different. I can't say I'd enjoy being followed like that. Then again, if the one following me looked like your man, I might enjoy it after all."

"Something like that." Emmie pushed the mug into Mags's hands. "I'm not sure what else you want to know about him." Or what she was willing to share. As long as she didn't talk about him, didn't share the information with another, she'd be able to keep him for herself.

"His name?"

"Theron Grave." That much she did know about him. Theron Grave, a strange name belonging to an even stranger man. But one she needed in her life. Where had his name come from? It sounded Greek; had she asked him about it? She couldn't remember right now. "He works in the city. Good man. He's been good to me."

Good. He'd been a miracle worker. Her body thrummed from his touches. Her core ached from something he had introduced her to. Never before had a man sated her and then left her wanting more at the same time. She glanced at the clock Just how long would it be before he returned? Maybe she could contrive to make sure that Mags would be gone, then tumble them both back into bed. Yes, she needed that. Wanted it. Her body should have been weary from his touch, but instead she craved him even more.

"Yeah, I can see that." Mags grinned over the rim of the mug. "How good is he?"

"I can't believe you're asking me that."

"Well, what else would I ask? Come on, Emmie. I've never seen you look so content and yet nervous at the same time. You're walking like, well, like a cat in a room full of rocking chairs after you just finished off a dish of cream." Mags settled onto the edge of the table, watching her closely. "You're a good friend to me; you've always been, for as long as you've been in town. So I'm curious about the man who's managed to put a smile on your face. I've been worried about you, about spending the rest of your life alone. You're a good woman. A great friend to me."

"You've been worried about me?" She blinked and stared at Mags.

"Yes, why wouldn't I be?"

"Because I'm not like that. I've never needed anyone before now." Emmie spoke softly.

"He's changed that, hasn't he?"

Emmie sucked in her bottom lip. Had he? Her heart said yes, her head said no. "I don't know."

"Yes, you do. You're just too afraid to admit it."

She was something special. Theron smiled and pulled on his helmet and settled onto the motorbike. He gunned the bike into life and turned out onto the street, following it through town and out toward the motel. Yes. A short time away from her would be enough to put his thoughts in order, and he'd be back at her side before she started to worry.

He glanced into his mirror, and frowned.

A truck. Dark blue. Splattered with mud as many farm vehicles would be. There should be nothing to worry about, but his instincts said otherwise. The hair on the back of his neck stood up, but he couldn't understand why the presence of the truck would leave him so unsettled.

The truck speeded up, kicking up dust in its wake.

Fuck. This wasn't good.

Theron's jaw clenched as he eased his bike closer to the side of the road, giving the vehicle extra room to pass, all the while splitting his attention between the reflection in the mirror and the view ahead of him.

The large Ford truck swerved toward him. Only the warning he'd been listening to, and his feline reactions, were enough to save him as he turned the bike off the road at the last minute. Every joint in his body jarred with the sudden move, and still it wasn't enough. The truck turned off the road, following Theron away from the road.

Shit.

At least on his bike he had the advantage of mobility, but would it be enough?

The shotgun blast knocked him off, into the dirt. He cried out in pain and rolled away from the bike, keeping his legs from being entangled in the wreck. His bike. His bloody bike. Whoever was behind this would pay for the damage done to her.

Move. No time to fuck about, worrying about a piece of metal!

Theron pushed up onto his feet and ran for the tree line. A second blast from a shotgun tore through the air, shards of shot barely missing his left shoulder, one scraping into his shirt, tearing it, leaving a shallow line of fire in its wake. It didn't stop him, not for a moment; instead, he ran, hard and fast into the cover of the trees. Only then did he turn enough to look back at the truck and those within it.

Two men.

The wind was coming from the wrong direction; he couldn't pick up on their scent. But when one stepped out of the truck the minute it stopped at the edge of the trees, he knew whom he was dealing with.

"She's mine. Got it? She's mine! Stay the fuck away from her." David took a step toward the trees. "You're not welcome here. You'll never be welcome here. I don't want to see you anywhere near Emmie again."

David. The sober and dangerous friend of the drunken grandson. Interesting. Just how had he found out about Theron's involvement with Emmie? Shot him? The idiot had shot him? Over a woman? No. Not over a woman. Over Emmie. A woman he would protect with his dying breath, if that's what it took.

A low growl rang out in the back of his mind. He'd do more than shoot someone who touched his woman. And this man, this human, thought that Emmie was his woman and that Theron had no right to touch her. Not now. Not ever.

Well, he was wrong. Emmie belonged to...

"What if he reports us to that fuckin' sheriff?" Jamie stuck his head out of the window. "We can't do this. I'm not going to end up in jail because of your temper."

"That's not going to happen." David grabbed the shotgun again and jumped out of the truck fully. "You're going to help me track the bastard down."

"This is murder. You can't expect me help you do this. I won't. I won't kill someone for you. I'm not going to prison for you."

"It won't be the first time that you've done something for me that's illegal. I'm not going to let that bitch boy escape from me."

"I can't..."

"You don't have a choice."

They could try and track him down, but it wasn't going to work. No. He had an upper hand that they could never have imagined. He slipped back into the shadows. Pulled his clothing off carefully. They wouldn't be expecting this. They'd be searching for a man, not a cat. Not a great beast. A smile tugged at his lips.

They'd made a mistake with him.

One they would pay for, dearly.

Chapter Twenty-One

A loud pounding struck her front door, and Emmie jumped. Theron? No, it was too soon for Theron to be back. Just what was going on? The hairs on the back of her neck rose.

"Your lover?"

"No, I don't think so." He stomach knotted. Sweat coating her palms. "He wouldn't be back yet. Not from the edge of town. Unless he found a way to break the sound barrier."

Emmie set the mug down and barely had time to walk into the living room before someone opened her door from the other side.

"Ms. Byron? We need to talk. Now." The sheriff's jaw tightened, his shoulders taut. Every inch of his body looked ready for a fight. Or to be the bearer of bad news, not something she wanted to face.

"Mike? Since when did you become so damn formal around me?" Her skin crawled.

"This is business." He tugged off his hat. "Morning, Mags. I need to ask you to step outside whilst I talk something over with Emmie. She's not in trouble, but it's confidential."

Mags rolled her eyes and wandered out of the house, taking the coffee mug with her. Great, one more thing she'd have to replace. A scowl settled over her brow as the door shut, and she turned her attention fully on Mike. "All right, just what's going on?"

"David and Jamie saw your friend leave."

"Leave?"

"Leave this house."

"And that's supposed to be a problem to me?" David and Jamie were nothing to a fully grown male shifter. He'd be able to handle anything the two goons threw at him.

"Are you blind? Don't you understand that both men are

infatuated with you? That David would knock down any man who so much as looked at you? Shit. I thought I'd have time to sort them out before it reached this point. But it's too late for that. Bad enough I have to haul them in for what they did to Aneta, but now they've gone missing. David's truck was seen hauling ass out of town, your man is missing, and now I'm left talking to a woman who doesn't even seem to know the power she can have over men."

Her stomach knotted. "I know very well what I'm capable of doing to a man. I just never took David or Jamie seriously." What did he mean about Aneta? Oh, God. No. "They attacked her?"

"Yes. Some sort of damn martial arts claws were used. Aneta finally came around enough to confirm what I believed. The claws are why it looked like an animal attack," Mike explained quickly. "They're called Tekko-kagi."

She stood there, blinking at him.

"Never mind, they're some sort of Ninja-type weapon. I had to look it up. Never come across them before."

Ninja? Great, she had a wannabe ninja, small-town bad boy on her hands. "Do we know who it belonged to?"

"David, which is what slowed things down. If it had been Jamie's, we'd have stumbled across it or others of his collection earlier. But Jamie's room is pretty empty. Doesn't look like he spends that much time there. It took a sales receipt before I had a reason to toss David's place. But he was already gone by the time I found that bloody thing."

Somehow that didn't surprise her. "And now they've gone after Theron?"

"Yes."

"And you're here why? You're a cop; why aren't you out, hunting them down? You should be stopping them, not standing here telling me what's going on."

"Because I need your help. If he's gone shifter on me, then I need you to pull him out. Especially if these idiots push him over the edge. They don't know how to -- I need your help." He took a deep breath and looked at her, his jaw set. "I know what you both are."

"Yeah, I know you do, wolfie." She flashed a grin.

Mike growled. "Fine, so he can't keep his mouth shut. I guess that's fair, as I know what you are. Okay, whatever. You've mated -- he's not going to take it well if David tries to claim that he owns you. He'll rip David to shreds. It's part of the nature of being what we are."

"Feline shifters don't mate. He wouldn't go over the edge, not the way you're suggesting. He might shift, though, if he thought they were going to attack him. And with good reason." Nuts. This was nuts. "But I'll try and bring him out of it. That's if it comes to it."

Mike nodded, the argument dropped as he grabbed Emmie's arm and headed for the door. "We might be too late already. I should have gone with my first instinct and dragged you right to the door, then explained later."

"So why didn't you?"

"Only a really dumb dog enrages a cornered cat."

Theron dropped the last of his clothing and gave himself over to the change. Pain rocked through his body. A low howl echoed off the trees, forcing the men to stop in their tracks. The wind shifted, their scent carried through the woods. They wanted to play that game, he'd face them. Bring them down. And scare the shit out of them once and for all. He took a deep breath and smiled.

Fear. They were afraid. Good. They needed to be. They'd disturbed a hunter. One who would not hold back. Not when it meant these beings, these creatures who claimed to be men, would go back to disturb and torment his mate. His woman. She'd be free of them, no matter what it took. Human males. They needed to learn where the lines were drawn when it came to women.

"What was that?" Jamie whimpered. "Sounded like a cat. A big one. But that's not possible."

"Why not? Didn't you tell me that you'd been attacked by one? Isn't that why we did the old woman that way? So the cat would get the blame?" David growled, shaking his head as his fingers tightened on the shotgun. "Well, now we can blame his death on the cat and then kill the fuckin' thing ourselves. It all works to our advantage."

"Kinda hard to blame it on the cat if we shoot him. So stop and think about it for a minute. You can't shoot him. Bullets are unmistakable. Even buckshot would give you away. Cut it out." Jamie hissed and turned back, walking back to the truck. "I don't want anything to do with this. You're nuts. I'd have never agreed to you hurting the old bitch if I'd realized just what you were going to do to her. You told me you were just going to frighten her into handing over a few bucks. Cutting her up like that -- she didn't deserve it!"

"Yeah, well, she'll croak this way, and we'll have it all. You can sell the house. We can get out of this dump."

"I don't want her dead. She's just an old woman!" Jamie protested.

Theron smiled, watching them through the trees, his claws extending into the dirt. Good. Fighting amongst themselves. It would make it all the easier to deal with them. They couldn't even keep quiet. Some hunters they were. And hurting the old woman? He'd be able to take that information to Mike, and he'd be able to look into it.

"Well, she'll be out of the way soon enough. No way that bitch would be able to survive that attack. Her heart will pack in on her." David grunted and took a step into the trees. "Are you coming or what?"

"No. I've had enough. I drink. I don't kill people. Thought you were just going to frighten her, frighten him. I'm not game for this!"

"Coward!" David turned and spat at his friend. "You're nothing but a drunken idiot. If you don't help me now, then I'll kill you as well." The metal *click-clank* of the shotgun being prepped stopped Jamie in his tracks. "I should of got rid of you years ago."

"You wouldn't…"

"After what I did to the old bat, you really think that? You know what I did. The blood everywhere. I had to ditch that shirt. I'll do the same, if not worse, to you."

Jamie paled and walked back into the trees. "You're insane."

"Just shut up and help me."

Theron took a step back into the tree line, his gaze narrowed on the two men. Even if this hadn't just become personal, he'd have been tempted to deal with David. Aneta, whoever she was, hadn't deserved the type of treatment that these two bastards had put her through. And they obviously believed the woman was dying, if not dead already.

But Mike hadn't said anything about the woman being close to death. The sheriff had been entirely too calm for that, which gave Theron some hope. If the woman was alive, then so much the better, but he'd still deal with these two. He had to. Or David would continue to stalk his Emmie.

A low, long snarl vibrated in the back of his throat, his teeth bared, tail swishing through the air. This man. This human who stepped into his way, this one who sought to hurt and claim a woman who would never belong to him, had pushed too far. He would die. Today.

"What the fuck does David think he's doing?" Emmie growled as she watched the road. She needed something to do. She couldn't just sit here, watching, waiting as Mike drove the patrol car out of town.

"He's taking out the obstacles in his way."

"And Aneta?"

"Another obstacle. This one to some money. Both through the house and a small amount she has in the bank. Both would go to Jamie if anything happened to her, according to the will. Jamie knew that. Odds are, he told David."

She frowned, shaking her head. "So this was all about money?"

"Yeah, money. Jamie is a source of money which David needs, but only through Aneta. If she dies, then Jamie would come into enough money to keep David happy for a few months." Mike turned the car out of town, kicking up gravel and dust into the air. "Are you sure he'd have gone this way?"

"Yes, the nearest motel is out this way. Pretty sure he said he was staying at the Six."

"He didn't head back to the city?"

"No. No, he'd have said if that's where he was going." Emmie peered out, searching for some sign of his -- oh, shit, she didn't even know what he'd been driving. "He had no reason to lie to me."

"It's going to be hard to spot his motorbike if he's turned off the road."

Bike. All right. Now she knew what she was looking for. Motorbike. Had to be. Why hadn't she seen a helmet? Or didn't he wear one? Cats were an odd breed. Some lived to take risks. Others laughed at what they saw as the foolishness of humans and took precautions when it came to things like helmets. It was one thing to rely on their own increased reaction times, but trusting humans on the road? That was sheer stupidity. What had her mom said? Drive as if everyone is out to kill you, because the odds are they're trying to do just that.

Her gaze narrowed on something. *There*. A scar on the landscape. A track of land that had been torn up by tires, leading away from the main road.

"There!"

Scars

"He can't have gone far. He doesn't know the area." David muttered to himself, and pushed farther into the undergrowth. "So where the fuck is he? He should be here somewhere."

"Maybe he can hear you coming" Jamie shivered and kept a healthy distance away from David, his gaze flickering toward the shotgun in his companion's hands. "We're not being quiet."

"Or the cat got him."

Or the cat is waiting for you; he's hungry and wants lunch. Theron smirked and edged slowly around the two men. *He's wondering just what man meat tastes like. Does it really taste like pork? Or perhaps more like chicken.*

"Come on, we should get out of here. If we cover things up, no one's going to believe a stranger. We'd need to hide the gun, that's easy enough done. Maybe head out to the city for a few days. Then we can come back and claim innocence"

"Sure, right, and end up with a warrant out for our arrests? Not my style. It's fine for you to do a stint inside. I'm not going there. I'm not ending up as a bitch boy to some over the top cellmate called Bubba."

Bubba. Now there was an interesting option. It was almost tempting to sneak away, change back into human form and report them, just so Bubba and his new lady love could meet. After all, he wouldn't want to keep a happy couple apart.

Theron sniffed the air, tasting their fear, the sweet, tempting smell that pulled at him, at the beast who now demanded to be let loose, on the men. It would have been so very easy to sink his claws into them, to rend and tear, rip them apart. Yes. All he would have to do was stalk them, launch himself at them, and then destroy them one by one. Their blood would pool beneath his paws before it sank into the hungry earth...

"Something's out here with us. Can't you hear it?" Jamie whimpered, shifting his weight from one foot to the next as he tried to back away another step. "I don't like it here. We should go. Before it's too late."

"Coward."

"With good reason!"

"Fine, get out, then."

No. Mine! Theron growled and darted out of the shadows, bowling Jamie to the ground, his tail snapping through the air.

Jamie screamed.

David turned, bringing the gun up, his finger tightening on the trigger.

Humans. Predictable. He let out a roar and launched himself back into the undergrowth, slinking out of their line of sight before David had the chance to draw full bead on him. *Too slow. Did you think you could out maneuver a hunter?*

"What was that?"

"That fucking cat I told you about." Jamie scrambled to his feet, turning, his eyes wide, the strong smell of urine filling the air. "It's back. God. It's back."

"Thought you were lying about that beast. Well, it doesn't matter. It's just a cat."

Just? Theron almost laughed. Oh, there was nothing *just* about him. His gaze narrowed, fixing on the pulse that throbbed in David's neck. The tempting expanse of white, delicate flesh that would rend beneath his claws called to him. And it was a call he could no longer resist

Mike pulled off the road, the back tires spinning in the mud. "Hold on."

Emmie gasped, her knuckles white as she grasped the seat belt. "Shit!"

"Not in the car, please." Mike smirked.

"What -- oh, God. Men!" The car swerved a foot away from the truck. Emmie scanned the ground for some sign of a motorbike, and caught a glimpse of what looked like one half covered by mud, in a mess of dug-up earth. Was he hurt?

She darted out of the car, the seat belt snapping through the air with a loud clunk.

"Emmie, wait!" Mike reached over, trying to grab her, but his fingers closed on thin air. "Women!"

It was only when her bare feet hit the ground when she realized that she hadn't put shoes on. She swore under her breath, but continued to move, lifting her head as she inhaled, searching for signs of Theron. Two men -- no, three -- but where they had moved to she couldn't be sure. They were downwind of her. That much she'd been able to work out without turning into a cat.

"Don't…"

She didn't even look back at Mike. Theron needed her. Whatever was going on, he needed her to bring him back into focus. She took a deep breath, trying to work out just where the men might be. Two figures moved, both human, one stumbling into view, the other nothing more than a shadow amongst the trees. The one walking toward them had lost all color from his face, his eyes wild, hair half across his face, the front of his jeans wet. Jamie.

"You can't g-go in there," he stammered, all but falling on his face at her feet. "There's an animal in there. A big cat. Teeth. Huge teeth. It'll go after you. Attack you. It went for me."

"I know." She didn't hesitate and headed into the trees. He'd be here. But so was David. And from the smell in the air, he was armed with a weapon that had already been fired at least once.

Theron kept close to the ground, his gaze fixed on David. He could chase down Jamie later. David was the real threat. Or he was for a little longer. That would change. Soon. Men like this one, this human, didn't deserve to breathe the same air as his Emmie. His mate.

He tensed.

Something familiar teased his senses. A scent he knew well. Emmie. His tail snapped furiously close to the ground. What was she doing here? How had she traced him? And why?

David turned; no sound, not a hint that could of alerted the man to Emmie's presence, yet he still turned and looked directly in her direction.

"Come on into the darkness and join the party, Emmie," David snarled, his fingers clenching around the shotgun. "Your boyfriend is somewhere out here, and I'm sure he'd be glad to see you. That's if that animal hasn't got a hold of him already."

Emmie didn't reply. Good. That had to infuriate David. He wasn't the sort of man who would take being ignored. She might be able to distract David long enough for a clear shot. Just one real opening. That's all it would take, and he'd have his teeth locked around David's throat.

"Get out here, where I can see you, before I start shooting to get your attention. You know I'll do it. Don't you? Come out here now, Emmie. I want to be able to see you."

"And what good will it do you? If you open fire on me, you'll end up dead. Either from the cat or Mike."

"I don't care about either of them. The cat, the sheriff, neither of them matter to me. They won't be able to help you. You'll be dead. So get your ass out here. Now, and I might just change my mind."

Threatening her. Didn't he know how much danger he was in? Of course not. David didn't care.

Emmie moved slowly into his line of sight, her smile calm. He couldn't smell any fear on her. No sign of terror as she walked toward David. Good. All the confidence of a cat. Nor would David now realize that he was trapped between two hunters, not until it was too late for him.

"What is it you want from me, David?" she whispered, her lips parting softly, one hip swung out as she lifted her chin.

"You. Just you. That's all I've ever wanted." He turned, bringing the gun with him, but for now he didn't aim it at her. "I've wanted you since the first moment I saw you. I thought I'd be able to get you out of my system by watching you, but it didn't get any better. Every time I saw you, it became worse. You burn through my blood. A sickness there is no cure for."

Theron edged closer, taking long, slow breaths, tasting the air. Yes. He could still taste the man's fear on the air, but it had become less, somehow. Strange. Didn't he realize how much danger he was in? His lips pulled back in a smile, baring his teeth. No, in focusing on Emmie, the idiot had forgotten about the beast in the trees.

"And you think a way to a woman's heart is by waving a gun at her?"

"No, but you didn't give me any other choice. God. Can't you see when a man is interested in you? I've tried. I've spoken to you. Talked with you. Tried to get you to look at me. But you just wouldn't. I thought it was money. So I started trying to get some extra money together so I'd be able to take you places. But that wasn't it, was it?" His hands clenched and unclenched around the shotgun he held. "You don't even date anyone around here, do you? Why don't you look at me, Emmie? The way I know you look at him?"

"Him? Who are you talking about, David?" She took another step closer to him, rolling her hips as she moved. "Is there someone you think I'm now with? I thought I was yours, David."

Smart. Keep repeating his name. He likes how it drips from your lips.

"That stranger. The one with the cocky smile and the bike. The one I saw leave your house. The one I know you're fucking," David growled, spitting as he spoke. "He was there all night. I saw him walk in. I watched as he left. I know what you two had to be doing all night. You were fucking him!"

"Are you sure that's what we were doing? Did you see us?"

"Well, no..."

"That's because it didn't happen. I wouldn't have sex with my own cousin."

"Your cousin?" David stood there, blinking. "He's your cousin?"

"Yes, isn't that what I just told you?" Emmie flashed a smile at him. "Theron is my cousin. We hadn't seen each other in years, so we spent the night talking, catching up with each other. Why would I have sex with my cousin? I'm not like that."

David didn't move.

Good girl. Keep him distracted. All the easier for me to rip out his throat that way. Theron crept forward, out of the shadows, toward David's back.

"You're mine. You know that." David's voice dropped a little; then he tensed, looking up. "Get the hell out o' here, Mike. Don't need you here. Just me and my girl, having a little chat."

"Is that what this is? Well, in that case, I'll be on my way. Just as soon as you hand over that gun of yours." Mike held out his hand. "If this is just a friendly chat with Emmie here, you won't need it, will you?"

Fuck, what was going on here? Stupid wolf. He should have kept out of this. His prey. Not the wolf. His hunt. No one else's. He wouldn't let anyone else get in the way of his prey. He'd tear into the man's throat, taste his blood, and hear his last breath rattle in his chest. His back tensed, back legs tightening as his tail stilled.

"Do you think I'm stupid?"

Emmie bit back a comment. Stupid didn't even begin to describe David. At least not in her eyes. The man had no clue the level of danger he was in. Was he high? She couldn't smell anything on him. No, just lust, stupidity, and nothing else. She could see Theron, his head, the sway of his tail. She knew Mike was behind her, David and Theron in front of her. She was caught in the middle of a bad situation that could go wrong at any minute if one of the three testosterone factories around her decided to go into overdrive.

Theron tensed, his tail went still, his back legs tight, body low to the ground.

Scars

Shit. He's going to…
The great black cat launched himself at David's back.
It all happened so fast.
Theron jumped.
David took a step forward.
Mike tried to grab the back of her shirt.
It all merged into one blur of action. She didn't think. She just reacted. Emmie stepped to the side, grabbing for the gun, twisting it up, pointing toward the sky as David tried to pull the trigger and screamed in pain. Blood. She could taste blood on the air. Claws struck skin, the weight of the cat striking his back enough to send them all tumbling to the floor.

God. She couldn't let go of the gun. She didn't dare. He might shoot Mike or Theron.

David screamed.

The metal of the shotgun became slippery under her fingers. The soft click of the trigger issued a warning. She twisted, forcing the barrel up as the shot rang out. Fire lanced through her fingers, the barrel suddenly hot. She screamed. She couldn't help it.
Pain burned through her hands as she let go of the shotgun and clutched her hands close to her body, tears streaming down her face.

Only when she tumbled away from David did she realize what was happening.

Theron stood over David's body. Blood marked his jaw, a low growl rumbled through the air, and David -- holding the shotgun -- had become silent.

Chapter Twenty-Two

"Theron!" Emmie pushed her way past David, tearing him from Theron's grasp. Blood flowed freely, pooling on the ground. Pain filled the air as David cried out, Theron's cries a sharp contrast to those of the human. "You can't do this. You'll lose yourself in the beast. Listen to me. Please!"

The large black cat growled at her, blood flecked across his jaw, his tail snapping back and forth close to the ground. He edged forward, growling his warning, the message clear. *Give me back my prey.*

"He's a human being, Theron. You can't do this." She barely even glanced at David, beyond a quick check to see if he was still alive. "You can't become the monster. Pull out of this. Please. For me." Her heart pounded against her rib cage; cold sweat coated her face. Her hands burned from the heat of the shotgun, but that didn't matter. Nothing mattered now beyond Theron.

The cat snarled, his teeth fully bared.

She reached out to him and then snatched her hand back when he snapped at her fingers. Nothing human looked back through those feline eyes; there was only the hunger of a beast who wanted his prey back. There had to be a way to reach him. A way to bring him back.

"Emmie, I have to get David out of here. Can you keep the cat off my back? Or will he attack you?" Mike kept his voice low as he edged forward. "If I don't move him soon he's going to die. Blood loss. I can't allow that. Do you understand?"

"Yes," she whispered, never taking her gaze off the growling cat. "Do it. I'll keep him busy. He won't attack me." How the hell was she going to do that? She had no idea if the cat would strike or not. She'd seen no signs of humanity in his eyes. Would she ever see Theron's warm smile again? It didn't matter. Not right now. She had to focus on distracting him long enough to allow Mike to drag David out of here.

Mike nudged forward a little more, tangling his fingers into David's shirt, muttering under his breath as he dragged the still breathing and heavily bleeding man, away from the cat.

Theron growled and took a step forward, his claws extended, still glistening with David's blood. Emmie edged closer to him, growling in the back of her throat. She could change, challenge him that way, but it might end up with both of them lost in the grip of the beast.

"Theron. I know you're in there, somewhere," she whispered.

The cat blinked, meeting her gaze, his teeth still bared.

"Remember what we shared only last night. The shower. The way my hands slicked over your body, the way I felt beneath your hands. Please. You have to remember that. Your lips against mine, how I tasted, sounded, and pressed into your caress. I need you to remember just how you held me. What the coffee we shared in the morning tasted like. How confused we both were by what has happened between us" Emmie kept her voice low, her gaze fixed on the cat's face. "I know you're in there. I can sense it. You haven't given up completely, or you'd have attacked me by now, or jumped Mike for taking your meal away from you." *Please, let me be right about this.*

Theron didn't move, but something flickered behind his eyes. Had she reached a part of him? Emmie couldn't be certain. Still, she clung to the hope that he heard her. That he and not the beast knew her, understood who it was that now tried to talk to him. If he didn't, then this would all be for nothing. She'd end up forced to change in order to defend herself from his attack -- no, he wouldn't strike out at her. If that had been a real option, he'd have already done it. She could only hope that, even before she tried to talk to him, there was something familiar about her scent, her voice, her presence. Just enough to keep him from doing something that they would both regret.

Mike dragged David's still form slowly out of the clearing, leaving them alone. Or so she hoped. She didn't know where Jamie was and couldn't risk turning around to see where the man might be. Her entire focus had to remain on Theron.

The cat edged forward a half inch, his head tipping slightly, ears erect, gaze focused on Emmie. A low, questioning sound, rang out, a cross between a growl and a whine. He lowered his belly down onto the damp earth, issuing the low sound once again. A glimmer of recognition flickered across his eyes and then vanished again.

"Theron?" There had to be something there of the man she loved. Her heart skipped a beat. "Don't leave me." Emmie reached out and cupped his face with one hand, her fingers playing over the soft fur. She took a deep breath, pouring her heart and soul into the next breath. "I need you. I need you in a way I never thought was possible. You're my -- my mate."

Light filtered into his eyes. Sanity, a touch of humanity, returning as she watched him. He turned, nudging his head into her touch, his tongue slipping out between his lips as he issued a low querying sound and lapped at her fingers.

"Change. Return to human form. You can't stay in this form forever. Come back to me, Theron. Come back to me so we can be together, not just for a short time, but for the rest of our lives."

Slowly it happened. The fur receded. His teeth returned to normal. Claws changed back into fingernails and human fingers as he collapsed, fully, onto the dirt. Pain filled the air in both animal shrieks and human cries as he was torn for a moment between the two forms. Fur returning for a moment, his gaze filled with pain, fear, and need. Then it was gone. The beast under control, leaving behind a naked, shivering man.

She shuddered, a low sob spilling from her lips as she ran her fingers through his hair. Safe. He'd returned to her. The beast gone.

"Welcome back, Theron," she whispered, tears spilling down

her cheeks, salt-heavy beads touching her lips. "Thank you. Thank you for not leaving me. Thank you for listening. For not leaving me alone. I've been alone far too long."

They clawed at him. Fingers coated in blood. Faces swam in front of him, death masks that he couldn't ignore; he couldn't shut them out. They reached out for him, tried to pull him close, to smother him as he lashed out at them. Where was she? Had she even existed?

No, why would she exist. Their kind didn't fall in love. She had to be a figment of his imagination. And now he paid for it. Lost. Lost in the rage of the beast.

He groaned, shaking his head, trying to push away the darkness that threatened to consume him. He knew it wasn't real. A part of his mind screamed that over and over again. He growled, struggling to pull free of the nightmare. Something wrapped about his body, it held him tight, until he found a way to kick free. He wasn't a caged animal. He needed to be free. They wouldn't hold him. He'd fight. Claw. Bite. They'd never be able to hold him, not even in a...

A sheet. It had to be a sheet or blanket. Not chains. He hadn't been captured. Not in the way he'd thought. He could escape bedding and the nightmares, if he kept fighting. Struggling. Blood. He could still taste blood. It coated his lips and tongue, but it wasn't fresh. He couldn't feel the flesh under his claws any longer. Where was he? No smell of the earth. No sign that he was still amongst the trees. And she was missing.

Theron growled, pushing up, forcing his body upright. The images, the dreams faded away as he stared around the room. Light blinked its way in through the drawn shades. A bed instead of the earth. One he knew well, and then there was her scent; it covered everything in the room. She was here. Close by. She had to be. She hadn't been a dream.

Thank you, God.

His legs shook as he tried to stand. His body protested at what he tried to do, but he had to move. He had to make sure he was up and strong. He'd attacked a man. Others knew about it. He had to deal with that now. It wasn't something that could just be forgotten.

Only when he stood up did he realize that he was naked. It shouldn't have surprised him. He'd been nude when he'd changed. Why would he be dressed now? He smiled slightly and pulled a sheet about his body, even as he stumbled toward the door. Why did he feel so weak? He'd been through shape shifts before; it wasn't the first time, but he'd never felt this weak or helpless. His hand shook as he took hold of the doorknob, pulling it open, sweat beading across his brow.

"Theron. God. What are you doing out of bed?" Her voice wrapped around him as a welcoming blanket. "You should be resting. You're exhausted. I'm not going to let you push yourself. Not today. I know how drained you must be."

"Emmie," he whispered, looking into her eyes. She was real. He'd thought, in one part of the dreams that had clutched him tight, that she'd been nothing more than a figment of his imagination. Now he knew she was real. He hadn't been creating fresh torments for himself as some form of punishment for what he had done. For losing control.

"Yes, it's me." She smiled, looking at him. "But you should be resting still. Hell. You need to sleep still. It's been a long day for you. Your body will need time to recover. You don't pull out of things like that so easily."

Recover. No. He'd been resting too long as it was. He blinked a little; there had been someone he had attacked He knew that. For a moment, the name, the situation, all escaped him. He could still taste the man's blood...

"David?" The name finally came to his lips. *Please, God. Let him still be alive.*

"He'll live. Which is more than he deserves after everything he's done."

Which offered potentially more problems than if the man had died. "What will happen? To him? To us?" *To me?*

"It's something that needs to be dealt with, but not yet. Not until you're strong enough." Emmie frowned slightly, looking up at him, her gaze narrowing. "You've been through a lot. You have to rest until you're strong enough to stand without wobbling."

Wobbling? Was he wobbling? His knees felt weak. Fuck. He didn't like feeling this weak. "Not sure what's wrong with me."

"Your body is fighting the aftereffects of the shift during anger. You let the beast loose." Emmie spoke softly. "You had good reason, but now it's taking a lot out of you."

The beast. Yes. He'd been in the grip of the beast. He could almost remember what had happened. The smell of the men. Their fear. The smell of the blood amongst the trees. And Emmie. His mate. There, calling him back to her. Had he thrown it off entirely, or did it still linger somewhere, waiting for a moment of weakness to again pounce out of the shadows and seek human prey? He had to keep this under control. He had to keep it bound and chained deep within until he was ready to change again. How had he allowed himself to be locked into the depths of the beast like that? If he had learned nothing else from his mother and brothers, it had been to never allow anger to take control of him whilst in cat form. He'd destroyed himself. "I don't know how you can stand to be near me after what I did. I lost control of myself. I nearly killed him. God. I wanted to kill him."

"But you didn't. Theron. You have to remember that. You didn't kill him."

But I wanted to. Needed to. I wanted to taste his blood running down my throat. I did taste some of it, but I wanted more. I'm the monster, and you're talking to me as if I'm a normal human being. A shifter who has always been in control of himself. I'm nothing like that. I'll never be like that.

He took a deep breath and let her turn him back toward the

bed; his legs shook. On that she'd been right; he wasn't at full strength, his body still torn in some ways between the need to be in human form, and the desire to revert back to the beast. He'd never felt like this after a shift. A price paid for the loss of control? Yeah. That made sense.

"Theron, you were angry. He was threatening my life. You reacted to that. He had a gun. You had every reason to lose control like that." Emmie sat down on the edge of the bed with him, tracing her fingertips across his arm. "If someone had been threatening you, I'd have done the same thing. You have to remember that."

It didn't make him feel any better. He'd spent the best of his adult life working to bring scum like David in safely or dealing with them before they became a problem. Instead of losing his sense of humanity, giving into the beast, he should have found another way.

"He'll live?" Had he already asked that? He couldn't remember. Not really.

"Yes, Mike got him to the hospital in time. He doesn't know anything more than a large cat attacked him. Shock seems to have wiped out any memory of the rest of us being there. Or blocked it for now. It gives us time to figure out what we're going to do."

"I'll leave. I have to." God. The words hurt. They lashed claws of their own into his heart, threatening to rip it to shreds. He didn't want to leave her, but he had no choice. By staying he'd bring her trouble, perhaps even place her in danger. He wasn't willing to take that risk with the woman he loved.

Loved. Wanted to be with. Needed to be with for the rest of his life. She was a part of him. Did she know that? Did she want to know that? If he spoke of it what would happen? Would she laugh? Or just ignore him? Maybe she would kick him out? He didn't want to leave her. Not now. Not ever.

"No, there's another answer. We just need some time to work it out." Emmie's fingers tightened on his arm. "I won't lose you."

Scars

Damn her. Why did she have to make this so difficult?

"Now, please, just rest. For a little longer. I'll get you something to eat, and we can talk about this when you're stronger." Emmie let go of his arm and pushed, slowly, to her feet, a slight quiver touching her lips. "I love you, Theron. I wanted to be able to deny it, but I can't. I have to believe that it's my love, our love, that brought you back out of the darkness. So, I'm not going to turn my back on what I'm feeling, what we share. I only hope you'll accept that instead of running and hiding from it."

Chapter Twenty-Three

Emmie leaned against the kitchen counter, struggling to control her emotions. Theron needed her. She had to keep calm, focused, and not lose it by sobbing hysterically over a pile of dirty dishes. What good would she be to him if she did the foolish woman thing by crying when she needed to be doing something useful?

Tears aren't a weakness. Remember that, Emmie. But neither are they a weapon to use against someone else. He used them. He laughed in my face before he walked out and never looked back. Don't ever let a man use your emotions against you. They'll find a crack into your heart and use it. Over and over again.

She growled at the memory of her mom's words and leaned over the sink, turning on the water. She splashed some onto her face, wiping away the traces of salt from the few rebellious tears that had slipped down her cheeks, then turned her attention to the dishes. *Picture of domesticity -- fuck. She'd have my hide for this.*

What would he think of her if he walked in now? Why did it even matter?

All right. Now she was being stupid. Why would he care if he saw her doing the dishes or not? It was just a simple household chore that had to be done. It didn't mean she was practicing being a housewife. God. Why was she getting so worked up by simple things?

Good question.

Because she'd just been through the ringer. She'd fallen in love with another shifter and had pulled him out of the darkness when he'd lost himself in cat form because of a man threatening her.

Fine, be so damn logical about it all. It's not going to do any good at the end of the day.

Scars

Well, what was wrong with being logical?

She tensed, a soft sound at the door drew her attention instantly. Her hands clenched as she turned and -- and caught the hint of Mike's scent. With a soft shudder, her nerves on edge, she relaxed and walked out into the living room. No one else in the town would have just walked into her home without knocking first. "Everything all right, Mike?"

"For now, yes. How is he?" Mike nodded toward the bedroom.

"Unsettled. Talking about leaving. He's ashamed of what happened. I can't blame him, either. I know it has to be hard, losing control like that. I'd be unsettled as well. I -- I don't know if I'd handle it as well as he's doing it."

"With good reason." The sheriff grunted and sat down on the sofa. "Losing control in the midst of a shift is one of the few crimes all of the shifter breeds agree on. It's a loss of self. He'll have to face an inquiry."

"With who?"

"The local elders. It's a type of court. They're normally called when something goes wrong. Didn't your mom ever mention them?"

"No." Court? More shifters? What else had she not been told about her kind?

"They don't meet often. Just when the need is there. A representative from each of the shifter groups attends it. The one up in the city has been called enough times recently over problems that hunters have been alerted. So the one out here is more cautious. There's no cat shifter there. No one approached you about it, I guess. Wonderful."

"Hunters?" What was he talking about?

"Hunters. Ah, guess you don't know about those, either. You've led a sheltered life, Emmie. They are the type of people I believe your Theron normally deals with. Hunters of our kind. Humans who keep trying to prove we exist. Then there are the problem children. Either shifters or humans who interfere with others. Rapists, abusers; we call in our own police force, though they'd be closer to bounty hunters, in order to deal with the problems. From what I've been able to find out about your man, he's a bounty hunter. Damn good one, from what little I've been able to find out. Many of the bigger shifter families know about him or have used his skills in the past."

"God. A bounty hunter. He never told me. He's barely told me anything about himself." He'd never had the chance, not fully; that was something they had planned to discuss after he'd returned from the motel. "How did you find out? Did he tell you?" Sure. He'd tell the local cops, but not the woman he was having sex with. Typical.

"We met earlier, before he came in to see you last night. He told me his name, and that was enough for me to do some checking. It's what I do, remember? I can put a name in the computer, maybe add some prints, and do a search. In his case, his name was uncommon enough that my other contacts in the pack were able to fill me in. He and a human called Buck work together in the city and other parts of the country. They're quite a well-respected team, which makes what he did all the more horrifying."

"I don't…"

"He lost control of everything that made him human, instead of an animal," Mike repeated patiently. "He can't be allowed to get away with this. The story will spread. Respect will be lost. The local court has to be made aware of the situation. They'll decide what his punishment will be."

"What will they do to him?" *Punishment?* Cold sweat coated her spine.

"I'm not sure. There are ways of -- stripping -- a shifter from their ability to shape shift. But it's nasty. I don't know if things will go that far. They'd have to find someone willing to do that. A witch with the spell at hand and the willingness to go through it. Not many will. It's not pleasant. Either for the shifter or the witch."

"He didn't mean to let it happen." Emmie folded her arms

beneath her breasts. "He didn't go after them on purpose. They attacked him. Ran him off the road. You saw the signs on the road. The wreck that is now his bike. He was lucky to walk away from that. He could have been killed. He should have been killed. A motorbike against a truck like that."

Anyone else might have been killed. She had to believe that his shifter senses, those of the cat, had given him fair warning. But they hadn't known he was a shifter when they'd attacked him. They still didn't know. Even now. Or if they did, Mike hadn't said anything about it.

"Mean it or not, he did it, and I can't just sit back and do nothing about it, Emmie. You know that." Mike sighed and looked away from her. "I'm bound. By the law and the rules the local court set in place. I'm screwed twice over. You know that."

"And I've seen how wolf shifters react to the point of attacking a threat to their mate. Hell, I grew up on those stories. So are you saying that you wouldn't have acted the same way he did if your mate had been attacked?" She looked him dead in the eyes. "Go on, tell me you'd have sat meekly by because of some damn rules. I dare you."

Mike opened his mouth to protest, then closed it again, frowning. "Fair point. I can't. I know what I'd do. What any wolf shifter I know would do."

"So what makes his actions a crime? He's beating himself up enough about this; why must we add to it? If you can't say you'd follow the rules or that any wolf you know would follow them, why is it expected of him? Of us? It makes no sense. You have to let this ride. I doubt any other shifter knows what happened out there. So why do you have to report it?"

Mike's jaw set instantly. "Because it's expected; it's my duty. I can't just sit back and do nothing. I have to report him. It-- it's my job. I'm sorry, Emmie."

"I thought you were a wolf, not a sheep." Her hands clenched into fists as she pulled them away from her body.

"I'm not a fuckin' sheep," he growled.

"Then stop following the route they expect you to; think for yourself instead of following the herd."

"Pack. Wolves have packs, not herds."

"Fine. Pack, then. But start thinking like a wolf instead of a sheep, following blindly on with the way things have always been."

He growled, the sound vibrating in the back of his throat. "Cats. You always think you know better than everyone else around you."

"That's because we do. Dogs have owners; cats own. Look around you, Mike. Ever seen a cat bow down to the wishes of a human?" Fine, he wanted to play this game, she'd drum the point home to him. "You've seen the jokes humans make."

"They're humans. What would they know?"

"Enough to look around and see the truth."

"Alley cat!"

"Stray mutt!" Oh, she needed this.

"Backyard howler!"

"Collared pet."

"Bet you're declawed!"

"Did your last owner snip your balls off?"

Mike's jaw dropped. "I can't believe you just went there."

Emmie smirked. "Well, I did. Shit, I needed that."

"You swear more than most women I've known." Mike shook his head and ran his fingers through his hair.

"As you said, I'm an alley cat. Mom tried her best with me, but I'm not a lady and don't pretend to be one. Don't try and make me into something I'm not."

"You're trying to fool yourself, Emmie." Mike took a deep breath and looked at her, his gaze softening. He almost reached out for her, his hand pulling back at the last minute. "All that swearing, the bravado, the way you needed to try and pick a fight with me, insult me, when simple logic would have worked just as well. I know what you're hiding. It doesn't fool me."

Scars

"What?"

"You're more of a lady than you'll ever admit. You swear, bluster, shout, but it's to keep people away from you. No, not just people. Men. You don't want them to get close, because they'll leave, so you make them leave before it even gets to that point. Or you walk out on them. Admit it, Emmie. You try to play the confident alley cat, but you're a scared little kitten hoping someone will come along, pick you up, cuddle you, and tell you it's all going to be all right."

Theron's head pounded. How long had he slept again? He could remember Emmie helping him back into bed. The feel of her arm draped about his shoulder, her lips brushing his in a soft kiss, and then -- then nothing. He'd passed out; that was the only possible answer.

But why?

He had been that tired?

He'd not done anything that hard on his system.

All right. So he didn't know just how a shift in that type of mood would truly hit him. Not until now. But it still shouldn't have...

Fine. Maybe he had been and had just refused to admit it, even to himself. Well, it was time he got his lazy ass out of bed and faced the reality of the situation. He'd screwed up. Dangerously so. Now he had to pay the price and face the local court of shifters. There was bound to be one. Most areas had them, and they liked to stomp down on visiting shifters, or at least, the ones he'd dealt with before had. By now Mike would have reported him. A cop and a wolf. Yeah, he'd have passed the report back up the chain like a good mutt. *Shit.* He couldn't stay with Emmie in case they decided to try her as well, though she'd done nothing wrong, and even if, by some miracle, Mike hadn't reported him, sooner or later David would remember what had happened out there.

God. This was a mess.

Only when he sat up fully and draped the sheet once again around his waist did reality finally hit him.

His clothing. He'd left it in the woods. And unless Emmie had sent someone to the motel, he now had nothing to wear except a damn sheet. *I'm fucked, and not in a good way. Unless I shift, I've got no way of leaving the house.* Shifting wasn't an option, not unless he could be certain that he would be able to keep the beast under control. And right now he wasn't sure of his own name, let alone anything else.

Why hadn't he thought this through when he'd changed?

Because he hadn't been thinking. He'd been reacting. As a male, protecting his female and screw anything else.

His stomach growled.

"I'm sitting here, contemplating just how big a fuck-up I've become, and you're complaining that you're hungry?"

It growled again.

"Fine, I'll get us some food. Then will you shut up and leave me alone?"

His belly rumbled in agreement.

Wonderful. Here he was. A master shape shifter, a wild feline, and he was being ruled by his stomach. Some hunter he was. He grumbled and pushed fully to his feet, the sheet wrapped tightly about his waist, before he stumbled toward the door. The smell of fresh coffee hit him and tugged him in the direction of the kitchen.

"Theron?" She peeked out of the kitchen, her long, dark hair tumbling around her shoulders. "Is that you?"

"You were expecting someone else?" Damn it, he still felt as weak as a day-old kitten. "Throwing parties whilst I've been sleeping?"

"Erm, no. Mike was here earlier, and I wasn't sure if he'd just walked back in. You know what dogs are like."

"Oh." Fine, well, maybe that damn mutt had been here for a good reason, like checking up on him? Or on Emmie? Well, they had been through a lot. Weapons had been fired. "And everything's all right? You look a little pale."

"Yes. Sort of. We had a fight -- er, discussion." Emmie turned and walked back into the kitchen. "Did you need something? Hungry? Thirsty? Shower?"

"Food?" He tried to smile as he settled down at the kitchen table. His stomach growled its approval, and the croak in his throat reminded him of something else he needed. "Coffee, as well? Please?"

"Sure. I kinda figured you'd be hungry when you woke up." She flashed a smile that didn't reach her eyes. "Eggs? Bacon? What are you interested in? I've not got a huge amount in the fridge, but I can always nip to the store."

"Eggs and bacon sound good to me. I'll be fine with that. Honest." The thought of her leaving, even for a short time, didn't sit well with him. He tried not to frown as she turned her back on him. What was going on? She'd been so supportive earlier, before Mike had shown up. What had that damn mutt said to her? Fuck. Did he have to track the man down and teach him a lesson? *Yeah, like I have the spare energy to do that. Good one, Theron.* "You and Mike had a long chat?"

"Something like that." Her shoulders slumped. "He wanted to report you to the local court."

"I figured that was coming." *Just not this quickly. How long do I have before they come for me? Or do they expect me to turn myself in like a tame little house cat?* "When is he going to talk to them?"

"I'm not sure he is. He and I -- we kinda -- I asked him not to do it."

"He's a cop. It's his duty to follow through with this." God knew he'd follow through with reporting a rogue shifter himself. He'd seen the damage a real rogue could do if he wasn't brought in check. But he'd never thought it would backfire on him like this.

"This isn't a human crime. His duty, as a cop, revolves around human crimes. Not shifter laws set up by some court system I didn't even know existed until today." She didn't turn around to look at him; instead she grasped the edge of the counter, growling under her breath. "Shit. Where were these ruling shifters when my mom died? When I was left alone with no one to turn to? I'm not going to bend down to some stupid court system that…"

"You didn't know about the courts?" How was that even possible? She'd been raised by a shifter, hadn't she? "I don't understand. How can you not know about them. Your mom must have known. She should have told you about them. Emmie. Stop and think for a moment. She must have told you about them at some point."

"Why? Why is there the assumption that she would have known? Or that she told me about them? She didn't. She never said a damn word. Don't you dare suggest otherwise to me." Emmie turned, her jaw set, eyes darkening. "She never mentioned them to me. I rarely saw other shifters until I was an adult, and by then, she was dead. We lived in a small place, and I never even knew my father. The only damn gift I have from him is my last name. So just why would I know about the councils? If female feline shifters are often left with their moms and that mom doesn't know about the council, who else would be around to tell them?" All the hatred, the anger at the way Emmie's father had vanished without so much as a backward glance, surged through those words. "She had a hard enough time trying to raise me on her own without suddenly knowing about everything else in the world. She got pregnant with me, and then my dad vanished. Shit. For all I know he never even knew he'd gotten my mom pregnant. He didn't even stay around long enough for that."

He opened his mouth to protest, then clamped it shut. *Shit, all right. Never thought about it that way before. If she doesn't know about them, how many other shifters are ignorant about them? It would explain a lot.* How could he have taken so many things for granted?

Because he'd been one of the lucky ones.

"I'm sorry. I didn't mean to snap at you. You've been through enough today. I didn't mean to add to it." Emmie shook her head and sighed, running one hand through her hair. "I'm just stressed, that's all."

"I can't blame you for that. You've been through a lot. Mostly because of me." He'd brought enough troubles on her shoulders without attacking her for things beyond her control. He only had one choice. Unless he wanted Emmie to be pulled into the middle of the mess with the court and everything else that would follow. "Emmie. I have to leave and soon."

"What?" She blinked and stared at him. "Haven't we been through this already?"

"Yes, but that was before I knew about the council." *Yeah, sure. I'm running away because of the council, not because I'm afraid of what I feel when I'm around you.*

"Maybe Mike won't let it go that far. He and I spoke for some time. I think I made some good points that he'll think about." Emmie peered out from beneath her mane of dark hair. Her bottom lip quivered even as she looked away from him. He could feel the pain his words caused radiating from her. He could see it in her eyes, the need to be with him, at his side, in his bed, and in his life. "I don't want to lose you."

I don't want to lose you, either, but what other choice do I have? Come on, man. Cut to the chase. Give her the line. Use it. Make her hate me. It will be easier on her this way. But who would it be easier for? Not her. God. He was fooling himself again. It wasn't for her benefit, but his. "It's for the best. You always knew I'd leave sooner or later, didn't you?"

The color drained from her face. "But -- I thought. After everything you'd said, in the diner, the night in the forest, and last night, for fuck's sake. What are you playing at? You said..."

"Emmie. Feline shifters always part company. It's how these things work for us. You know that. Your mom warned you." He spoke slowly, forcing a smile across his lips. He gave a slow shake of his head, hoping it looked as though he were mocking her. "You said it often enough. That you expected me to leave you once we'd fucked a couple of times. So, why are you so surprised about it now?" His gut knotted as his heart turned into a piece of lead and threatened to sink into his feet, but somehow he kept smiling. Knives dug into his gut as he forced the new words into life. The new lies to scar her soul. "Oh, you're a sweet kitty, I'll give you that. But just why would I hang about this dead-end town? You're a good lay, but not that good."

A low growl sounded at the back of her throat. Her hands clenched. Eyes turned black. Her lips pressed into a tight, thin line before she managed to let out two hate-filled words. "Get out!"

"Sure, just as soon as I have something to wear." *Forgive me. Please. I have my reasons. Just don't forget this. Don't forget the hatred you feel now. Hold onto it. It's better than being in love. Easier. You'll understand that eventually. Please, God. Let her understand this one day.*

"You can leave wearing that sheet or buck naked for all I care. Get out. Now. Before I call Mike and have you escorted out. You're not welcome here." A twitch worked its way across her cheek.

"Then call him. I'm not walking out of here in a sheet or naked." He couldn't walk out at all, not unless he had someone helping him. Every fiber of his being screamed at him to stay with her, to be with her for the rest of his life, but staying would only make matters worse for them both. This was the best thing to do, for both of them.

Chapter Twenty-Four

Emmie watched, her arms folded beneath her breasts, as the police cruiser pulled out of her driveway. Only when she knew for certain that the car had turned out of the road did she let go of her scant control. Tears seeped down her cheeks, a low, gulping whimper rang out, escaping before she could prevent it. She turned and walked away from the door, her knees giving out before she'd made even two steps across the room.

A long, low howl of sheer pain filled the room. Sobs wracked her body. She pressed her hands against her face, covering her eyes, salt coating her face, lips, and fingers. Pain. She'd never felt this type of pain before. It wasn't supposed to be possible to feel this amount of pain and still live.

Is this how her mom had felt when her dad had left? If so, she finally understood what her mom had warned her against. All the pain. The cruel words. The look in his eyes.

Theron. How could he be so cruel to her? He'd said -- he'd told her that he wanted to be with her. Now this. Just what was going on? He'd walked out on her. Left without a backward glance. How could she have been so stupid? He didn't love her. This was nothing more than a way for him to get laid more than once by the same woman. How many times had he pulled that stunt on women? And she'd just been another notch on the belt for him. Another stupid female who had fallen for his lines.

How could she have been so stupid?

Because he was good at this. Good at seducing women and...

No. The look in his eyes, that hadn't been faked. No man had the ability to act that well. Not when he was naked and in bed with a woman. And she'd pulled him out of the grip of the beast.

Hadn't she?

What else could have tipped him over the edge but the way

she had been threatened by David? Who else could have brought him back into the realms of sanity but the voice of his mate in the first place? Her heart throbbed, wounded, pain seeping into every corner of her being. No longer sharp, no longer the knife digging into her chest, but the dull ache that rippled through her being. She'd let a man hurt her. Allowed him to use her -- and it wouldn't happen again.

She'd learned her lesson. However painful that had been. It wasn't a mistake she would make again. She scuffed the tears away from her face and forced herself back up onto her feet, stumbling across to the bathroom. Cold water helped. It at least washed the tears away from her face and soothed her sore eyes. It did nothing for the pain she felt within The hurt she would find a way to hide rather than let anyone else know what she had been through. She'd been a fool. It didn't mean she had to plaster it across her face for everyone else to see.

Emmie tried to focus long enough to pour herself a mug of coffee, but when it slipped from her grasp and shattered on the kitchen floor, splattering her with the heated liquid, she finally accepted that she wasn't going to hold it together any time soon.

Theron. He'd walked into her life. He'd wrapped his claws around her heart. Taught her to feel, to accept him, to welcome him fully. Then, with a smirk, he'd walked out again, wearing little more than one of her sheets.

God. What a fool she had been.

Emmie sank slowly down onto the floor, hugging her knees to her chest, her hair falling over her face. The idea of burning the bed, the bedding, and everything connected with him, appealed to her far too much right now. The call to destroy it, and anything else he had touched, was too potent for Emmie to risk moving from the kitchen until she could get a grip on her emotions again.

It would have been easier if he'd been killed by David's gun. At least then she could have just grieved instead of blaming herself for everything that had happened.

Scars

"Mind filling me in on just what the hell is going on?" Mike glanced over as he turned the car out from the end of Emmie's road. "I get a call from Emmie to come and get you. You're standing there, wrapped in a sheet, acting like a fool. Smirking and telling her goodbye, that she should have known this was coming. Then I get you in the car, and you look like death warmed over. What happened in there? What sort of sick game are you two playing?"

"It's over." Theron forced the words out from between clenched teeth.

"What?"

"Between Emmie and I. It's over. Done with. I'm getting out of town."

"And you're going to do that how? Your bike is trashed, or didn't you realize that?"

He hadn't. "No, I didn't know. I don't remember much about what happened out there. Okay. Fine. I'll find another way out of town."

"You were forced off the road, or you turned off it to try and avoid them," Mike explained slowly, keeping his gaze on the road. "Jamie isn't talking. And David is in no fit state to talk. Right now the man's in the psychiatric ward. He keeps gibbering on about a large black cat trying to maul him. No one believes him. Especially after the news that he faked a cat attack on Aneta. Seems that backfired on him."

"That isn't far off what happened." He almost smiled. "Just hope he doesn't start putting the pieces together. That's why I have to leave. I can't sit here, waiting for the council to bring down sanctions against me. I can't put Emmie through that." No, she deserved something better than that.

"Ah, so that's what's going on. You're trying to protect Emmie. Did you even stop to think about that? She's a grown woman. She had the right to make that decision for herself." Mike shook his head, his knuckles white on the steering wheel. "Bloody cats. You're all alike there. You think you know better than anyone else around you, including other cats."

"You arrogant son of a bitch!"

"Yes, I am. But it's still the truth. Both you and Emmie are the same in that respect. You think you know better than everyone else around you."

"Emmie would have insisted I stay with her."

"You two need each other. You can't just walk out on her life." Mike pulled the cruiser off to the side of the road, then turned to face Theron. "She's in love with you. You love her. So just what's the problem?"

"It would have left her in a dangerous position if I stayed with her. She's too good for that," Theron growled. "I'm not going to put her at risk just because I -- well, I'm not about to take that risk."

"It's not just your choice to make, why can't you see that, if only for a minute?" Mike's jaw clenched, and he forced his hands away from the steering wheel. "When someone loves you, truly loves you, they're willing to walk through the fires of hell with you. But you have to be willing to give them that chance."

A chance to do what? Die at his side? Find herself ruined as she was called before the council to answer for his sins? She didn't even know what the court would do to him, or what they could do to her if they decided she had something to do with his actions.

"Stop thinking about the court."

"Why?"

"Because they're not going to know about it. I'm not about drop you and Emmie in it. She's too good a woman to be ruined like that."

"So you're protecting her?"

"No, I'm thinking for myself. Emmie was right. I needed to stop acting like a -- well, forget it. I didn't see a need to report you for something I'd have done myself. If someone had been coming on to my mate, then I'd have attacked them as well. It's part of our nature. I don't know why we've had to suppress it for so long when it's programmed into us."

"Because we're not animals. We change into the form of animals, but it doesn't make us like them. Not unless we lose control." Theron repeated the mantra that had been drummed into him since childhood. "If we attack without reason, we lose that thread that makes us human."

"Theron, haven't you ever sat down and thought about it? No, obviously not. I didn't until Emmie took me to task. Animals don't attack without a reason. Human beings are the only ones who do that."

He wanted to argue, to tell Mike that he was wrong, but the words wouldn't leave his mouth. He'd seen far too many humans attack and kill without reason. Sure, they rationalized it, putting it down to fear, or greed, or the desire to protect, and there were some cases that fitted those excuses. But there were others, far too many others, that had no reason whatsoever. Men and women who killed without thought or mercy, enjoying the smell of the other person's blood hitting the air or the spray across their face. The death of that often nameless victim was, to them, a sheer pleasure.

It made sense.

But it wasn't enough to change his mind.

"If I stay, sooner or later I'll bring trouble down on her. If not via the council, then something else. I'd have to leave for work at times, and if one of my targets then tracks us down, they'll try and use Emmie against me. I can't expose her to that."

"Bullshit."

"What?"

"You don't want to stay with her because the longer you're with her, the more you'll feel for her, and you're afraid of just how deeply you'll fall in love with her."

His throat tightened. Was it that obvious? He'd tried to

hide it from himself, rationalize it that he was doing this for her protection, but the truth was blatant, and still he fumbled over the lie. "I just can't risk it. I can't stand the thought of someone using her to get to me."

"She's a strong woman. She knows how to shift. She can protect herself. Just stop treating her as if she's made of glass." Mike sighed and rubbed the heel of his hand over his eyes.

Theron's stomach knotted

If someone like Lloyd or one of the other scum bags he dealt with on a regular basis got their hands on Emmie, then he'd be lost. How far would he sink in order to protect the woman he loved? Far enough that he knew he might not be able to come back. Or he'd sell his soul to do whatever they wanted, just as long as they didn't hurt Emmie. God. He was a mess. He knew, somewhere in the back of his mind, that she was strong, a shifter, with the ability to protect herself. But somehow that wasn't enough to silence the fears, the doubts, the images of her prone and bleeding on the floor. He couldn't take that. He didn't have what it took to face that possibility.

"Maybe it's me who isn't strong enough."

Chapter Twenty-Five

"Theron? Hey, anyone there?" Buck waved his hand in front of Theron's face. "Hello, ground control to Theron? Come on. Give me some sign of life."

"Sorry. I -- err. Never mind." He blinked and looked out of the windscreen, staring at the drizzle of rain that turned the sky grey. A week. Seven long days since he'd left Emmie behind in that small dead-end town. He should have snapped out of it by now, but it didn't take much for Emmie to slip back into his thoughts. Would it amuse her? If she'd known just how he was taking all of this? He'd never know. *Focus, man. Work. Come on.* "What's he supposed to be wearing?"

"Jeans, shirt, boots. The usual Friday night crowd-pleaser. Seems to be the code for this part of town. Earrings. Studs. Both ears. Nothing fancy. No tats, either." Buck shook his head and turned his attention back to the door of the bar. "He walked in there about an hour ago. We've got a bird watching the back."

"Owl?"

"Barn owl. He owes us a favor from a while back. Good kid -- little nervous, but good. Didn't see the harm in having him act as lookout. If he ever gets over his fears, he could be a good repeat backup for us."

Theron frowned. "He has a family?"

"The mark?"

"No, the owl."

"Yes, don't you remember? We helped his mom out a few months back. The stalker issue? Nice family -- mom, pop, three kids? He's the eldest. What's up with you? I've never seen you this out of it. Normally you're at the top of your game when we head out on a job." Buck glanced back at him, his brow creased in a deep frown. "You've been out of it ever since you came back into town. It's just not like you. And what the fuck happened to your ride? You never did tell me. You loved that bike, so there's no way you just left it behind."

"Long story. One I'm not in the mood to hash out."

"Mood or not, you need to snap out of it before you get one -- or both -- of us killed. I'm worried about you. You're not with it. And that's not like you. Last time I saw you like this, you were running a high grade fever. Are you sick again?"

"I'm not sick, and I can do my job."

"Like hell you can. Bird boy out there would make a better partner than you right now. You're not focused at all."

"Fuck you."

"Not my type." Buck stopped for a minute, then formed his next words carefully. "It's a woman, isn't it? You got yourself laid, and she's stuck in your system. Never thought I'd see the day that happened to you."

God. The man didn't know just how close he was with that. Emmie. Just why couldn't he get her out of his mind and his heart? *Because she belongs in both. Not just as a one- or two-night event.* That wasn't the point. She didn't have a place in his life. The danger to them both was just too great. He wasn't about to risk her, and -- and he was still acting like a man with a serious case of the L word.

"Who is she?"

"You don't need to know." Emmie. Goddess. Lover. Mate.

"Sure I do. Sooner or later you're going to wander off and try to find her, so I reckon it would help to at least know her name, especially if I want to find you again," Buck muttered. "Shit, okay, he's on the move. Hey! Theron. Focus, will ya!"

Focus. On what? Who? Damn it. He couldn't go on like this. He needed her. She was still under his skin. He couldn't shut her out, the smell of her, the taste, the way she sounded when he...

"I can't do this."

"No. You can't. That's the first sensible thing you've said in the past week." Buck sighed and turned the engine on.

"What the fuck? Where are we going? We've got a job to do. We can't just walk out on a case."

"Not like this, you haven't. I'm not about to get myself killed because you're not focused on the job. Look, whoever she is, either get her out of your system or go back to her. You're useless to me right now. We can't work this way until you're back to your normal self."

He growled, his hands clenched, knuckles white as Buck turned the car out, away from the bar. "Just who in hell's name do you think you're talking to?"

"The man who's been my partner for the best part of the last five years. A man who I thought I could trust with my life. The man who came back from some small town as little more than a shadow of himself. So I'm not sure who you are. But you sure as hell aren't the man I knew only a week ago."

"Bastard!" His nails extended into claws before he realized just what he was doing. No. He wasn't going to let this happen.

"Cool it. Now," Buck snapped. "You're losing control. Theron! Get it under control."

"Pull over." He couldn't let this loose, not on Buck. Not on his friend.

"Where?"

"Anywhere. I don't care. Just pull over. I've got to get out of the car before I do something I'm gonna regret." He couldn't do this. Not with Buck of all people. "I'm not going to hurt you. But if I don't get out of the car and get some fresh air into my lungs, I'm not sure what I'm going to end up doing to myself." *Yeah, sure I won't hurt him. Just as long as he keeps a healthy distance from me. Fuck. I'm a mess.*

"Hold on," Buck muttered and turned the car off the main street before he pulled off into a park. "Will this do?"

Theron didn't even give him enough time for the car to come to a complete stop before he yanked open the door and darted out. His chest hurt. Muscles ached. He needed to change. To bite into something. Taste the blood. See it pooling on the damp earth. Or -- or just see her face again.

"Breathe." Buck exited the car. "Just breathe, damn it. Don't let this thing, whatever it is, win. You're stronger than that."

Win? It had already won. Her eyes. The way her skin had felt beneath his fingers. He couldn't get her out of his mind, his system, his heart. He'd lost himself in her, and there was no coming back. Some strength. He'd been run over by an eighteen-wheeler called Emmie.

"Shit. Man, I don't know what to do. I've never seen you like this."

No one had. No one would again. He had to put a stop to this. Even if it meant turning himself into the shifter council and telling them what he'd done.

"Emmie! Open the damn door! You can't stay in there forever. He's not worth it!" Mags pounded on the door with a clenched fist. "If you don't let me in, I'm going to call Mike and have him break the door in! I'll tell him I smelled gas. Or smoke!"

Emmie groaned and threw the cushion she'd had over her face across the room before she rolled off the couch. Would it take a lie from Mags to get Mike to force the door open? "Fine. Just give me a minute."

"Sure. Not one second longer, though. I'm watching the countdown."

"Bitch." Emmie muttered under her breath and stumbled to the door, unlocking it before she pulled it open. Mags stood there, her gaze fixed on Emmie, her full lips twitched into a half smile. "Look. I'm okay. I'm just not in the mood for company. I'll be fine in a couple of days."

"Right. You're not in the mood for company. Uh-huh. I get it. You're in the mood for that hunk to walk back into your life so you can fuck him senseless, then dump him, instead." Mags walked in and closed the door calmly, giving Emmie no room to argue with her. "I don't blame you. I'd be pissed if he'd dumped me. Men. What is it about them? Shit. Can't they let us do the dumping on occasion? I'd love to drop one of them into it. Just once. Just to see the look on his face. But it's a guy thing, right?"

Emmie trembled, a laugh bubbling up from her gut. "God. You've no idea how funny that is." How many men had she used and walked away from over the years? Too many to count. In human terms, she would have been a slut. In cat terms, she was a mature female getting what she needed from a male before walking out on them.

"So. Fill me in." Her friend strolled past her into the kitchen. "Shit, woman. When was the last time you did anything in here? The place is a dump."

Fine. So, the place was a mess. She knew that. She didn't care. "Don't remember." Sure she did. The dishes she'd done the day he'd trashed her heart and walked out of her life. "Does it matter?"

"You'll end up with flies in here." Mags leaned down and picked up a dirty plate, dumping it into the sink. "It's not like you to let things get like this."

Well, at least she'd have something to swear at. "And?"

"God, woman. What are you doing? You're letting him push you so far down you won't be able to come back up. Is he really worth it? You're better than this. Stronger. You can't let him destroy you. Shit. He's just a dumb man."

Yes. No. How was she supposed to know right now? "Did you want something, or are you just here to make my afternoon a misery?"

"You're my friend, Emmie. Just because you've decided to hide away from the world for a few days, that doesn't change the fact that you've been here for me. Now it's my turn to be here for you. I don't care if you want me to leave. It's not happening. I'm not walking out on a friend who obviously needs me. If I have to shake you a bit to get you to see sense, then so be it."

Need? Since when had she ever needed anyone? *Anyone except Theron. Come on, I still want him. Need him. I still smell him on my sheets. I can't even bring myself to change the bedding.* "I'm fine. Whatever I'm sick with, it will pass. Soon." It had to.

"Sick? Yeah. I guess you're sick. Love has been known to act that way with some people." Mags looked over the kitchen and pulled out the coffee pot. "You need coffee. Or something stronger."

"Stronger wouldn't be good on an empty stomach." No matter how tempting it sounded right about now. "Fuck. Coffee, then. More later." Yeah, a lot more. Maybe she'd get drunk and crawl into a hole for a few days. Forget he even existed. No. That wasn't possible. But she could at least numb the pain.

And do what? Become the town drunk? *Wonderful fucking idea. Not.* She wasn't going to let him push her that far down. A few drinks, fine. More than that and she'd be starting down on a path she wasn't sure she'd have the strength to pull back out of.

"You've got it bad." Mags shook her head and filled up the pot, adding an extra scoop of coffee. "Can't say I blame you. That man is a dish. But he still had no right to dump on you like that. I'd have thrown something at him. No, you have to call the cops and get him driven out of here. Did you ever get your sheet back?"

Emmie groaned. "You know about that?"

"The entire town knows by now."

Heat flushed across her face. "I'm never stepping outside again."

"Yes, you are. It's not that bad."

"Try looking at it from here. If the whole town knows, then -- God. I can't stay here." Emmie turned, looking around the small kitchen. Despite her insistence on never fully unpacking, the small house had become home to her. The thought of leaving unsettled her. "They're going to think that I'm some sort of..."

"That you're a woman, who fell in love with a jerk. Welcome

to being human."

Except she wasn't human. She never would be. She could pretend. Play the role. But it wouldn't change what she really was. "I'm not going to deal with this."

"You've got to. You're a grown woman, Emmie. Act like one. You're not about to let this man walk all over you. I don't care how good he was in the sack; he's not worth all this."

Yes, he was. Is. God. If he walked into the house right now and asked me for sex, I'd drop at his feet. "I just don't like the idea of everyone looking at me, feeling sorry for me."

"Unfortunately, that's also part of being human. Don't worry. The whole thing with David and Jamie is the big gossip around town. David's insane, did you know that?" Mags reached up and pulled down two clean mugs. "He's been put in a secure facility. They had no choice. He bit one of the nurses. It's all over the diner. They say he'll never be normal again. Still, it's saved him from doing time in the state pen. Aneta's healed up enough to confirm that David was behind the attack. Oh, and Jamie's locked up as well, for his part in it. He didn't hurt Aneta, not physically, but he was there when it happened, and he didn't do anything to stop it."

Wonderful. Well, at least Theron would be safe. Good. That was one problem she didn't have to think about. Shit. Why did she even care about the bastard? He'd fucked her and left! Her heart didn't care. She still loved him, still worried about him. He was safe for now, and a part of her wanted to sing her relief.

The rest of her still wanted to scratch his eyes out.

"You love him. Even after everything, after this past week, you still love him, don't you?" Mags's voice dropped into a low whisper. "Oh, Emmie. I didn't realize you still had it that bad. I mean -- well, hell."

"Yeah, I know. God. I'm fucked."

Chapter Twenty-Six

It hadn't passed. No matter how he had tried to channel the anger it still hadn't faded. Buck had stayed around, waiting, watching as Theron had shifted and paced through the park. Yet it hadn't helped. Maybe he needed something else? A different piece of tail to fuck. Not a shifter, though. Not this time. He'd made that mistake once already this month. Better to pick out a pretty little piece of human ass and ride her until she screamed.

Oh, yeah.

A blonde this time. He was done with brunettes for a while. Something like the barhopping, skimpily dressed college girls who hung around this time of night. Or a professor. Uptight. Fed up with students. Someone old enough to know what they wanted from a man. Yeah. He could go with that idea.

There was just one problem with that idea. He wasn't in the mood to get laid. No matter how pretty the human might be or how willing -- and it had nothing to do with Emmie.

Sure it didn't.

Buck hadn't left. He wouldn't leave. Theron had growled at him, bared his teeth, even slashed through the air with extended claws. But the man still wouldn't go. Just what was it with him? If he would just get back in the car and...

All right. If Buck wouldn't leave, then why hadn't he turned and vanished into the night. He was a great cat, for fuck's sake. He could turn, slip through the trees, and there would be nothing Buck could do about it.

So do it. Vanish. Go on. It's easy. Isn't it? I did it with Emmie. Just take to the shadows. Run and never look back.

No. Not anymore. He couldn't just walk away. No matter how much he wanted to. He had to work through this. Find a way to get it under control. Then he could shift back into human form and find himself a sweet piece of ass to sate his need with. God knew, there would be enough women in the bars, and he'd never lacked for the skill to reel them in when he really wanted to.

"Theron, are you done yet, or do you need a little longer to prove you're acting like a complete moron?" Buck leaned against the side of the car, his gaze fixed on the prowling cat. "This isn't impressing me."

Theron growled.

"Obviously not. Well, I can wait here all night if I have to." He shook his head, a wry smile tugging at the corners of his lips. "You know, I thought you were the smart one out of the pair of us. It's kinda nice to see that you're still human, though. That you make mistakes, really big-ass, stupid fuck-ups. I always wondered what it would be like to be around when you finally screwed up. Well, now I know. You're just as much of a screw-up as the rest of us. Reassuring in some odd way."

Theron bared his teeth and sat down, his tail swishing through the air with an almost audible snap. *Humans. Always thinking they are better than everyone else around them. He'd show him. He'd...*

"Sure, hiss at me. Go on, growl, howl. Do something. You want to attack me? Shit, who could stop you?" Buck parted his hands, spreading his arms wide. "But I don't think you really want to do that, do you?"

No. He didn't. That was part of the problem. He wanted to run. Sprint. Find his way back to the small town where he knew she would be. She called to him. Even now her soul, her heart, called to him, tugging on his senses, demanding attention. He couldn't shut it out, even though he knew he had to.

"Are you just going to sit there all night?"

Maybe. What else can I do? She's left me impotent.

"Fine. If you're going to be an ass, then I'll have to do what a friend would. I'll sit here and wait for you to wake the fuck up and stop acting like a kid who just had his favorite toy taken away from him. Stop sulking and do something."

I'm not sulking. I'm just -- just upset about all this.

He pushed up to his feet and stalked away into the shadows of two of the trees, but no farther. He couldn't leave. Buck's words continued to play in the back of his mind. He was sulking. Him? A grown man. Stalking into the darkness as a beast, instead of looking his best friend in the eyes.

God. What had he become? He wasn't acting like a man. He wasn't even acting like a wounded animal. He was acting like a child, just as Buck had said. It had to stop. Now. Before he lacked either the strength or the courage to do something about it.

Slowly he stepped forward, back into the soft circle of light offered by the moon. Pain wracked through his body as he returned to human form and stood, shivering, in front of the car.

"Ready to talk?"

"No. I'm ready to do something about this. Before it grows out of control."

"Oh? Are you trying to tell me it hasn't already reached that point? I don't know who you're trying to convince with that, but it's not working on me. I know better." Buck reached into the car and grabbed a blanket. "Fine. Just what did you have in mind?"

"Emmie."

"Ah, at least I now have a name to go on. And what did you plan on doing about this Emmie?"

"I need to go back to her. Find her. Talk to her. Explain -- no. Apologize to her." If she would even open the door to him, and she'd have every right to slam the door in his face, call the cops, and tell him to get the hell out of town and never look back after what he'd done to her. Even if the door never opened, he'd be able to yell through it, explain, cry, beg for her forgiveness.

Beg. He'd never thought he'd be reduced to begging a woman for anything.

"That's if she'll even agree to see me."

"Ah, just what did you do to her?"

"She's a shifter. Like me."

Scars

"Oh, fuck. You didn't?" Buck groaned and hung his head. "After everything you've told me about women of your kind, you went and made that mistake. You fell in love with a cat?"

"Yeah." _Did the entire world know how badly he'd fucked up?_

"You'll be lucky if she doesn't tear out your throat. And if she feels anything for you at all, then -- oh. God. She fell in love with you, didn't she?"

"So she said." Theron stalked toward the car.

"Man. You're fucked."

"I know."

"So you're going to your own funeral, then?"

"Yep."

"Well, least we can do is have a decent wake before you get your balls ripped off."

"You need a good night out." Mags shoved another cup of coffee into her hands. "A trip into the city. Those always did you good. We can head out. Cut loose for a bit."

Right. Go into the very city where she knew Theron would be? Not the best of plans. "No. Not this time. I just need a little space to get my thoughts together. I'm not ready to face people again."

"And that means you want to hide away in here for a little longer. Sorry. Not happening. Not on my watch." Mags flashed a grin. "We're going out if I have to drag you out kicking and screaming. Get your ass in the shower. I'll pick something out for you to wear. Then we're going out."

Going out to do what? Get laid? Thanks, but my heart can only take so much. The sick part was if it had been that part of her cycle, that feline time of the month, she'd have jumped at the chance. Just as she had only what? A week ago? Nine, no, ten days? Now she didn't want to leave the house. The thought of facing all those people, even ones who hadn't known, would never know, what she'd been through, was just too much to cope with.

"Emmie. You can't just sit here, waiting, watching the clock, and hoping he'll come back. He's not coming back. You know that. He wouldn't have walked out if he felt anything for you." Mags settled down on the edge of the couch, watching her closely. "Emmie. Please. You have to put him in the past. I don't like seeing you hurt so badly. He's a man. Just a man. Nothing to waste your time over."

Waste? No. He had never been that. "Fine. We'll go out. Just not the city, all right?"

"Why?" Mags locked her gaze on Emmie. "Oh, God. Yeah. He lives there doesn't he? Fair enough. We won't go to the city. Where then? Hey, what about that blues place, about ten miles south of here?"

"Sure." Little too close for comfort, but she wasn't about to look for a sex partner there. No. This time she'd do something fun. Dance. Get drunk. Flirt. Do all those normal things a woman did. "Sounds good. Just give me a little time to get showered and ready for it."

"Just make sure that's what you're doing." Mags smiled slightly. "I don't want to have to come in there and drag you out of the shower."

Yeah. A night out. Drinking. Dancing. Something to take her mind away from everything that had happened. That's what she needed. A normal night on the town, in the bar, with someone she could trust. And she could trust Mags. The past few days had taught her that much.

Mags didn't move from the couch as Emmie walked through the house to her bedroom. With fresh towels in hand, clean clothing, she made it to the bathroom and turned on the shower. What was the old song? Wash that man right out her hair? Well, if that's what it took, then so be it.

She stripped off her rank clothing, only now realizing just how badly she smelled. The scent of stale sweat and despair clung to her flesh, taunting her with what she had become. Lost. Foolish.

Scars

She needed to shake herself up. Take herself out of this place. Her hair. God. How had she tolerated the smell and feel of her skin, her hair, the very way she looked?

Hot water hit her body in a merciless wave of pain and pleasure. Soap cut through the grime, shampoo washed out the lank, greasy feeling of her hair. How had she tolerated it? She? A cat? A creature that would find a way, always find a way, to clean itself. How had she lived like this for even a short time?

It wouldn't happen again.

Not for Theron. Not for any man.

Where had her pride gone?

Down the drain, along with the grime that had coated her body. Well, it was time she pulled herself up, once and for all.

It was twenty minutes later, wrapped in warm towels with her hair piled up on top of her head in a clean, fluffy, white towel that Emmie finally walked back out into the living room with a smile on her face. "All right, so tell me about this place we're going to"

"The Blue Moon. Nice place. I went there a couple of weeks back." Mags smiled; relief filtered across her face. "Good bouncers there. They keep the trouble to a minimum. According to Mike, there's been no real trouble there since it opened up."

Mike. There was a name she didn't want to hear right now. That man knew too much. "Okay, well, I'll take that as a good sign, then. Music good?"

"The best. The place is clean too. Owner keeps the drugs out. He's made it clear that anyone coming in with drugs isn't welcome. Rumors have it that he took one guy out back and beat the crap out of him for trying to deal in the club." Mags slipped off the couch and grabbed a brush, walking over to Emmie. "He's something of a poetry fan too. Spouts off with shit from Byron to anyone who'll listen." She tugged the towel away from Emmie's head, letting the long, dark hair fall down around her shoulders. "Good-looking man. I wouldn't mind waking up to him in my bed."

Emmie almost laughed. She'd known a few men like that. *Yeah, like Theron.*

No. Oh, not just no, but hell, no. She wasn't even going there. There was no Theron. He'd never existed. He would never exist. *Sure, and there is no spoon, either.*

Chapter Twenty-Seven

"So, you do need me to drive you there?" Buck grinned as Theron walked back out of the shower. Clean. Dressed. His hair caught in a ponytail. "And fuck. I've never seen you look this slick. I hope she'll at least open the door to you."

"Yeah. I need you to drive." Fine. If he was going to do the impossible and admit to a woman that he needed her, then he could also admit to his best friend that he couldn't go through this alone. "I doubt I'd be able to keep my focus on the road, even if I did have a ride of my own." Shit. That was one thing he'd never forgive those bastards for. The damage to his bike. The damn thing was a write-off.

"Good. You'll need to tell me just where I'm going, then." Buck brushed off an invisible flake of skin, or something, from his sleeve, then blinked as Theron repeated the name of the small town. "That place? It's a dead-end joint. What's the head count there? A thousand? Two?"

"Tops."

"What were you doing out there?"

"I followed her out the night I left town."

"Ah, okay." Buck frowned, then shook his head. "Never knew you'd follow a woman, even one of your own kind, without a damn good reason."

"She was in heat. She knew I was there that night, and she ran from me."

"And you followed her?"

"Well, yeah. She ran. It's like waving a naked piece of ass under a man's nose. I couldn't ignore that. I -- you ever seen how a cat will chase something if it wriggles and moves?" Theron waited until he saw Buck nod. "It's like that. I had to follow. It's instinct."

"But. You're not a cat. Not fully. Couldn't you control it?"

"If I'd stopped to think about it, sure." *Yeah. Sure. Let the human think I can clamp down on generations' worth of instinct.*

"But you didn't?"

"Nope."

"Sucks to be you, doesn't it?"

"Right now, yeah." He didn't have to be so damn smug about it, though. "So, are you going to take me there or not?"

"Ready when you are." Buck grabbed his jacket. "If you're going to back out, now would be good. Before we make that drive out there."

"I'm not about to change my mind." *Oh, God, but I want to, though. She's going to tell me to get the hell out of her life again. And I don't know if I can take that.* "She'll listen to me. She has to."

"I hope so. For your sake," Buck muttered and headed out of the door.

Yeah. So did he. God. If Emmie did slam the door in his face, he'd be lost. And he'd deserve it. How had she coped after he'd walked out of her life? Had it hurt? Of course, it had. Fuck. He was an idiot.

Theron shook his head, slipped on his jacket, and followed Buck out into the night air. She'd see him. She had to. Or all of this would be for nothing. He glared up at the clouds, daring it to do something like rain on him and make things even worse. Trying to apologize to a woman when he looked like a drowned cat would just about push things over the edge for him. Still, Emmie would get a kick out of it.

Buck watched him over the roof of the car. "You can always change your mind."

"It's not happening. She deserves an explanation and an apology." Yeah, and a man who didn't run away from his own feelings only to blame it on trying to protect her from -- from whatever came to mind at the time. "Come on. Before I really do change my mind about this."

The drive out of the city went by too quickly for comfort.

Scars

Neither man spoke much, except to mutter occasionally at the other drivers on the road. Even that didn't provide enough of a distraction for Theron to settle his thoughts. When they turned off the freeway and toward the small town, his stomach suffered an invasion from what felt like annoyed snakes.

"You look green."

"I feel green," Theron muttered and tried not to throw up. "I have to do this. If I'm going to be able to look myself in the mirror again, I have to do this."

"So it's a pride issue."

"Sort of." It was a hell of a lot more than that.

"Yeah. I know." Buck grinned. "You want her."

"Need."

"All right. You need her. But have you thought just what you're going to do if she doesn't need you?"

"I don't even want to think about that. Not yet."

"Right. So if she says no, I drag you to the nearest bar, get you drunk, then pour you back into the car."

"Something like that." Theron stared out at the town. "Turn right here."

"Sure."

Here. She had to be...

A car pulled out away from her house and headed down the street, going back the way Buck and Theron had just come. "Shit, that's her."

"What?"

"Turn the car around!"

"Weird. I could of sworn that was Theron."

"It can't be. You're daydreaming." Mags turned down Main Street and headed out of town. "Stop thinking about him. He's not here. So let's just go and get blasted. Well, you get blasted. I still have to be able to drive us home."

Well, that was one question answered. At least she didn't have to worry about how she was going to get home. "You're right. It couldn't have been him. He's back in the city or someplace else. Not here."

"He doesn't exist. Just get that firmly fixed in your mind."

Sure, easier than it sounded. Fine. She could do this. Theron wasn't worth the effort; he'd walked out of his own free will, and the matter was done with. There'd be other men at the bar. Men who might be able to distract her. So, she'd have to deal with the rumors, but it didn't matter. She wouldn't be living here much longer. Too many bad memories now. One night out, and then she'd turn her attention to the important things in life. Like packing up and moving on.

That had been part of the problem. She'd become too attached to the town and the area. It was time to leave. Find a new quiet spot to live. A new city nearby to prowl for men when the need hit her. Just as long as it took her away from here, away from the house that still held his scent.

"The club, what time does it stay open to?"

"One."

"Good, that should be enough."

"Enough for what?"

"To find a man, get drunk, get screwed, and then fall over in a corner."

Mags laughed and pressed her foot down on the gas. "The sooner we get there, the better. I've never seen you let loose before. This could be fun."

"You've no idea." If she strolled into there in full prowl mode, the men wouldn't know what hit them. *I'm not in heat. I don't have to do this.* But she wanted to. God, she wanted to. If for no other reason than to wipe Theron out of her memory and her arms. "I'm going to knock them dead."

"Dressed like that, with your attitude. Oh, hell, yeah. You'll have no problem." Mags laughed and took a turn off the main road toward the small glow of lights. "Looks like it's busy tonight."

"Good."

"Plenty of interesting men around, with any luck." Mags pulled the car into the parking lot.

"Should be." She could smell them even as she opened the door. Men. Hungry for sex. Eager for anyone or anything that might cross their path. The noise that filtered out from the bar beckoned her closer. A low, throbbing beat, the music something she didn't recognize, but it pulled at her soul. "Damn. That sounds good."

"Doesn't it just." Mags locked the car and hurried over. "Shall we?"

"That's what we came here for."

"I think we lost them." Buck grumbled. "How the hell did we do that? This town can't be that big. Where the fuck did they go?"

"No. We haven't. Stop the car a minute. I should be able to follow her scent."

"In a car?"

"Trust me. I'll be able to trace her. I just need to be able to take a few breaths." Sure. I can track anything I've fucked if I'm within a mile or so of her. Please. God. Don't let them be any farther away than that. He waited only long enough for Buck to stop the car before he stepped out and inhaled deeply.

She had to be there. Somewhere. He closed his eyes, sifting through the smells carried by the night air. Here and there he caught a touch of her. Older though, not the fresh trail he now needed. Damn it. He was a cat, not a wolf. Sure, his sense of smell was good, but it wasn't enough. Not this time.

Too many confusing trails. She'd lived in the area for long enough that he'd be able to trace her to her home and favorite haunts with his eyes closed, but this -- this one time when he needed to be able to find her, the wind and rain that threatened in the air all combined to battle against him.

"Looking for someone?" The police cruiser pulled up alongside him. "Ah, thought so. Well, now, this is going to get interesting." Mike leaned out of his window. "I wasn't expecting to see you again -- at least, not quite so soon."

"Where is she?"

"Now which *she* would that be?"

"Emmie. Who else would I be talking about?" Theron growled, turning his full attention on the sheriff.

"Ah, Miss Byron is out with her best friend. I believe I saw the car take the turn off to the new club. Nice place. You might want to try it out sometime." Mike smirked and nodded a hello at Buck. "You must be his partner. Well, good to meet you, though your friend here's a bit of a loser letting someone like Emmie go. Maybe you should smack him around a time or two?"

"Ignore him. He's just a dumb dog," Theron growled.

"Ah, so you're a werewolf?" Buck smiled. "And don't mind him. He's a grouch right now. Think he needs to get laid."

"He had the chance to do that more than once with Emmie. And damn, she's fuckable. I'd do her, if she wasn't a cat."

Anger flashed through his body, building rapidly, surging out of control as it threatened to override his being. "Don't you ever talk about her like that again. She's mine. She's not some fuck toy. She's my mate."

"Good. It's about time you realized that."

"I thought cats didn't mate?" Buck spoke up, the grin all too clear on his face.

"They don't. Not normally. But there are always exceptions to the rules." Mike looked back at Theron. "Now, are you going to start acting as if you're her mate, or keep up with the pretense that you're nothing more than a dumb alley cat fucking anything that comes your way? Because I'm not about to let you fuck her around again. She's a good woman, even if she's a cat."

"I wouldn't be here if I hadn't made up my mind to tell her the truth." Theron's jaw clenched. *Fuck. Hard enough to do this around Buck, let along that smug dog.* "I'm not about to hurt

Scars

her again if I can help it. I can't promise that she won't hurt me, though. She'd have every right to after how I treated her."

Chapter Twenty-Eight

Sweat. Lust. Alcohol. It all combined into one intoxicating wave that threatened to send her to her knees. Music pumped through the building, vibrating through her being as she walked farther into the bar. Dozens of men at the bar turned to look at her, hunger alive in their eyes, their gazes tracing her body, lingering on her breasts and legs, barely even touching her face.

The Blue Moon offered it all in one neat little package.

Yeah. This she knew. This she understood how to deal with. Men and their lusts. She'd handled this through most of her adult life.

"I knew you'd like this place." Mags nudged her before sliding one arm through Emmie's and tugging her toward the bar. "The owner is a dish as well. Dark hair, living sex by the way he moves. God, he's a hunk. Older than I normally like, though."

Older might be exactly what she was looking for. Someone more stable. Who wouldn't expect anything from her but...

A scent hit her. One she knew well. Male feline shifter. Oh, God, not here as well. Did she have enough time to leave before he cornered her? What was another shifter doing here? Had it become preternatural central? It wasn't Theron, but there was something vaguely familiar about the smell. It taunted her memory, teasing her closer. Not in the sensual way that Theron's had, but something almost comforting.

"Are you all right? You look a little pale." Mags leaned in closer. "Maybe I should take you home. I'm not sure this is such a good idea."

He stepped out from behind the bar. Long, dark hair touched by occasional silver strands whispered across his back, bound at the nape of his neck with a cord of black and silver leather. His black gaze focused on Emmie's face, a smile twitching at the corners of his lips; his voice dripped with love and sensuality both. "Welcome to my club."

His voice. She knew that voice. Why did she know that voice? "Thank you."

"And Mags, good to see you here again. The Blue Moon just isn't the same when you're not here."

Emmie frowned. Just how often had her friend been here that the owner knew her name.

"Emmie needed a night out, Byron. I figured this was the best place for her to let off some steam." Mags slid away from Emmie's side and wrapped both arms about the man's neck. "You have to admit this is a good place for that."

"Ah, yes. But I think I'd like to talk to your friend first."

Byron. His nickname. Wasn't that what Mags had told her?

"What's she got that I haven't?" Mags pouted.

"Now, now. No sulking." The man cupped Mags's chin and brushed a light kiss across her lips. "Your friend, Ken, is somewhere close to the stage. I know he'll be glad to see you again."

"Ken? Hmmm. Good. You'll look after Emmie, then?"

"She's perfectly safe within my hands." Byron flashed a smile and patted Mags on her rounded cheeks. "I'll be over at my table, with your friend."

"No woman is safe in your hands, but maybe you can chase away a few nasty memories for her." Mags flashed a saucy grin and slipped away through the crowds.

"You're quite safe with me, but I think you already know that, don't you?" Byron smiled and escorted her through the crowd, which parted easily before him.

This man. Her instincts knew this man. Her heart knew this man. But why? *Stop being stupid, you know how, and you know why.* But that wasn't possible. It didn't make sense. Why had he walked back into her life? Shit, he'd never been in her life to begin with.

"You're confused."

"Yes." She didn't resist as he escorted her to the table.

"With good reason." He settled in at her side.

"I know you."

"Yes, though I've never been allowed to speak to you directly before." Byron turned to look at her. "I wanted to, though. I tried so hard to convince your mom that you needed to know who your father was."

"You can't be him." Her heart pounded against her chest. This wasn't happening. Her father would never have wanted to come anywhere near her. So just why was he pretending to show an interest in her now? "Mom would have told me if you'd been close or wanted to see me."

"She hated me." Byron shook his head and looked away from her. "With good reason, but she used that as a way to keep us apart."

"I don't believe you." Her lips dried out. How could her mom have kept them apart? It just didn't make sense.

"She told you that I walked into her life, fucked her, and left -- leaving her pregnant with you -- and then never looked back?"

"Yes." Oh, God. Why would her mom hide him like that?

"That's almost true. I did just that, but I came back when I realized what a fool I had been. She wouldn't give me another chance, though. I can't even blame her, not truly. I'd hurt her more deeply than anyone ever should."

It was a hurt she understood. She'd been through it. Theron had hurt her, perhaps just as deeply as this man, her father, had hurt her mom. But, had she truly turned her father away when he'd tried to step up and be more than a sperm donor? "She told you to leave?"

"Yes. I tried over the years to get close to you, but she refused. When she died, and you moved on, I lost track of you. It took me six months before I tracked you here, and when I realized you weren't moving on for a time, I opened the club and decided to stay close by in case you needed me."

"But I didn't pick up the scent of a shifter. Not even when I wandered out of town into the woods." Why hadn't she known he was here? Had there been some hint, some trace of him when she'd taken her runs through the trees? Had she missed it? Had she truly been that lost in her presumed safety in the area?

"I kept away from the town itself. And when I had to be closer to you, I used a charm an old witch had given me. It wasn't something that I wanted to do, but I knew that, because of what your mom had told you, you'd never let me near you. When you walked into the club, my heart almost stopped. If Mags is the reason you walked into my club tonight, I'm going to be forever grateful to her."

Emmie rubbed her fingertips against her brow. "I should have known you were here."

"I made certain you would not know about my presence, Emmie. I didn't want to frighten you away." He leaned closer, brushing his fingertips across her cheeks. "You're just as beautiful as your mom was. It hurt me, deeply, when I knew she was dead."

"Why?"

"Because I never stopped loving her. I took no interest in feline shifter females after that. She was everything to me, even if she denied it. I wish it had been different, that she had accepted my apology, but she was too angry, too frustrated with what had passed between us."

That part she could believe. Her mom had never been one to forgive and forget. She'd spilled her tears and hatred into Emmie's ears and done everything possible to foster her daughter's distrust of male feline shifters. It had been with good reason. Now she faced her father for the first time -- her father. The man who had helped to bring her into the world and then walked away from them both without so much as a backward glance. Only now she was being asked to accept that it hadn't been that way at all.

Had it all been a lie?

No. Not all. He'd confirmed some of it. It was the rest that she was left uncertain about. "You kept trying to get in contact with me?"

"Yes, until you vanished when you were an adult, when she was dead." Grief washed through his voice. "I was distraught when I found out. I never thought she would die before me. I loved her far more than I ever admitted, even to myself. I miss her. God, how I miss her."

Mom. Why didn't you tell me? Why couldn't you tell me the truth? It would have made things so much easier for me.

"I think she didn't want to lose your love, the way she thought she had lost mine. I know, when I tried to return to her, she thought I was trying to play some cruel game with her heart. Nothing I said, or did, changed her mind. And I tried. I truly tried to see you when she lived. She kept moving, keeping you away from me whenever possible. When she thought I had strayed too close to your school, your home, she packed everything up and took to the road again."

No, there had been some trace of a shifter. She'd caught a hint, every now and then, just a hint on the wind. Could that have been her father? Or someone else? Did it even matter now that she knew her father existed and now had the chance to talk to him, to find out just what had happened, how he had come into her mom's life, and just what had followed after they had parted company?

"We were always moving," she mumbled, trying to put her thoughts in order. "I've seen you before, somewhere. Not fully. Just a memory. A glimpse caught out of the corner of my eye. Outside school once. The play another time, the Christmas play. Then, there was my first hunt. I was being shadowed that night, mom chased the shadow away, but that was you, wasn't it?"

"Yes. I stayed close, when I could."

"But?"

"She made certain I never got too close." Byron looked away

from her. "Perhaps she had good reason. No. I know she did. She wanted to protect you from men like me."

"She failed."

Chapter Twenty-Nine

"Busy place," Buck muttered as he turned off the engine. "How are you going to -- Hey. Wait a minute!"

Theron slammed the door shut on the car and walked toward the entrance of the club. He could smell her now. Taste her on the air. She was here. In the club. Was she already with someone else? No, she wouldn't be. Not this soon, it wasn't her way, unless she'd gone into heat early? Except he'd have been able to pick up on that. So, why here?

Her friend? She hadn't been driving, so someone must have brought her here, the human woman; what had her name been again? Mags? Sure. That made sense.

"Theron, wait! You can't just walk in there without thinking this through." Buck caught his arm, pulling him to a halt. "You need to stop, think, and work this out. If you walk in there half-cocked, then you'll make a fool of yourself, and you don't want to do that. I know you don't. No matter how pissed off you are."

Pissed off didn't even begin to describe it.

"All right." He turned and looked at his longtime friend. "You're right. I'm going to go in there, find Emmie, and talk to her. I'm going to crawl. Apologize however it takes and hope she'll listen to me. If that doesn't work, I'll do a different set of crawling, into the bottom of a bottle and hope you'll then drive me home when I hit rock bottom."

"You're not going to drop like that. If she turns you down, you'll turn around, walk away, and we'll head back to the city. If you want to then lose it away from her, fine. But don't let her see that she…"

"That she what? Gets to me? Sorry, I might not have that level of control left. Not if she turns me away." His voice -- it didn't sound like it belonged to him, not anymore. How could she have such power over him?

"Fine, we'll deal with that when and if it happens. I'll be right with you. Just let me know if there's anything I can do when we find her."

Theron nodded and took a step toward the door. She'd be there, they'd talk, and she'd either tell him to fuck off, or they'd find a way through this. "At least the music sounds half decent in there. Blues?"

"Yeah, sounds pretty good"

Something else. Hidden amongst the scent of alcohol and human sweat, something that set his teeth on edge and made him question just why she had come to the club. Shifter. Male. In his prime. *No. She couldn't have come here because of -- not Emmie.*

Mine, roared the beast. *Mine. Not someone else's. Take her back. Fight. Claim.*

Not if she told him to go away and leave her alone. He had no right to lay a claim on her, not without her consent. He wasn't David or Jamie to press a woman into doing something they didn't want.

I'm stalling. God. Theron took a deep breath and walked in through the door of the club. The sound hit him like a wall. So many men and women here, he almost turned back; they'd all witness his humiliation.

"Is she here?" Buck leaned in as they walked through the bar.

"Yes." Where, though? He could smell her, but trying to see her through the crowd of people was difficult at best. He inhaled slowly, searching for her. "Near the back of the bar, I think."

"Theron?" A woman's voice cut through the crowd.

"Damn, is that her?" Buck tugged at her arm.

"No."

"Good. If she's not your Emmie, that means you won't hit me for trying to..."

"Yeah, that's you, isn't it? Theron Grave. What the hell are you doing here? She doesn't want to see you."

"Mags? I'm guessing you must be Mags."

"What about it? You're not going anywhere near Emmie. I've only just got her out of the house. I'm not about to let you waltz back into her life and turn it upside down again." The small, blonde woman poked one finger into his chest. "Turn around and walk away. Now. Before I call one of the bouncers. Or better yet, the owner. He's with Emmie right now, and he doesn't like trouble in his club. So leave her the hell alone."

"I'm not here to hurt her, Mags. I need her. I love her." The words spilled out before he could stop them. "I'm here to apologize to her. Not to hurt her. If she tells me to leave, then I will."

Mags didn't move, not for several long minutes. Her gaze hardened, jaw tight, one finger still rested on his chest, ready to punch him again.

"He means it. He's a wreck without her. I had to drive him here myself just so he wouldn't have an accident on the way here." Buck moved to one side. "Let them sort it out between themselves. I'll stand nearby and watch; you can stand with me if you want. If it looks like it's about to get nasty, we can break them up."

Mags didn't move. Not for several long seconds. "I don't like this."

"Do you honestly think that the bouncers won't step in if there is a problem?" Buck pushed a little more.

"Well, no. But she's been through enough recently. I don't think that -- she shouldn't be left alone with him."

"I'd slit my throat before hurting her deliberately again." Theron stepped forward, his gaze locked on Mags.

"Then you..."

"Leaving her the way I did, I knew it would hurt. I wanted her to hate me. To curse me and never want to see me again."

"It worked. She doesn't want to see you again."

"So, she can tell me to go to hell, and I'll walk away from her without looking back. Fair?"

"Fair." Mags nodded.

Theron breathed a sigh of relief. "Thank you."

Buck patted his arm and then led Mags away to a nearby table. At least that was one problem out of the way. Mags would make sure that, no matter what happened, Emmie would be taken care of.

The scent of the other male shifter hit him hard. The man lifted his head up, looking away from Emmie and their conversation, the lines around his eyes hardening almost instantly. Strong. Yeah, a shifter like that was a strong bastard. Shit. This was going to get interesting and not in a good way.

Then she turned, her eyes widening, jaw tight, relief, hope, and hatred flashed across her eyes in quick succession before she even spoke. Fuck. This wasn't going to go well.

"What are you doing here?" Emmie's voice little more than a growl.

"I thought that would be -- never mind." Theron took a deep breath and tried to calm down. Diving head first into a fight with her was not what he had in mind. "I'm sorry."

"For what? Breathing?"

"All right. I deserved that." Maybe he did, but fighting back in front of this other male shifter might only push her closer to the newcomer. "I'm sorry that I lied to you, hurt you, and walked out on you. I shouldn't have -- but I was afraid, and I let that fear get the better of me."

The other shifter, the male, the one who sat too close to Theron's mate, smiled. "He's trying, Emmie."

"He's that and more."

Weird. A rival should be trying to push him away, not giving him a chance to speak at all. It didn't make sense.

"Give him a chance. It takes a lot for a male cat to apologize. We don't like admitting we made a mistake. Why would we? We're gods, after all." The older shifter flashed a smile.

"I don't want to give him a chance. He doesn't deserve one."

"Emmie, don't let your anger get the better of you." The male reached over and squeezed Emmie's shoulder. "But I know what living with that regret is like -- would it really kill you to hear him out?"

Emmie sucked in her bottom lip, tears welling in her eyes as she looked away, a soft shudder playing through her body. "Fine. But if I tell him to leave after we've spoken, then he's to go."

"Agreed." Theron didn't even hesitate.

"You've been tossed a lifeline; I suggest you use it carefully." The older man slipped out of the booth and walked toward Buck and Mags. "I'll be within calling distance and keeping a close eye on what's going on here."

Sure. Of course, he'd be watching. He'd want to see the new male fuck up again. Shit. This was going to be hard enough without another male watching. Wonderful, he was going to make a fool of himself, and the other male would laugh and move in for the kill.

"Well, what did you want to say?" Emmie scowled, folding her arms beneath her chest.

"I'm sorry. I had no right to leave the way I did. I..."

"Look. If that's all you have to say to me, then you can leave now. I'm not interested. You got your claws stuck in me once; it's not going to happen again." Twin points of color blazed across her cheeks, her nostrils flaring slightly, anger blazing in her eyes.

God. Okay. So this wasn't going to be easy at all. He deserved it, of course, after how he had walked out on her. Still, he'd hoped it would be easier than this. "I don't know how many times I can say sorry." Every fiber of his being screamed at him to reach across the table and pull her into his arms. *No, not yet. She's not ready -- she'll scream for help and laugh as I'm escorted out of the damn club.*

And the other shifter would smirk the entire time.

"I thought that leaving was the only safe option."

"For who?"

"Me."

Emmie blinked. "Okay. I -- I thought you'd say it would be safer for me."

"No. I left because I thought it would be safer for me. I tried telling myself otherwise, sure I did. It's what men do. Women too, no doubt. Shit. I'm not making sense." How big a hole was he digging himself into?

"So you did it to protect me? But then you changed your mind?"

"Yes." Yep. Big hole. Humongous. Was that even a word? Well, it was now.

"Why?"

"Because I realized I was wrong." The words weren't as difficult to say as he'd thought they would be. Odd. "I should have given you the choice. I assumed that you'd be better off with me out of your life -- that the court would be called in, and all hell would break loose. I didn't -- I thought I didn't want you drawn into the middle of that, but I realized that it was me I was protecting, not you." Did that sound as lame as he thought it did?

Emmie looked away from him, her hands closing around a half empty glass. "And what were you protecting yourself from? What were you so afraid of?"

"You."

She turned, her mouth falling open, the color draining from her face as she tried to speak and nothing came out. She looked away from him again, blinking. When she finally spoke, her voice was little more than a whisper. "How could you be afraid of me?"

Chapter Thirty

Afraid. Of her? What sort of game was he playing? One that she didn't need to be a part of, that she was sure of -- mostly -- well, maybe -- shit. Not at all. It didn't make sense. She had to get to the bottom of this, or at least get a grip on the rolling emotions that threatened to spin her life out of control. "I don't understand."

"I've never met a female like you, Emmie. You wormed your way into my heart and buried yourself there in a way I never thought was possible." Theron's hands shook, and he shifted his weight on the chair. "Finding out that I had fallen in love, when that just doesn't happen to male shifters, was a shock. I didn't know how to handle it. I still don't. I just know I can't be without you."

"And if I tell you to leave?" Her heart threatened to lodge in her throat.

"I'd go."

Would he? Sweat coated her palms, and she rubbed them over her skirt. He'd leave. Walk out of her life forever. *But I don't want him to leave. God. I need him. I -- I can't go through this again.*

"The other shifter, he's your new male, isn't he?" Theron's hands clenched, knuckles white.

"Him?" Emmie swallowed a laugh. "Erm."

"Yeah, I guessed as much. He's old enough to walk in and sweep just about any female shifter off their feet. Shit." He slumped in the chair. "I know it won't mean anything to you, not after what I did, but I love you, Emmie. I'll never stop loving you. I'll go, if you tell me to, but I won't be able to turn off what I feel. God knows I've tried over the last week, it didn't work. I just ended up miserable and unable to focus on my work."

She didn't know if she wanted to laugh, or cry. He looked lost, his gaze lowered, shoulders slumped, his hands in his lap. One part of her wanted to hug him tight, the other wanted to slap him silly and set her father on him. *God. Her father.* That was another complication she hadn't been expecting to deal with. Fine. She'd find a way to deal with him, with both males, and it would be on her terms. Not theirs. She leaned over the table and cupped his chin, looking into his eyes as she spoke. "He's very special to me."

Theron groaned. "I see. Fine. I know where I stand, then. Did you want me to leave now, or wait until your male has returned? Er -- what's he doing with Mags? I thought that -- God, Emmie, he's making a move on her. I'll kill him. He's got you, and he's..."

"He's not my male. Ah, Theron. Byron might be many things, but he'll never be my male."

Theron opened his mouth, his lips moving wordlessly.

She leaned closer, enjoying the moment. "He's my father."

Theron blanched, closed his mouth, and stared at her. Good. He didn't know how to take the news.

"Your father? How? I mean -- oh, shit. He's going to kill me. He knows, doesn't he? About us. How I -- okay. Fine. I'll take what he dishes out." He frowned, his gaze shifting back and forth from Emmie to Byron. Then the penny dropped. "Hold on. Didn't he do the same thing to your mom?"

"Yes and no." Emmie let go of his chin and settled back into her chair. "He left, then came back, the same way you did, only mom wouldn't let him back into her life. He tried to keep an eye on me when I was younger, but mom kept him away, no matter what he did. He lost track of me for a few years, then we stumbled into each other tonight."

"And are you going to tell me to leave, just like she did?"

Was she? *Tell him to get the hell out and never look back! He'll only hurt you again and again. Remember what mom said? They aren't to be trusted.* But her dad had watched out for her, he'd come to find her, been upset when he'd been kept from her, so it wasn't like that. She had a chance, a chance to be happy with him, if she could only find the courage to take that risk.

Risk. Hope. Taking chances. What if it all came crashing down around her ears again? What if she spent the rest of her life wondering how it could have been if she sent him away?

All she had to do was tell him to go, and he would.

"No. I'm not."

Relief washed over his face. "Thank you."

"But that doesn't mean you're moving in, either." *Not yet, anyway.* "That will take time."

"Yes," Theron nodded slightly, hope returning to his storm cloud eyes.

"Yes."

"Perhaps a long time."

"I understand."

"Good."

"It could take a few days, maybe even a week, before we reach that point." A wicked light danced within his eyes.

"What?" Emmie stared at him.

"Well, I don't know about you, but I plan on getting you back into bed as quickly as possible, and I'd feel better sleeping with you after I've reacquainted myself with every inch of your body -- my days, or nights, of slipping off into the darkness after fucking you senseless, are over."

Her nipples hardened, pressing against her clothing, heat flowed through her core, every inch of her body tingled, waiting to hear more as she watched him. A smile tugged at the corners of her lips. "And I'm just supposed to accept that this is how it will be between us?"

"You could always challenge me."

"We both know where that leads." *Yes. Him. Her. Naked beneath the stars.* "And maybe that's just what I want."

"Or need."

Need. Yes, that was something she could agree with. "And your friend?"

Scars

"I think he's taken with Mags, or will be when he can tear her attention away from your father." Theron frowned, shaking his head as he watched the odd combination of shifter and two humans. "Unless their tastes run to being shared."

"With Mags, that could be a possibility."

Chapter Thirty-One

She ran beneath the stars, the breeze playing through her fur, tail snapping through the air. He was here. Somewhere. Hidden within the trees. He'd find her, come for her, claim her in a way she needed beyond anything she'd ever known before. Her core throbbed, aching for his touch, but the cat wanted to run and enjoy the hunt, to find out if he had what it took to chase her down.

He'd find her. She had faith in that, but just how long could she keep ahead of him? The longer she ran, the sweeter it would be when he...

A twig snapped. The sound of something moving through the trees, could it be him? No, he wouldn't be that careless. He'd find a way to get ahead of her. Emmie stopped, her tail snapping out through the air. He was here. She knew it. She could almost taste his presence on the air.

Where?

She turned, slowly, her ears flat against her skull, the hair on the back of her neck lifted. She wanted to be caught, but making it easy on him wasn't part of the plan. What male could respect a female who made it easy for him? All right, some did, but he wasn't one of them. No. He wanted a challenge.

Instinct flattened her to the ground. He dived over her, her quick move barely enough to keep her out of his grasp. She rolled, growling, coming back up to her feet as she watched for him through the darkness.

He stared at her, his teeth bared, the low growl carrying easily through the night air. Time to fight, good. She was ready for this. The question remained, was he?

He darted toward her. A dark flash of slick fur and muscle. She knew just how powerful he could be, how strong he was, but she wasn't going to be a pushover for him. Not this time. She twisted, avoiding his teeth, snatching herself out of his grasp a second time. Joy washed through her body, her claws tearing up the ground, every ounce of muscle tight, ready to turn again.

His eyes narrowed, lips parting in a smile. A low growl filled the air, his chest rumbling. Joy danced within his gaze and through his body. He was ready for this. So was she. But not like this. They'd start in this form, but when it came to sex, that would be done another way. Human form. Yes. When it reached that point, they'd shift to human form. She'd never seen the fun in having sex as a cat. Not when she preferred to enjoy him in his delicious human form.

He growled -- a warning. She tensed, her gaze locked on him as she shifted her weight. He jumped. She rolled, scrambling to be free of him. She didn't move fast enough. His teeth fastened onto the scruff of her neck as he forced her onto her belly on the ground.

Heat blossomed through her body. Even in this form she couldn't help but be aroused by him. He ground down against her, his erection felt even through the fur as she arched up toward him and began the return to human form. It hurt, but with his presence, his body pressed against hers, pain turned to pleasure as the fur retracted into her body. He growled once more, then began to change as well. His teeth no longer pressed into the back of her neck.

His cock slipped between her thighs as the last of the fur and animal form stripped away from both of them. "You gave me a good chase this time, kitty."

"I told you not to call me that." She growled, bucking under him, her nails digging into the damp earth.

"But you are my kitty, aren't you? Mine and no one else's. Never again will you need to search out a male to satisfy you during your time of hunger, of heat. I'll be there for you. Ready and willing."

And able. So very able.

"Just don't call me kitty."

"I will, again and again. And if you ever want me to stop, then you'll have to beat me in a fight."

Bastard. He knew it wouldn't happen. Not any time soon. Her inner walls clenched, rippling closed, hunger growing deep within her being at each passing moment. She lifted her hips, pressing them against his body, trying to capture his cock between her thighs. It wouldn't take much, a roll of his hips, the pressure against her shoulders as he pushed her farther to the ground and then claimed her.

"Tell me what you want," he whispered against the back of her neck. "Tell me all the things you want me to do to you."

Emmie shivered under the touch of his lips and tongue along her spine. Her core tightened, liquid heat coating her inner walls. Her nipples tightened, crinkling into points that brushed against the sparse grass beneath them. The soft tips tickled her belly and inner thighs, adding a hundred tiny fingers of sensation to her growing pleasure. Her hips rolled back, heat playing through her core. Her body tightened. Every inch of her being cried out for his touch.

She tried to press against him again, seeking a way to pull him within her core. He refused to comply. She bit into her bottom lip, struggling to find another way to entice him, but each time she lifted up for him, each time she parted her thighs and wriggled against him, he pulled away. The head of his cock trailed over her tender, eager flesh, his heavy sac brushed over her taut thighs, his soft breath teasing the back of her neck.

Please. God. He can't leave me hanging like this.

But he did. She needed him, wanted him to push into her body, to feel his cock throbbing against her inner walls, but still he didn't claim her. Why was he doing this to her?

She knew why, and knew all too well what he wanted. A soft shiver ran through her body. Was it really so much to give him when he'd braved her scorn to find his way back to her? She turned, looking back over her shoulder at him. His gaze locked with hers for an instant, lips parted, wet from his own tongue, breath heavy against her taut flesh. A deep quiver ran through her being as she forced the words into life.

"Fuck me."

"Is that all you want?"

"Yes, please. Just fuck me." She tried not to groan; her body ached for his touch, for the feel of his cock deep within her walls. "Theron, I need you."

He shifted his weight, his body positioning behind her fully. The tip of his cock brushed along her heated sex. She groaned, lifting her hips that little bit farther. "I've missed you, my sweet and wicked little kitten. And you will always be that to me, mine. Be it as my kitten or my tigress. You're my mate. My female -- all you have to do is say the word."

"The word?" What did he want to hear from her? "I need you, Theron. Please, don't make me wait any longer."

"Then tell me you need me in your life. Not just in your bed. Tell me you want me for your mate, not just a male to tumble with through the grass." He nipped along her back, tasting her salt-coated skin.

Mate. Not just lover or friend, but mate, for life. "Yes, I want you as my mate. God. How could I not? Please. If you'll have me, I'd be yours, forever. I love you. I've always loved you." *What -- oh, God Why did I tell him that?* Because it was the truth. She did love him. She had since the first moment he'd taken her into his arms. "I love you, Theron. My mate. My heart."

"That's all I needed to hear from you." He growled, the sound vibrating against her back. He shifted, pressing the tip of his cock between her slick lower lips inch by torturous inch. "Don't move. Not a hair, my mate."

She whimpered; the need to move tugged at her being. She wanted nothing more than the ability to press back against him.

He slipped slowly into her willing body, stretching her inner walls, and still she struggled to remain still. Sweat beaded across her body as she struggled to hold position and welcomed him deep within her core.

Her fingers curled into dirt, a low moan slipping free from her lips. Her inner walls clenched against his thick erection. He had to let her move and soon. She couldn't stay like this much longer. Pressure built slowly within her belly as he began to ease in and out of her tight, heated body. He groaned above her, his fingers grasping her hips, holding her in place.

"Please, I need to move."

"Not yet."

Emmie shuddered, her head hanging low, long strands of dark hair forming a midnight veil over her eyes. How could he do this to her? He had to know she wanted to move, to rock against him and enjoy every moment they shared.

Each slow thrust of his cock within her body only added to the fire that threatened to burn out of control in her core. Sweat beaded across her breasts. Her limbs shook. Muscles tightened and threatened to spasm. A war raged between her desire to please him and remain still, and the urge to thrust back against him.

Theron slipped one hand slowly down over her thigh, tracing light patterns across taut skin with his nails. "Beautiful and all mine."

His. Yes, oh, God, yes. She'd never wanted to belong to someone before, but now that she did, it felt right. "Mine," she growled back over her shoulder. A mutual ownership, she'd make sure he remembered that.

"Yes, I'm yours." He chuckled.

Emmie arched, a low gasp tearing through the night air as his fingers caressed her slick, silken skin, settling on the small bud between her thighs. "Have to move."

"Not yet." He tapped against her clit. "You're not ready."

Ready? Ready for what? A volcano exploding? "Theron!"

"Soon."

Not soon enough, not with the way her body shouted out its demands. "I can't do this."

He didn't answer. Not this time. He tapped one finger lightly against her clit. Each touch shot a jolt a pleasure through her core, her inner walls rippling on his cock. Once, twice, three times more he tapped his finger on the small, slick bud.

Emmie growled. Her instincts kicked in. She wasn't some submissive little creature who would bow down to whatever he wanted. She was a cat. And she wanted him. Fully. Her hips rolled, inner walls claiming his erection, holding him deep within her core. "Mine," she growled afresh.

"God! Emmie!"

A low chuckle slipped from her lips, her fingers spread, digging into the dirt, her thighs edging farther apart as she arched her back and danced against his body. "My turn."

"For what?"

"To take control." She bucked, all but kicking him off, away from her back, his cock sliding free of her body. Her core protested, her body tight, hungry for his touch, but she ignored it as best she could. Just long enough to turn and press him against the earth, her hands resting on his shoulders. "Your turn to stay still."

"Evil..." Whatever else he had been about to say was lost in a low hiss as she lowered her hips down across his body. He groaned, his eyes closing, thick lashes caressing his upper cheeks. His lips parted, back arched as he pressed his heels into the dirt as she circled her hips down on his cock, trapping it, claiming him Her walls rippled on his cock, holding him, massaging his erection as he lifted his hips, trying to press deeper into his body.

Beautiful. He'd laugh, or scoff, if she called him beautiful to his face, but it wouldn't change the fact that he was beautiful. His muscles tightened across his belly and chest, his hands fisted on the ground, he moaned, his breath coming in soft, low gasps.

A slight frown flickered across her face. He wasn't supposed to be moving, but she was enjoying it too much to protest. "I love you."

His eyes flashed open, a light dancing within them, his smile instant, full and unshielded. "I love you, always."

Her core rippled along his cock. She groaned, tipping her hips, her bottom tight, her sex massaging his thick length. Slowly she danced on his cock, circling, rocking deep, her thighs clenched as she tried to torment him with her body. Her breasts ached. Nipples tingled. Pressure built between her thighs, in the pit of her belly, even her toes tingled.

"Dance for me." His lips twisted into a sensually wicked smile.

Emmie blinked. "What?"

"Dance. A lap dance. Make me groan for more. Make me beg."

Beg? Oh, hell, yeah! She could do that. Emmie shivered and traced her fingers up over her own thighs. "Don't move. Watch me. Feel. But don't move."

He nodded, his eyes wide, liquid with desire.

Emmie lifted up, until only the head of his cock remained within her walls. He groaned beneath her, his hands pressed tight to the ground, his hips thrust down as he struggled for control. He wanted her to do this, but he knew, he had to know, just how hard it would be for him.

His cock throbbed, a pulse that vibrated through her core, even with just the head between her lower lips. He wanted a dance. He'd get one. And one he'd remember until his dying day. She trailed her fingers slowly over her belly, slipping one between her thighs as his eyes grew wider. Her gaze locked with his. Her fingers parted her silken flesh until the erect nub was bare to the night air.

"God." The word little more than a hiss.

She brushed her finger tip over the tight nub, her hips rolling beneath her own caress. Her need filled the air. Nothing more than the head of his cock within her body. Each wave of pleasure that pushed through her body only added to the pressure that grew within her core. She tapped against it. Once. Twice. Three times. A low whimper slipped free from her lips with each delicious touch.

"Wicked!"

Yes. And she knew it. Emmie pushed slowly down over his cock. Taking it deep. Her slick walls clenching on his thick erection as she eased her way down. Her thighs shook. The strain of taking things slow added to the sensual pain that rolled through her being.

She trailed one finger along her body, cupping her left breast as she teased her other, glistening finger in a teasing path along her flesh, until she captured it between her lips. His eyes widened. A low rumbling growl played through his chest. Her thighs tensed. Hips tipped. Her inner walls clenched on his cock, milking it in sensual waves. She twisted on his cock, teasing it with her firm grasp.

Twist. Tip. Tighten. Turn. She moved slowly. Taunting him. No. Not just him. It teased her as well. Her body wanted to let loose. To just give up and ride him. Fuck him until he gasped for breath, and they both came in shuddering waves. She sucked the taste of herself from her finger and whimpered. Hunger danced within his gaze. His thighs were tight. Quivers ran through his muscles. Each soft vibration only added to the pleasure that claimed her body.

She swallowed hard and closed her eyes. Music played out in the back of her mind. A song from *Dirty Dancing* -- "Overload." Her body settled into a low, sensual rhythm, following the words of the song in her mind. She didn't question why this song settled into her mind. Or why it was so easy to follow the beat and let that set a pace for her body. She surrendered to it.

This overload!

"Please. God. I have to move."

"Not yet." God. It almost killed her to tell him that. *Won't you help me cure...* She groaned, giving herself back to the song. A little longer. Just a few more lines. No. She couldn't. Her control slipped. A single word tearing from her lips. "Now!"

He bucked, thrusting into her core. His fisted hands left the ground and grasped at her hips. Pressure. Sweet, intimate, pain-touched pressure tipped her toward the edge of sanity. His scent filled the air. Her desire mingled with his, filling the small clearing with the heady aroma of lust.

"Need you," he groaned.

"Love you."

"Mine."

"Yours," she cried out.

"Come for me. Now!"

Emmie opened her eyes. She couldn't breathe. Her body tightened beyond her control. Pleasure. Pain. Pressure. Hunger. She didn't know where one ended and the next began. Now. She had to -- *Oh, God!*

It burned through her. Controlling her. Ripped her senses from her body as she writhed above him. Time lost meaning. Thought fled. Nothing more than pleasure remained. Her body. His. Together as they rocked as one.

A sound tore through the clearing. Their voices joined. Merging just as their bodies locked together. Mated.

Chapter Thirty-Two

"So, you've made a decision?" Buck leaned against the hood of his car.

"Yes." Theron ran his fingers back through his hair. "I need to be with her. I think you knew that already, though."

"Yeah, just needed to make sure you'd put the pieces together fully. Come on, man. You've not exactly made some wise choices recently."

He couldn't argue that point. Not after some of the stunts he'd pulled. "She's the one. Not that I thought, a couple of weeks ago, that there'd ever be a one. But, yeah. She is." Emmie. His Emmie. At least she'd welcomed him back into her life, after they'd sorted out a few small details. There'd be other problems to work through, as they settled into each other's lives, but they'd do it together. Together -- he was still getting used to that idea. It would take a while to smooth off all the rough edges of their relationship, but they had a decent beginning.

"She's a good woman." Buck looked away for a moment. "So is Mags."

"Ah -- I thought I'd seen you spending time with Mags." Theron shook his head, a grin pulling at his lips. "She's protective, though. Something you need to think about, she'll tear the throat out of anyone you mess around with."

"I'm not the type to cheat. It's not my style." Buck frowned, his gaze narrowed. "I'm not like you..."

"Like I was. Fuck a female. Maybe a second time. Then on to the next. Yeah. You've always been the steady one of the group. But I'd say you have a rival for her."

Twin points of color flushed into Buck's face. "Byron."

Emmie's father. That was going to make life interesting if the older shifter decided to make a serious play for Mags. "Byron --

he's a good man."

"Cat."

"Okay, he's a good cat." The hair on the back of his neck stood up. "He came back for Emmie. For her mom. He's not the sort to give up on a woman he loves."

"And does he love her?" Buck's voice choked.

"I don't know. Something you'll have to find out. Cat shifters are straightforward. If you ask him outright. He'll answer you." Would the answer help him though? He'd seen the look in Byron's eyes. Subtle at first, then something stronger. A wave of emotions that would not be easily denied, yet Buck was someone he knew, trusted, and respected. Mags was a wonderful woman; the choice had to be hers.

Just as it had been Emmie's.

"Soon. I'll look for him soon." Buck lifted away from the car and shook his head, sticking his hands in his pockets. "Take care of her. She's a rare one. Never thought I'd see the day when a woman brought you back down to earth."

"She didn't."

"Oh?"

"She gave me wings."

Emmie looked around the bedroom that had been her sanctuary for so long. Would she ever become used to the idea of sharing it? Not just on rare occasions, but on a daily, and nightly, basis?

She inhaled, tasting his scent on the air. Her body reacted instantly. Heat rippled through her being. Her thighs tightened. Nipples crinkled and pressed against the soft cups of her bra. It didn't matter that she knew they would spend the night in each other's arms. Her body craved him now. Not later. She smiled, shaking her head softly, tendrils of hair tickling a path over her face and neck. He'd opened her eyes and her heart to a world she'd denied could ever exist for her.

Scars

The ghosts of the past had been laid to rest.

The car pulled out of the driveway, taking Buck with it. Just Buck. There was another problem. She'd seen how the man had looked at Mags, but the way her father had watched the woman had also been clear. But that was a mess that would have to sort itself out. As much as she loved Mags, getting into the middle of someone else's love life just wasn't a good idea. Not unless she knew how to fix things.

Which she didn't.

The front door opened and closed behind him. Her mate. Theron. She could almost taste him, his passion, the need that he carried with him. Hunger coated him, filled the air as he walked in through the house. Her body responded. Before he'd even opened the door of the bedroom she was ready for him. Craving him.

"Emmie." The single word little more than a growl. His erection pressed against the outline of his jeans.

"No regrets?"

"About leaving the city? None at all. I can work just as well from here as I could from there." Theron closed the gap between them, wrapping his arms about her waist. "There will be times I have to leave. But you can come with me, on some of the trips at least. It won't be easy. It might even be dangerous."

"I'm strong. Stronger than you know yet. If I'm working alongside of you, then you can trust me to look after myself."

"Yes, I've come to realize that. But looking after you is my job." He pulled her closer, tracing one hand down her spine until he cupped her ass. "By my side, then. Where you belong." He leaned down, brushing his lips against hers.

Emmie shivered, parting her lips beneath his. Heat surged through her body as she leaned into his kiss. The touch of his tongue against her lips was all she needed to lean fully into his caress. She wrapped her arms about his neck, pulling them closer, her nipples hardened as she growled into his kiss.

His tongue slipped into her mouth, stroking, exploring, tasting her. Every inch of her body came alive beneath his caress. She belonged with him. Not just for a short time. Forever.

His mate.

Terri Pray

Terri Pray is a stay at home wife and mother currently living in Iowa with her second husband. She was born in England, only moving to the States in 1999. They have two children together and share a love of writing and role-playing that brought them together via the Internet. Together they not only run a chat site, Dark Fantasy Chat, but also work in the RPG industry and Terri can often be seen at such conventions as ValleyCon, Gen Con and Origins at the Final Sword Production booth.

Visit Terri on the Web at www.terripray.com.